KOBI SWITCHED ON HIS flashlight and walked down the main corridor, heels squeaking on the floor as he made his way to the doors in the gray half-light. When he reached them, he carefully peeled away the duct tape and slid back the top and bottom bolts. Only when his hand was on the handle, about to push it open, did he hear the voice in his head.

"Whatever you do, never go out alone."

"Like you did," he whispered to the empty hall. "No choice, Dad."

He opened the door onto a morning alive with the chatter and rustle of insect sounds and bird cries. The parking lot was a forest of Douglas firs, rising five hundred feet tall.

When he was satisfied it was all clear, he took off at a sprint.

Also by Michael Ford

Lost Horizon

FORGOTTEN CITY

MICHAEL FORD

HARPER

An Imprint of HarperCollinsPublishers

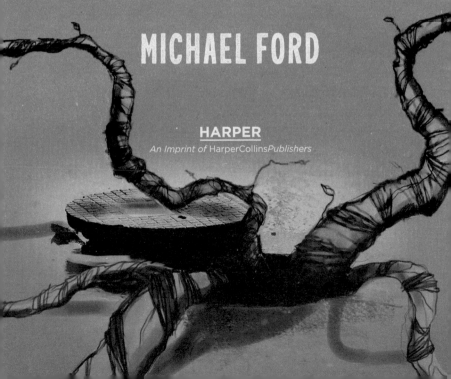

Forgotten City

Copyright © 2018 by Working Partners, Ltd.

All rights reserved. Printed in the United States of America.

No part of this book may be used or reproduced in any manner whatsoever without written permission except in the case of brief quotations embodied in critical articles and reviews. For information address HarperCollins Children's Books, a division of HarperCollins Publishers, 195 Broadway, New York, NY 10007.

www.harpercollinschildrens.com

Library of Congress Control Number: 2018939985

ISBN 978-0-06-269697-7

Typography by Michelle Taormina

Interior Art by Michelle Taormina

19 20 21 22 23 PC/BRR 10 9 8 7 6 5 4 3 2

First paperback edition, 2019

PROLOGUE

KOBI'S DAD WAS DYING before his eyes.

He wasn't about to drop dead in the next few minutes or hours or even days. With the right drugs, the correct dosing, the perfect balance of nutrition and exercise, there was no saying exactly how long he would make it. But slowly, inescapably, the poison in his blood was killing him.

Neither of them ever mentioned it, of course. Talking about it wouldn't change a thing. Kobi couldn't help noticing the signs, though. His dad's spindly wrists and bony fingers unfastening the tape that sealed the school's front door. The thinning hair Kobi could see when his dad bent to unfasten the bottom bolts. The slight yellow tinge to the whites of his eyes as he turned back to face Kobi.

"Remember to double up on the tape, okay?"

"I want to come with you," said Kobi, though he knew exactly what the answer would be.

His dad chuckled. "Not this time, kiddo. When you're—"

"Older, sure," Kobi interrupted. "How old will I actually have to be? Like, thirty?"

"Older than you are now. You're still just a kid." Kobi straightened until he was a fraction taller than his father. "Okay, a big kid." His dad ruffled Kobi's mess of dark hair, then placed both his hands on Kobi's shoulders. "Maybe next time, all right? Just sit tight, follow the protocols, and wait for me. I'll be back in ten days. Two weeks max, if things take longer at the lab."

"But..."

A flash of impatience crossed his dad's face. "Son, please. It's hard enough leaving you without the guilt trip."

"But I can *help*," said Kobi. "You know what I'm capable of. I'm strong, Dad, and you're..." He didn't really know how to put it.

His dad smiled, revealing slightly pale gums. "Thanks for reminding me. That's why I need to get to the lab. Look, I know you don't like being here alone, but it's just too dangerous going all the way across the water. I'm not going to risk your safety. End of discussion. Right?"

Kobi gave in and shrugged.

"Good," said his dad. "Now you've got plenty of food. Don't forget to check the windows and doors, three times a day."

"I *know*, Dad," said Kobi with a roll of his eyes.

"And take your vitamins."

"I read in one of the science journals that nutritional supplements are a con by pharmaceutical companies."

His dad smiled but then said firmly, "Kobi, I'm serious. You can't be complacent. Morning and night. You need to keep your body healthy. Got it?"

"Got it."

"And reset all the traps at every external door."

Kobi forced himself to smile. "Just go, will you?"

His father nodded, released Kobi's shoulders, and pulled up the small flap in the cardboard that covered the front-door window, placing his eye to the hole. "Okay, all clear. I'll see you soon, Son. Oh, and one last thing—no wild parties while I'm gone."

He opened the door quietly, just enough to slip through, then closed it behind him.

"Can't promise that," muttered Kobi.

He quickly fastened tape across the seal, smoothing the edges down with care. Then he sprayed the anti-Waste aerosol liberally around the door. Finally, he peered through the hole himself. His dad was already making his way down the front steps, toward the trees. In a matter of seconds, the jungle had swallowed him. Kobi kept staring for a little while, scanning the trees for any sign of movement. Anything suspicious at all. The green stared back, giving nothing away.

Kobi closed the viewing hole and slammed an open hand into the wall. *I should have insisted. Pushed him harder. He's too weak to go out on his own.*

He walked down the hall slowly, dread sitting like a rock in his gut.

Ten days. Two weeks max. He just had to wait.

Fourteen days stretched ahead like an ocean of time.

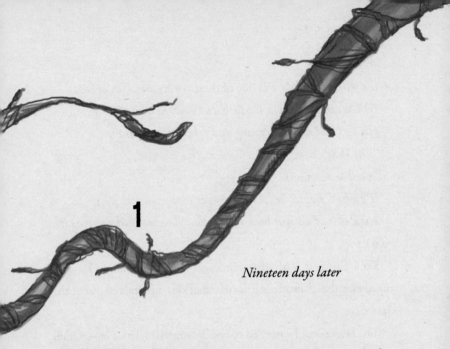

1

Nineteen days later

THERE WAS A WINDUP crank for setting the bear traps, but Kobi didn't need it. He forced open the metal teeth with his bare hands until the mechanism clicked, then slid the trap carefully into place beside the fire door to classroom 9C. He was sweating. Following all the security protocols—moving from room to room—took a good hour on his own. But it felt good to be doing something—anything—to keep the gnawing anxiety at bay. Next he methodically checked each window seal. Maintaining an impervious barrier against Waste-carrying spores and pollen was a constant battle, and without the precaution of reinforcing the seals with duct tape, it wouldn't be long before the school was overrun. At every possible contamination point, he sprayed the pesticide his dad had formulated.

As he worked, he tried and failed to ignore the scrawled writing on the white board. It was one of their last lessons—calculus.

"What's the point, Dad? Math won't get rid of the Waste."

His dad had stopped writing and taken off his glasses.

"The Waste won't be here forever. And when it's gone, the world will need to be rebuilt."

"By who?" Kobi asked. "We've never seen anyone else."

His dad had turned back to the white board. "Just concentrate, smart ass."

Kobi finished with the windows, then took the eraser and angrily scrubbed away the lines of equations. He stalked out of the classroom.

The last rooms he needed to check were the science labs. Of all the rooms in the school, these were the ones that reminded Kobi most of his dad. He'd spent most of his time in there, carrying out his Waste experiments. A fridge hummed in the half-light, connected to solar generators on the school's roof. Through its glass door, Kobi saw the vials of Waste cleansers in their stand. His dad had taken four with him. The cleanser couldn't repair damage to Waste-contaminated cells, but it cleared Waste from his system, temporarily at least. His dad described it like a war. He could beat the enemy back from their land, but each time the land was ravaged further.

And the cleansers couldn't prevent recontamination. Out in the city it was only a matter of time before his dad inhaled Waste spores, or drank water that wasn't 100 percent purified, or Waste entered his system through small cuts or insect bites. Even in the best-case scenario, one dose might last six days. Twenty-four days' worth. That meant his dad was five days from a death sentence. Soon, the enemy would overrun him.

But he told me to stay. What if he comes back and I'm gone?

In the woodwork room, which his dad had long ago commandeered for weapons and equipment, Kobi checked the doors and windows quickly. Dozens of half-finished contraptions were strewn around the place—experiments they'd been working on. A spare generator dual powered by solar energy and the wind turbine on the roof, a smoke-bomb launcher, a water purifier, the cobbled-together radio receiver that had never received anything.

Kobi didn't want to look, but his eyes traveled to the corner occupied by the Snatcher, the single biggest thing in the room. It was about the size of a small car and looked like a giant metal spider, with its eight legs curled up beneath its carapace. This one had only a single wing, because the other had broken off in a collision with a tree about three hundred yards from the school. Kobi's dad thought its navigations systems must have malfunctioned because normally Snatchers didn't head this far out, and they certainly didn't crash into things. The drones' programming and microjets allowed them to cut intricate flight paths through the city terrain, moving silently and stealthily to capture their prey—any living thing that crossed their sensors.

Kobi approached the contraption, letting his gaze travel over the battered titanium shell and the solar panel array lining its remaining wing. Underneath its head, a number of wires spilled out. His dad had deactivated it straightaway to make sure it couldn't send any signals back to its hub in the city. Its multitude of black "eyes" stared back at him. Apparently they detected across the visual spectrum, including infrared and ultraviolet. A perfect hunter. Kobi trailed his fingers over its cold shell. Along the side of its "head" were scrawled five letters: *CLAWS*. The name fit, given the segmented appendages curled up beneath its main body. Dad said the Snatchers' mission was simple—to patrol the city, scoop up any Waste-infected fauna, and take it for disposal. Dogs, cats, deer—whatever they spotted from the air.

People too, if they weren't careful.

Whoever built the Snatchers was long dead, but the drones were automated and solar charging. They'd fly until the hardware broke down.

Nineteen days. I haven't got a choice, Dad. You said two weeks max.

Kobi turned away from the Snatcher, set the door trap, checked the seals, then opened the fridge and took two vials of cleanser.

I'm coming for you.

In the changing room, Kobi lit the candles they left around the windowless room, then reached into locker D22 and grabbed his Kevlar vest, scavenged from the local police department headquarters a few blocks away. He slipped it on and tightened the straps, followed by his backpack. He hooked the police Taser into the janitor's old utility belt, then loaded his water flask, flashlight, and compass as well. He fastened the sheathed machete to his left hip. Last of all, he took out his preloaded crossbow—courtesy, like the bear traps, of Big Hank's Hunting Supplies—and slung it over his shoulder. He was about to shut the locker when he remembered the scent masker. Bear musk.

"We're lucky there are no girls left to impress."

He smiled and shook his head at the memory of his dad's words. Kobi used to hate it when he made jokes like that, but he would have given anything to hear his dad's voice right now, echoing down the corridor with apologies and excuses for taking longer than expected.

Kobi sprayed the can back and forth over his clothes, then slipped it into his belt.

Candlelight flickered over the holographic photo tacked to the inside of the locker door. It showed the previous owner of D22. Maxwell Trenton looked like a nice kid. Maybe a year or two older than Kobi himself, he was scrawny, with braces across his teeth. Kinda goofy. He wore a Seahawks hat and was standing between two hulking linebackers in front of a huge crowd at the city's GrowCycle Stadium. The football players looked like they could have broken Max in half like a twig, but they were smiling for the camera. Kobi guessed the signatures hovering across the bottom were theirs.

Maxwell was dead, of course. So were the linebackers in the photo, along with the rest of the 2029 Seahawks team, and all the unsuspecting spectators in the background. Plus the janitor, every cop in Seattle, and even Big Hank, if he was ever a real person in the first place.

But not my dad. No way.

People had always thought it would be nuclear war or climate change or a meteor strike that would destroy the world, not a food company. His dad had told Kobi the story so many times. By the late 2020s, climate change had begun to severely affect the world's ability to produce enough food to feed the growing population. The answer was GAIA, a fertilizer GrowCycle developed to grow crops quicker. People thought it would be humankind's savior, but something went wrong. The scientists pushed things too far. Some genetically engineered hormone spread through the environment, altering organisms' DNA. Animals, humans, plants . . . they all began to *change*.

The rest was history. *"Or the end of it,"* as his dad had joked.

On the bench in the middle of the locker room, Kobi spread out his map, showing the familiar outline of the bay and the grid of streets.

"Where are you, Dad?" he whispered, and his voice choked up in his throat. He reached automatically for one of his vitamins that he usually kept in his inside pocket. But he'd left the pills back in the gym. He hadn't taken any since his dad had left. To

Kobi, it felt like one small act of protest against his dad for leaving him there alone.

All around Bill Gates Memorial High, toward the map's left edge, hundreds of hand-drawn circles littered West Seattle. Each was labeled in his father's familiar hand: *F* (food), *M* (medical), *W* (weapons), *H* (hardware). All the food sites on this side of the bridge were crossed out. Exhausted of supplies. There were plenty more locations marked, but they were all on the other side of the bridge. There was even an *L* all the way on Mercer Island, though his dad said that that particular lab would always be impossible to access. Mercer Island was Waste ground zero; the most contaminated place in the world. Before the disaster, GrowCycle had dumped a load of Waste on a vast site sown with a range of botanical specimens as a PR stunt, intending a new park to spring up overnight. It didn't quite work out that way.

The closest labs were a day away on foot, in the old university a few blocks off the I-5. If his dad had made it that far. Kobi had never even crossed the bridge, despite pleading more times than he could count. The excuse was always the same. *"You're not ready."*

Anything could have happened—that was the problem. There were other predators in the city besides Snatchers. They'd found bear droppings close to the school a couple of months ago, and Kobi didn't even want to think how big a Waste-infected grizzly might be. The Waste affected all creatures differently. In the initial contamination period, 99 percent of fauna had died off.

Those that didn't, and managed to breed, spawned all manner of mutated offspring.

Or maybe something as mundane as an accident had kept his dad from returning home. Maybe he'd fallen and hit his head. Thing was, time out in the Waste affected his father badly, even with his cleansers. Just a few hours of prolonged exposure would leave him frail.

And he wasn't in great shape even when he left. . . .

Kobi's stomach cramped up, and he waited for the spasm to pass. His last meal had been the day before—a can of Barkz dog food. Not bad, if he kept his eyes closed. It was nutritious—40 percent protein, plenty of fat and fiber. All that mattered, when it came down to it. But the longer he waited, letting the hunger gnaw at his stomach, the weaker he'd get.

If he was going out, it had to be now.

Folding the map, he blew out the candle and left the locker room, grabbing his backpack on the way.

Bill Gates had once had a student body of about fifteen hundred. Their lives echoed silently around the corridors and classrooms, on the bulletin boards that announced sports news and the upcoming prom, in their assignments displayed on the walls, in the graffiti scrawled onto the bathroom stall doors. In the thirteen years the school had been his home, Kobi had come to know every inch. He and his dad had broken into hundreds of lockers, every classroom cupboard, and every teacher's drawer in their attempts to scavenge things useful for survival. Mostly a waste of time. A pointless sifting through forgotten lives.

Kobi switched on his flashlight and walked down the main corridor, heels squeaking on the floor as he made his way to the doors in the gray half-light. When he reached them, he carefully peeled away the duct tape and slid back the top and bottom bolts. He put his eye to the viewing hole, to make sure there were no nasty surprises. Only when his hand was on the handle, about to push it open, did he hear the voice in his head.

"Whatever you do, never go out alone."

"Like you did," he whispered to the empty hall. "No choice, Dad."

He opened the door onto a morning alive with the chatter and rustle of insect sounds and bird cries. The parking lot was a forest of Douglas firs, rising five hundred feet tall. Other trees, not quite as towering, grew among them, sycamores and maples. Sunlight filtered through the canopy above. A few bikes rested in the branches of a red oak, about 150 feet up, carried there by the force of nature as the tree had grown from seed to sapling to megaflora. Kobi's father had used a book from the school library to teach him the names of all the plants in the city. Though some of the newer, deadlier ones weren't listed in any books.

More cars lay abandoned among the trees, some like miniature metal greenhouses, busted-out windows sprouting shrubs. Across the road, the football field's goalposts were twined with vines and the turf was invisible under dense knots of sprawling weeds. Kobi tried to imagine Maxwell Trenton and his friends squaring off against a rival team, but he just couldn't.

He listened for a moment, eyes trailing across the vegetation for any sign of predators.

"Always be patient. Better slow than dead."

Kobi turned toward the sky. Snatchers rarely came this far from the city center, but it paid to be cautious.

Satisfied that nothing lay in wait, Kobi stepped into the open, took more duct tape, and lined the door from the outside. He fastened the padlocks, then made his way down the cracked steps and along the path he and his father had cut toward the road. Despite being hewn back just a few weeks earlier, the grass had already grown back as tall as Kobi himself. He hacked at the stray tendrils with his machete, all the while glancing over his shoulders, covering the angles.

"Two pairs of eyes are always better than one."

"So why didn't you let me come with you, Dad?" he murmured.

Kobi moved through the grasses quickly, stepping carefully over a centipede the size of his arm. Then he made his way into the thicker forest, where the light was dim. He darted from tree to tree, pausing at each to check his surroundings.

"Situational awareness, Son—always know what's around you, and always have an escape route."

He wished sometimes he could switch off his dad's voice—but his rules were deeply ingrained after so many expeditions together. Kobi clambered over a fallen trunk, pausing against the side of an overturned school bus. The intersection ahead was pretty exposed—a hundred yards of bare asphalt. It was always a risk to cross it. He watched the vine-covered houses across the street. Anything could be lurking in those doorways—and he'd be right in their line of sight.

When he was satisfied it was all clear, he took off at a sprint. His dad had always moved too slowly for Kobi's liking. He reached the safety of the trees on the far side within seconds, glad of the foliage overhead.

"Stay under cover when you can. Don't be visible from above."

Vertical gouges marked the nearest tree trunk. Cougars probably. They'd practically stumbled into one a few months back—hyperaggressive like most Waste-infected predators. It had taken three crossbow bolts to bring it down. Kobi still remembered how he'd felt as the adrenaline drained from his veins. His dad said the animal was better off out of its misery, and as he watched it die, Kobi thought he saw some relief in the creature's yellow eyes.

Moving between the massive trunks, Kobi passed the rusted chassis of a taxi lying on its back in the middle of the street like a stranded turtle. Foliage grew through the windows, and vines threaded over the front and back axles. Kobi waited behind it for a few more minutes, then pressed on, hurrying beneath the sign telling him he was on SW Genesee.

The street to the south was clearer, a wide expanse of crusted earth, with mounds of dirt pressed up against crumbling buildings. A dark scar ran across the road ahead, blocking the way. Kobi had come this way before, with his dad. Sometime in the past, a water tower had collapsed, causing a mudslide across two blocks, flattening several houses. As it had dried, a crack had opened up. Coming closer, Kobi realized the crevasse had grown since the last time he'd been there. It was now twenty feet deep and fifteen across. He peered over the edge. The pit below was filled with Chokerplants, vines covered in spikes slithering slowly over one another like giant anacondas. Wrapped in the coils of one were the remains of some large, fur-covered animal, its limbs at crooked, unnatural angles. Kobi shuddered. Plenty of bones littered the chasm—other creatures unlucky enough to stumble in.

His dad would never have been that dumb though.

"We'll skirt around it," he said. *"Never take risks you don't have to."*

But the detour would be much longer now, and take Kobi into a maze of residential streets he didn't like the look of. He took a few steps back from the edge to get a running start. "Sorry, Dad," he said, picturing his father's horrified expression. But Kobi knew he could make it. The tests they'd done in the school gym proved his abilities were increasing on every metric. Unnaturally so. Strength, speed, endurance, and cell regeneration were off the charts for a kid his age. They weren't sure why, but Dad said it was likely down to Waste exposure pre-birth—Kobi was showing the same enhanced physiology that Waste-infected creatures did, but without the negative side effects.

He sprinted toward the gap, imagining a football in his hands and a row of those Seahawks linebackers blocking his path. At the edge, he pushed off, feeling the power drive through his muscles. He came down on the other side with room to spare.

He allowed himself a grin and lifted his hands in the air.

"Touchdown," he muttered under his breath.

He took two more steps before something snagged around his ankle.

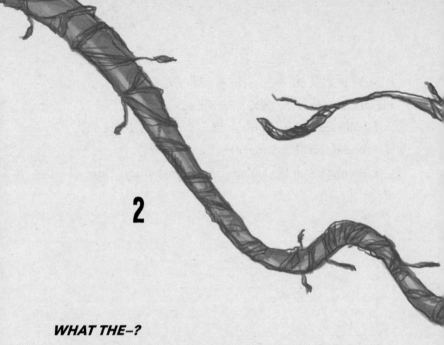

2

WHAT THE–?

Kobi's foot jerked from beneath him and the sidewalk rushed toward his head. He just managed to cross his arms to protect himself before slamming into the ground, but the breath burst from his lungs. Looking back, he caught sight of a yellow vine, as thick as his wrist, wrapped around his sneaker.

It was pulling him toward the edge of the crevasse. Kobi's body thrummed with panic as he struggled to get his breath. He tried to tug free and hissed in pain as the Chokerplant's barbs sank through his pants and into his flesh. He scrabbled for purchase, but there was nothing to grab a hold of.

Kobi rolled onto his back and yanked the machete from the sheath, aiming and hacking. The first slice missed, drawing sparks off the asphalt. The second hacked three-quarters of the way through the vine. Yellow sap oozed from the wound. Kobi swung again, severing the vine. The broken end reared like a snake, then slid back over the edge.

Kobi scrambled up, letting the dead coils slip off his ankle. He was breathing hard.

He pictured his dad's face again and felt blood burning his cheeks, trying not to imagine what he would say if he were here.

"Idiot!" Kobi growled at himself.

He pulled up his pant leg and saw the rows of bleeding puncture wounds. It would heal soon enough, but he'd be slowed for a while.

And there were things out here that could smell blood from miles away.

Limping slightly, and moving with extreme caution, he continued through the dense forest. Streams and wet ditches crisscrossed the mossy ground, and lichen-covered cars looked like massive boulders. Here and there, Kobi caught sight of the houses set back from the road. Some had skeletal branches growing through them, and others were covered in explosions of exotic flowers. It would be easy to get lost there, but he knew a few markers from his trips out with his dad. A mailbox at an angle with the number 3321; an old basketball net still standing among the trees; someone's speedboat, rearing up like it had caught a wave; the old filling station with a sign reading "NO MORE GAS!" Dad said that people panicked and tried to get out when the Waste really took hold. But by then it had been too late—there was nowhere to run to.

Kobi passed it all quickly but on high alert, checking the map whenever he could find cover.

It took a couple of hours before he neared the river, where the roadway ramped up and the apartment blocks grew more substantial, giving way to industrial buildings. Many had collapsed in on themselves years before, though a few chimneys remained, standing defiant against the tide of organic matter that swarmed up their walls. Closer to the bridge, the Duwamish waterway had burst out of its banks in places, making a swamp below. Several Walmart trucks lay stranded on their sides in the marshland like the corpses of beached whales.

West Seattle Bridge was still standing, though its stanchions were covered in vines, and the road had sprouted grasses like a wild meadow. Kobi wondered how much longer the structure would last before it gave in to the forces of Waste and nature. Beyond, rising through fog, the cityscape appeared. Skyscrapers swathed in green, like strange columns of vegetation, and above them all the delicate spire of the Space Needle—the only place where the plants hadn't completely taken hold, thinning toward the top. He'd seen plenty of pictures of the old city, and even a few films from the school's archives. Sidewalks teeming with people, buildings aglow with light, signals and billboards flashing, thousands of cars. All gone.

Kobi paused at the edge of the bridge, taking out the map again. This was as far as he'd ever gone with his dad. As far as he'd ever been *allowed* to go. Over the bridge, in the city proper, there were untold dangers.

His plan was simple. Head to his dad's lab at the university. And try not to get killed, of course.

With a tickle of dread across the back of his neck, he began to cross the bridge, darting quickly between cars and bushes, ignoring the stinging pain in his ankle. The water below and the bay beyond were dark and choppy. Kobi didn't know if anything in the sea had survived the Waste. If it was the same as on land, it wasn't worth thinking about the mutated monsters that might be lurking under the surface.

He got most of the way across the bridge in a couple of minutes. Toward the far side, a truck was jackknifed across the highway, its rear doors hanging open. He was creeping around it when his eyes spotted a glimmer of metal in the sky. Terror spiked through his chest.

Snatcher.

"If you see a Snatcher, drop whatever you're doing and find cover right away. I mean it, Kobi. No ifs. No buts. Just hide."

He skidded underneath the truck and held his breath. If it had picked up his heat signature, he had to be ready to run.

After a few seconds, he peered out. The thing was heading slowly toward the north. Its ten-foot wings were spread wide, and birdlike metal talons glinted from its underbelly next to an array of cameras and scanners.

Hiding under the truck, Kobi's every instinct screamed to turn around and head back to the school. A crossbow and Taser were no match for a Snatcher.

I've come this far. I can't give up on Dad now.

He peered up, saw the sky was clear, and dashed to the railing at the edge of the bridge. It was ten yards to the lower road, and the drop would have broken his dad's legs, but Kobi swung his legs over and lowered himself as far as he could before releasing. He landed in a crouch, cushioning the impact on his knees. The puncture wounds on his ankle burned with pain, but he forced himself not to cry out. His eyes searched for trouble on the lower level, but there was no movement.

Staying under cover where he could, Kobi moved beneath overpasses and between looming warehouses suffocated in rogue vegetation. There was little to attract big predators here, but he still heard the occasional bird shriek or patter of paws. Each animal sound brought his progress to a halt as he waited for the noise to move past.

Checking back to the map every couple of blocks, sometimes stopping and taking stock of his surroundings for several minutes at a time, Kobi finally reached the first of his father's *F*s—a minimarket. He couldn't see inside the store because there were leaves pressed up against the glass. The automatic doors, he noted, were open a fraction. Normally Kobi and his dad would have taken the time to scope it out tactically—going solo was dangerous.

Kobi took out his machete, which would be better for any close-quarter encounters than the crossbow. As he approached, there were no obvious signs of any predators inside. No movement or sounds. He stepped around a sidewalk—Chokerplants lurked below many, and they sensed their prey through vibration of the ground. He pulled open the door farther and pushed aside a snaking tendril of ivy. The place was warm and musty, and he could just about make out the cash register beyond the broken bottles littered across the floor. It was dark because of the plant life blocking the windows, so he flicked on his flashlight, moving the beam across the interior.

The shop had already been looted, that much was clear. Probably in the chaos after the first wave of contamination, or maybe by later survivors until they, too, succumbed to the Waste. But not everything had been taken. Plenty of stuff was just dust in packets now—bread, potato chips, candy. There were dried soups, but they had almost no nutritional value. An old refrigerated cabinet was sprouting huge colonies of mold and fungi. Rounding an aisle, Kobi's heart leaped as he saw cans on a shelf. He started to rifle through them. One thing his dad had taught him a long time back—"best by" dates meant nothing.

"If the seal's good, what's inside is good."

He found a few cans of macaroni in tomato sauce, and some beef chili that made his mouth start to water. Vegetables—carrots and potatoes and beans.

He started loading up his backpack, calculating rations already. There was enough for several weeks. He could return with his dad, though it might take a couple of trips to get it all back to the school. Then Kobi found some canned pineapple hiding behind a row of canned mushrooms and couldn't help himself. He cracked open the top with his Swiss Army knife and tipped the can to his lips. The juice was the sweetest thing he'd ever tasted. Opening it up the rest of the way, he shoveled the fleshy pieces into his mouth, barely stopping to chew. He belched.

"Pardon me," he said, grinning.

Then he heard the rattle of metal, and the grin vanished.

Kobi kept his body completely still, pineapple juice dribbling over his chin.

There was a shuffling, scraping sound coming from nearby.

Inside the store . . .

Kobi swallowed, and even that seemed horribly loud.

It might be nothing. Just a plant shifting. A draught. Or it could be Dad. . . .

He heard a deep, snorting breath, and his insides turned liquid.

The sound definitely wasn't human.

The shuffling noise edged closer, and Kobi slowly turned to track the sound. It seemed to be coming from somewhere at the back of the store. He glanced toward the exit, making calculations. He could make it, but not silently.

It might just be a rat. They could be aggressive but on their own weren't much of a threat. And they were edible, at least for Kobi, with his immunity to the effects of Waste. Kobi slung the crossbow off his shoulder.

A crashing sound, and the whole shelf wobbled suddenly, as if something had bashed into the other side. A sweat broke out across Kobi's upper back.

A rat couldn't do that.

The breaths were getting closer, and it sounded like they were coming from something *massive*. Something that could smell him through the bear musk.

Or something that wasn't afraid of bears.

Kobi made a quick assessment. His backpack was too far for him to reach. Slowly, he picked up the half-empty can of pineapple.

Please, let this work. . . .

He hurled it to the back of the store. It landed with a rattle of metal, and the shelf beside him shook again as the creature's heavy feet broke into a run in the same direction as the distraction. Kobi lunged for the exit.

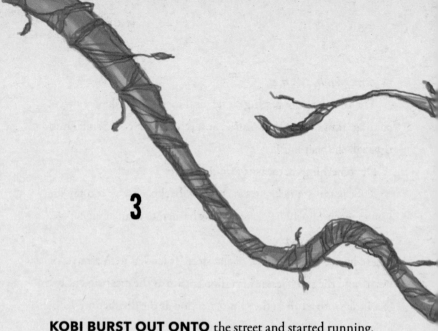

3

KOBI BURST OUT ONTO the street and started running.

A moment later, he heard a crash. Looking over his shoulder, he saw a huge four-legged shape skid out onto the sidewalk, raining shattered glass from its gray fur. Another shape followed, slightly smaller. As Kobi took them in, his blood turned cold. Wolves, the bigger one six feet tall at least. They'd come straight through the glass door. Claws curled and jagged, scraping the ground. Bellies bloated from hunger. The creatures' eyes gleamed a Waste-infected sickly yellow.

Kobi scanned his surroundings. He was out in the open with no shelter in sight, and he knew he couldn't outrun the wolves.

"In a life-and-death situation, make a decision quickly and don't change your mind."

Kobi stopped and turned to face the wolves, which were maybe fifty feet away. His arms felt heavy. *Move!* he commanded himself.

He reached for his crossbow and leveled the sight at the smaller creature's head. For a second he imagined his dad looking over his shoulder like when they used to do target practice in the gym. . . .

"Always go for the body. It's the biggest target."

He dropped his aim and pulled the trigger, but his hands were shaking and the bolt thumped into the wolf's foreleg. It jerked back, then reached down with its jaws and gripped the shaft between its teeth. With a sharp tug, the bolt tore loose.

Waste didn't only make some creatures larger. It made them smarter too.

Kobi's crossbow reloaded automatically. He fired again, and the second bolt embedded in the larger animal's neck. It let out a strangled, guttural growl and came to a stop. The other creature halted and turned to its companion. Kobi aimed for the smaller creature's chest and pulled the trigger once more, but the bolt mechanism jammed. The wolf took a loping pace forward, and Kobi knew it was a split second from attacking. He was stuck. If he ran, he'd be taken out in no time. A shadow fell from above, along with a whir like a nest of hornets. The larger wolf shrank back as a Snatcher descended, gleaming and hovering on air jets that blasted the foliage. The Snatcher's legs scooped up the smaller predator. For a moment all Kobi saw were legs scrabbling through the gaps, accompanied by a terrified yelping, then the Snatcher shot vertically from the road. The whole thing had taken less than a couple of seconds.

That could have been me. . . .

Kobi shouldered the crossbow and fled. He didn't look back. Didn't need to because he could hear the wolf's paws pounding fast along the road behind him. He concentrated on the road ahead and on driving every last ounce of power into his legs.

No rules for this. Just survive at any cost. Buildings blurred past on either side, then he plunged into a thicket of trees. Twigs whipped his skin and lashed his clothes as he stumbled over roots. The crash of foliage at his back grew closer. The machete in its sheath bounced against his leg.

Still running, he pulled the bear-musk can from its holster and drew his machete. He slammed the blade into the can and an explosion of scent misted out in a cloud. Kobi tossed the can over his shoulder, hoping it would fall somewhere in the wolf's path.

Sure enough, the paws slowed. A tree lay across the road ahead. Kobi vaulted it, then veered left, doubling back. He pressed up against a thick trunk, fighting for air. He heard nothing but his own heavy breathing. Risking a look, he saw the creature with its muzzle to the ground, moving around the misting can. The stink of bear was overpowering.

If I get out of this, I promise I'll never be careless again.

The wolf lifted its head from the can, swaying its massive shaggy head back and forth. Kobi could see its nostrils flaring. Then it moved slowly forward, dipping its head every so often.

I did it. I fooled it!

The wolf was walking away, putting distance between them.

Twenty feet, twenty-five. It jumped onto the same log Kobi had leaped over, and paused, staring intently at the ground for a good few seconds. Kobi realized what it was looking at. His footprint. A skidded smear of mud as he'd made a turn. The wolf turned too, looking toward his hiding place, and Kobi froze.

He couldn't tell if the creature could see him through the thick foliage. But the wolf's gaze was unyielding. The wolf took a pace in his direction. Kobi didn't know whether to move or sit tight. Another step. Then another, quicker.

It broke into a run.

Kobi shoved himself away from the tree and took off. He splashed through a muddy gully, ducked under a hanging branch, and then suddenly he was clear of the trees. His sneakers were soaked through, squelching with every step, as he headed up a narrower street. An old traffic signal lay at an angle, collapsed onto the roof of a delivery truck. Kobi ducked beneath it, keeping his stride on the far side. He could run the sixty-yard dash in under seven seconds, but he was pretty sure a Waste wolf could do it faster. In a storefront window he saw the reflection as the wolf flew after him, eating up the ground with its uneven strides. How long could he keep going? *Where* was he going?

And what would it do to him if it caught up?

His breaths were ragged, choked up and near sobbing with fear, but then he saw it ahead.

Fire escape!

Its grated metal platform was a story up against the side of a large white building. Fifteen feet until he could grab hold of the lower section. *Can I make it? If I don't . . .*

The wolf snarled, and he could have sworn he smelled its fetid breath.

Kobi launched himself into the air and knew at once it wasn't enough. He hit the wall, and reached, fingertips a fraction short. His feet scrambled, and somehow the toes of his sneakers found some grip, giving him an extra push. His fingers closed on metal and held on. He pulled himself up. Then he heard the snap of the wolf's teeth and his arms screamed out at a sudden extra weight. The creature had its jaws fastened on the sole of Kobi's sneaker, its front paws reaching up as it reared against the wall, straining. Kobi wailed and yanked up his foot, and the wolf dropped back, the shoe a tiny morsel in its mouth.

Kobi rolled up onto the fire escape's platform. Below, the wolf dropped the shoe and launched itself again, but it couldn't reach. It growled and tried once more, eyes rabid with hunger and mouth drooling. Finally, it settled back, prowling with angry strides up and down below him. The bolt still protruded from its neck, trailing blood over its thick fur.

Though his pulse was racing, Kobi's breathing slowly returned to normal. As it did, he began to process. His knapsack was back in the supermarket, and there was *no way* he was going back there. But he still had his weapons, luckily, and the map.

Kobi took it from his back pocket, trying not to think of the pacing wolf below, and tried to work out exactly where he was. From his vantage point, there were no landmarks—everything he saw looked like jungle. He traced his finger up the block from the supermarket. Had he taken a left or a right? How far had he run?

Then he saw the SODO Medical Center, marked with one of his dad's *M*s. It was three blocks from the supermarket. He looked up at the modern building rising above him.

This could be it.

The fire escape looped all the way up to the roof, five floors above. Leaving the wolf to its frustrated pacing and snarling, Kobi climbed the ladders and worked his way up two more stories. Blinds were drawn across most of the windows. He chose a window at random and drew his machete. He knew he couldn't risk heading all the way up to the roof itself. Up there, any Snatchers within ten blocks would spot him.

He slammed the machete's hilt into the glass, and it spider-cracked. It felt wrong to be making so much noise, but there was no way around it. A second blow sent the glass fragments tumbling over the frame. A few shards sprinkled three floors down to where the wolf was waiting. Kobi used the blade to knock the remaining pieces out, pulled up the blinds, and looked inside.

The window opened into an office lined with books and dominated by a large desk. Several old potted plants had burst from their confines and spread up the walls and across the ceiling.

Kobi threw his leg inside and climbed in. The computer terminal on the desk was covered in sprouting fungus, as was the back of the tall desk chair.

A nameplate on the desk read "Dr. Miriam Argento."

So this is the hospital.

Kobi walked toward the door, one foot in just a sock. He was probably safe inside the building, and there was a chance he'd find food somewhere there. He couldn't stay inside forever, of course, but he might also source some basics like morphine, antiseptics, and bandages. Clean syringes were always a bonus too, for his dad's anti-Waste shots. Despite everything, Kobi started to feel positive. He could eat, lie low, and then head out again at first light.

As he was passing the desk, he noticed the wastepaper basket and a copy of the *Seattle Times*. Curious, he picked it out. He'd seen a couple of newspapers before, but years ago, before he could even read properly. His dad had never liked having them around. Kobi guessed that seeing them made him remember the painful stuff. *Like Mom.* She'd died just a few days after Kobi was born, and his dad *never* spoke about her. Whenever Kobi tried, his dad just shut down, so in the end Kobi simply stopped asking.

The print was still clear, and the date across the top was March 19, 2031. Kobi knew from his dad's history lessons that this was about a month after the outbreak. The headline read: HOSPITALS OVERRUN: POLICE URGE RESIDENTS TO STAY INDOORS.

Fascinated, eyes scanning the text, Kobi went to sit in the chair.

With one hand on the back, he spun it around.

His heart jumped into his throat as a decomposed body slid off the seat, crumpling at his feet. Kobi leaped back, tripping and crashing into one of the plants. He tried to push himself farther away but found himself pressed against the wall, staring into the eye sockets of a skull.

4

DR. ARGENTO WAS STILL wearing a suit, but the parts of the body that Kobi could see were only bone. Spindly wrist and hand joints. One foot still wearing a high-heeled shoe.

Kobi was panting.

It's just a body. It can't hurt you. She's dead. . . .

He dropped the newspaper and stood up, eyes glued to the corpse, then backed out of the door. The hospital corridor was empty, with several glass partitions at regular intervals. Trying to forget what he'd seen, Kobi wandered vacantly over the linoleum floor. There were plants there too, but the overgrowth wasn't as dense as in some other buildings he'd entered. He guessed it was because the environment in the hospital had been so sterile to start with. Signs above the doors pointed to other departments. Some of the words made no sense to Kobi—*endocrinology, oncology, pediatrics. Dad would know what they mean.* Through the glass he looked into the forested wards. More skeletons lay on rotting beds, not quite as shocking now that he was ready for it. They looked at peace, with their sagging nightclothes, or moth-eaten blankets pulled up to their chests. He'd seen dead bodies before, but never so many in the same place. Like this, they all looked the same.

Kobi reached a bank of elevators. Peeling back leaves from a sign attached to the wall, he saw what he was looking for on the second floor: "Cafeteria." Elevators had long ago ceased to work, as the grid stopped generating power, but he gave the call button a hopeful press anyway, and when it didn't come he took the stairs. The cafeteria looked like a jungle, the counter and cabinets sprouting giant ferns, tables and chairs like islands of lush shrubs. Kobi heard his dad's voice in his head, making the same joke he always did when they scavenged a restaurant or diner.

"The service in here is nonexistent!"

"Food's a disappointment too," muttered Kobi. The menu promised waffles, bacon, eggs done any way, burgers and hot dogs, fresh fruit salads, and a dozen other things that Kobi had never eaten yet still made his mouth water. But in the kitchen the only edible remnants he found were canned sweet corn and maple syrup.

Better than Barkz dog food, I guess.

There was still gas in the pipes, so he sterilized water over the stove, taking some to refill his canteen and enjoying some slightly stale chamomile tea with the rest. By the time he had finished, it was getting late in the afternoon. Getting back to the school before dark fell would be possible, if risky, but he hadn't come this far just to turn back. The labs where his dad had been heading weren't too far—maybe twenty blocks or so.

If he ever made it there.

Kobi pushed the doubts away, but they lurked on the edge of his consciousness, threatening to break back in and fill his mind with outright despair. Another night on his own. Another twenty-four hours his dad would have to survive without his medication.

And what if they'd somehow missed each other, and his dad had made it back to Bill Gates?

Kobi hadn't even left a note. How dumb was that?

"Don't worry about things you can't change."

He heard his dad's voice, kind and calm, and it soothed his worries. Still, the idea of sleeping in the hospital, among the dead, freaked Kobi out. He headed back upstairs, this time to the fourth floor, looking for somewhere to bed down in peace. At first, it seemed that most of the floor was operating rooms and offices and a couple labs filled with scanning equipment. There was less vegetation than on the other floors, and there wasn't a single body. From the window at the back of a waiting room, where puzzle books and magazines sat curling in a stack, Kobi caught a glimpse of the sun setting over the forested Seattle skyline. In the distance, rising taller than anything else around, was the disk-shaped summit of the Space Needle.

His dad said it used to be an observation tower, with thousands of tourists taking the elevator to the top every day. After the outbreak the military had commandeered it to launch the Snatchers, and after each patrol the seizure drones would return to it like birds to a roost. Kobi saw them now, black shapes circling like vultures.

He considered settling into one of the chairs to sleep, but they looked a heck of a lot less comfortable than his makeshift cot back in the school gym. He decided to try the top floor instead and took the final flight of stairs. At the top, the moss-covered door had been pushed off its hinges by thick vines streaming through an air vent. He stepped over it.

Some sort of transparent plastic curtain hung from the ceiling a few yards up the corridor, fixed to the walls on either side to provide a barrier. Everything beyond was blurred, and a sign above read: "Quarantine zone: biohazard suits must be worn beyond this point."

Kobi walked toward it. There was a door to the left, and inside he saw the suits themselves hanging on pegs. White overalls with integral hoods and visors. Something about them, hanging there like weird second skins, made him shudder, but he found a pair of sneakers roughly the right size and changed into them.

Next, he turned his attention back to the sealed area. He unzipped the plastic and stepped through. What he found inside wasn't at all what he'd expected. The walls were pristine white. No plant life whatsoever. The air tasted warmer, and stale. That at least made sense, if this was a Waste-free zone.

He found himself looking into some sort of medical lab area

filled with computer stations, large dark-screened digital displays, and desks littered with papers. He saw models of molecules that looked a bit like those in the science rooms back at Bill Gates, plus chambers that resembled futuristic coffins. There were shelves filled with lab equipment and what may have been medications. One wall was entirely covered by something like a school whiteboard but ten times the size. Fixed to it were photos of individuals, plus close-ups of anatomy Kobi couldn't fathom. Long equations had been scrawled down one side.

They were trying to figure out how to treat the effects of Waste. I wonder if Dad knows about this place.

Through glass partitions at the back of the room was another ward, with six beds, each surrounded by an array of complex monitoring tech. None of the beds, Kobi was pleased to see, were occupied.

His stomach didn't feel great, and he wasn't sure if it was the odd dinner he'd eaten or just the anxiety chewing at him. This place looked safe; that was the main thing. In the ward, he shut the door and pushed one of the beds up against it.

Just in case.

Then he settled onto another, pulled a sheet over him, and tried to ignore all the weird equipment.

Tomorrow I'll keep on looking.

At first light, he'd leave the hospital and continue toward the labs. And this time, he'd be *a lot* more careful.

"I'm not quitting, Dad," he said to the white ceiling.

And, despite thinking that he'd never be able to sleep, it took only a minute before he drifted off.

Kobi lay on the bench, gripping the bar above. Chalk dusted his palms. His dad stood above him, watching with a frown. "Just don't hurt yourself, Son."

"I won't," said Kobi. He took a deep breath in, then pushed. His pectoral muscles contracted, and he eased the bar off its hooks. His arms straightened, elbows locking. His dad had his hands ready in case he dropped the weight, but Kobi sucked in another breath as he lowered the bar to his chest. Another breath out and he lifted again. His arms were shaking as he slotted the bar back into the hooks. He sat up.

"Kobi, that was three hundred pounds!" said his dad, shaking his head. "Most full-grown men couldn't press that."

"I think I could lift more," said Kobi, flushing with pride. "Let's put another twenty on."

His dad was making a note on a clipboard. "Not today," he said. "You're making amazing progress, but I don't want to push you too hard without knowing what's going on with your physiology. Have you taken your vitamin supplements today?"

"Of course," said Kobi. He stared into his dad's eyes. "We know what's going on with me. It's Waste."

His dad nodded. "Seems to be." He looked worried.

"What's wrong?"

His dad set down the clipboard and laid a hand on Kobi's shoulder.

"We already know your body can handle the contamination, and we know it's made you stronger and faster than a normal kid. But knowing it isn't the same as understanding it. I need more blood for the lab tests."

"Sure," said Kobi. He stretched out his arm, and his dad opened a clean syringe. Kobi turned away.

"Even after all this time, you still don't like it, huh?"

Kobi nodded, closing his eyes. His dad took blood every few days to monitor changes. He'd done it a thousand times, but there was something about seeing the needle go in . . .

But it didn't. And when he tried to lift his arms, there were leather straps over his wrists, pinning him down. His head was held in place by something out of sight. He strained his neck but couldn't move at all. He wasn't on the bench anymore, but a gurney.

"Dad? What's happening?"

But his dad had gone too. And the gym. A hooded figure in a white suit leaned over him, then another, their faces hidden behind shining visors. Kobi tried to kick with his legs, but they were strapped down as well. He tried to scream, but there was something down his throat. He couldn't breathe. One of the scientists stooped lower, and in his hand Kobi saw a gleaming scalpel.

No . . . please!

"Don't be afraid," said a voice. A boy's voice.

But he was afraid. He was terrified. The scalpel neared his face, and behind the mask he saw the scientist's cold, dispassionate eyes.

Oh god oh god oh god.

He felt the cold steel touch his skin, then the edge pressed down, biting . . .

Kobi opened his eyes to semidarkness and saw the shadows of the hospital ward. He wasn't sure, but he wondered if his ears were picking up the dying notes of a wolf's howl. He glanced around.

Alone.

No scientists, no scalpel.

Of course not. Everyone's gone.

His head throbbed. It wasn't like a normal headache. It felt like the inside of his skull prickled with something like a static charge, and the backs of his eyes felt hot and heavy. He threw off the blanket, breathing hard, then remembered where he was—the quarantine zone on the fifth floor of the SODO Medical Center. He'd never spent a night out of the school, and maybe he was feeling the effects. *Should have taken those vitamins . . .* he thought wryly. He reached for the flashlight on the cabinet and flicked it on. Something had changed. It took him a few seconds to realize what it was. Green threads of moss laced the inside of the door and a few shoots were coming up from the mattresses, even the one he sat on.

He'd forgotten to zip the hatch behind him. Waste spores must have found their way in. It never took long. Didn't matter though—he wasn't staying.

Kobi crossed the room, toward the window, and looked out over the dark city. Still night, but what time was it? He wondered whether the wolf was really out there, waiting, or if that howl had been part of the dream too. He killed the flashlight and stared, letting his eyes adjust, as the sweat dried on his skin.

What the heck was the dream about, anyway? The stuff with his dad was just a memory, but what about the second part—the doctors, or scientists, or whatever they were? The voice that sounded like a boy's. Some nightmare brought about by seeing the biohazard suits, maybe?

There was no way he could go back to sleep now.

He saw something outside—an arc of light shining in the darkness across the roof of a building a block away.

Kobi's whole body seemed to seize up, heart thundering, the unease from the dream immediately swept away by a roaring hope. "Dad!" he said, his breath clouding on the window.

In a moment, his excitement melted into fear. *Why is he on the roof? The Snatchers will—*

Another flashlight joined the first. Then a third.

Kobi gasped and pressed his hands against the glass.

Impossible . . .

The lights vanished, but Kobi knew he hadn't imagined it. The flashlights, the way they'd moved . . . it could only mean one thing. People. Actual *living* people. Kobi's insides felt like they were being squeezed. His dad was certain that everyone in America had been wiped out, and if other survivors existed, that they were out of reach. Trying to find them was a lost cause. Kobi had never thought his father could be wrong about anything, but he was. Entirely wrong.

Kobi tried to control himself, think rationally. If his dad were here he would tell Kobi to be wary. Stick to the rules. But what if these people could help Kobi find him?

Without another thought, Kobi grabbed the utility belt resting on the floor, fastening it hurriedly. He threw the crossbow over his shoulder and with shaking hands unfolded the map, trying to work out which building the flashlights had been coming from. Then he ran for the door.

I'm coming, Dad.

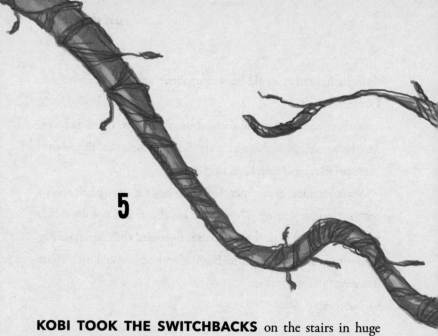

5

KOBI TOOK THE SWITCHBACKS on the stairs in huge bounds, feet slapping into the stairwells. He ran through the hospital lobby, then burst out though the door before forcing himself to slow. Night was perilous. If a Snatcher got him now, it would *not* be funny.

The flashlights hadn't been far, but he couldn't see them now. He thought about shouting, but that might alert predators, so instead he hurried along the front of the buildings, pausing every few feet to search the darkness for danger. The more he thought about it, the surer he was—there were survivors. They must have found his dad. *Why else would they be out here searching?* Maybe they'd gone back to the school and found him missing, then followed his trail here. His heart was beating so fast, and his skin felt electric. *Real survivors!* He wondered where their base could be. How many more might be living there?

He was almost at the intersection when he heard a growl and stopped dead. He saw the wolf crouched on the other side of the intersection in the doorway of a former bank. It was looking right at him, its flanks panting up and down. The arrow was still in its neck, a trail of dried blood caking its fur.

Panic flooded Kobi's veins. How could he have been so reckless! Keeping his eyes locked on the wolf, he slowly brought the crossbow around on his shoulder. The wolf's lip curled back as Kobi raised the sight. He'd have to take it down in one shot. Then the wolf stood up and padded off, and a moment later Kobi heard muffled voices.

He ran a few feet on and took shelter behind an old street stall smothered by a thornbush. Peering through the knot of branches, he couldn't believe what he was seeing. There were nine of them, five in full-on biohazard suits with headlamps, but three in simple gray outfits, their heads bare. And though he couldn't be completely sure, he was pretty convinced they were kids. Like him.

Kobi was ready to step out when he spotted the rifles hanging from the adults' shoulders. Big Hank's had been raided in the early days of the pandemic, so there'd been no guns left. Kobi wondered where these had been scavenged from. They looked kind of high-tech anyway—almost military. The adults had sleek black batons hanging from their belts too.

They were casting their arcs of light everywhere, like they weren't even worried about the Snatchers. Surely they had to know about them if they'd survived this long—so why were they being so careless? Kobi threw glances at the sky, expecting the gleam of metal at any moment. Had these people come from a place where the scanning drones didn't operate? Maybe another country. Or had they just emerged from some nuclear bunker after years underground . . . ?

The group moved slowly, carrying out a careful search. Every so often the flashlight beam would land on one of the kids, so Kobi got a good look. Two girls. Kobi could barely believe they were real, like they had walked out of one of the posters in the classrooms at Bill Gates. One of them waved, and for a second Kobi thought she had spotted him, until a figure on Kobi's left, near where the wolf had been, ran out from behind a car. It was a boy, younger that Kobi. He joined the two other kids. One girl stood out because she was the tallest. She looked of Indian descent maybe, though it was hard to tell from this distance in the dark. She stopped quite suddenly, like she sensed danger, and the others kept walking. They were heading right toward one of the sidewalk grates.

Kobi couldn't stay put. He rushed out. "Hey, watch it!"

Everyone in the group turned to face him, and five rifles lifted too. Kobi couldn't see faces behind the dark visors.

"Don't move, kid!" one shouted, then to the others: "D-One settings!"

English. They were speaking English. With American accents. Kobi blinked, backing off, lifting his crossbow over his head.

"Freeze or we'll shoot!" yelled another.

The boy looked scared, head jerking around, and he moved

toward the taller girl and one of the adults. Kobi felt pinned to the spot.

"I'm looking for my dad!" he called back.

The suited figures edged closer, their guns trained right on him. One bent his head to his lapel. Kobi didn't understand for a second, and then realized he was speaking into some kind of communication device, like in action movies Kobi had watched on the salvaged projector at Bill Gates High. "Target acquired . . ." A pause, then, "Yes, alone."

The speaker passed onto the grate.

"Get off there!" shouted Kobi. *What are they doing? Don't they know* anything?

The man looked across to his companion, then nodded. "Okay, take him down. *D-One.*"

"No, wait!" Kobi shouted. A soft *pfft* sounded, and a rifle flashed. Kobi jerked aside as a small projectile buried itself in the thornbush at his back. Somehow he'd dodged it.

Another *pfft*.

Kobi felt something stab into his leg and clutched his thigh. A dart was sticking out. He tore it loose. "Please, I'm . . ."

The grate in the pavement erupted, throwing the two adults in the air. Another fell back, trying to get away, as colossal Chokerplant vines emerged from underground. A guard on the ground fired from his back but missed, and a thick tendril snaked down and scooped him around his waist. Kobi watched in horror as the man was dragged through the gaping hole in the street, screaming. One of the leaders was snatched too, his weapon skittering away as he tried to claw free. The Chokerplants pulled him down mercilessly beneath the sidewalk.

One of the remaining adults turned and ran.

"Hey, wait!" cried the smaller girl. She had olive skin and short dark hair.

Kobi stayed back, still clutching the dart in his hand. If it was some sort of tranquilizer, it didn't seem to be having an effect on him yet. The two remaining adults were backing up, moving toward the kids, guns raised and firing at the Chokers in rhythmic bursts. One scored a hit, and the huge tentacle shrank back, tip quivering. But with a crack, another grate opened up on the other side of the strangers. Chokers came from that way too, forcing them to turn. The smaller girl screamed as the adults were swarmed by vines. One tried to run but was snatched around both knees and pulled across the asphalt into the hole. The other was caught between two plants—one had his arm, rifle dangling uselessly, the other his leg, and they lifted him into the air. For a horrible moment Kobi thought he'd be ripped in two, but the larger Choker tore him free. It held him aloft for another second or two, headlamp throwing out crazy spills of light, before wrapping him more tightly in its coils and withdrawing beneath the road.

The other kids were frozen in place as the Chokerplants emerged again, tentacles searching. It wouldn't be long before one of them found the kids—and then it would be a slaughter.

"Run!" shouted Kobi. "Come on!"

The kids began to move but headed away from him. Kobi, not knowing what else to do, ran after them. He caught up quickly—they were slower than him. The smaller, olive-skinned girl was stalling, looking back toward the hole.

"They're dead already," he yelled, grabbing her arm. She gave in and ran too.

The road trembled beneath them as they made their way up the street, and Kobi saw cracks splitting the surface. The tips of the vines were breaking through everywhere, and he realized the plant below must have been monstrously huge. "Stay behind me!" yelled the taller girl, and she led the way, slaloming between the emerging Chokers, switching direction sometimes just in time.

It's like she knows where they're coming from, thought Kobi.

A heavy vine lashed toward him, and he dropped to a skid, sliding beneath its bulk. The whole street seemed to be coming alive. Ahead of them it was worse—an entire line of plants awaited, twitching their tendril tips in anticipation of a meal.

Most of the buildings around them were absolutely coated in vegetation, but at the front of one, Kobi saw a smashed door at the top of a small flight of steps. "This way!"

The girl he was hauling along didn't resist, and the other two followed. They plunged through a curtain of greenery and found themselves in the vestibule of some sort of apartment building. The air smelled chemical and bitter, and Kobi saw a large pile of dried bird droppings next to the bottom of the stairs and more smearing the walls. *That's good. Birds wouldn't roost here if there were predators.* He pounded up the stairs first and realized the others were still waiting at the bottom.

"We need to get higher," he said. Almost on cue, the first delicate frond of a Chokerplant entered through the door behind them. The darker-skinned girl pushed past quickly, but the taller one used her body to shield the boy. Kobi led them up the first flight, then a second, then another. He wasn't sure how high Chokers could reach, but the one in the street had been massive. The taller girl was helping the boy, whose breathing was labored. As they passed the third floor, a shriek and a crack of wings made them all jump. Two huge birds, each a couple of feet tall, flapped past, scattering yellowing feathers.

At the top of the fourth set of stairs, the plant life wasn't as dense. Every wall was still covered with moss, and the stairs sprouted patches of mold, but here and there one could almost imagine what the place had once looked like before the outbreak. Pictures hung at angles from the walls, and there were dull metal numbers visible on some of the doors. The one marked *43* was open a fraction, so Kobi pushed it farther. Nothing stirred within, so he nodded to the others and led them inside.

They found themselves in a small apartment. The furniture was rotting under bushes, and massive fern leaves spilled from the kitchen. A cockroach as big as Kobi's foot scurried away into the green recesses of the bathroom. A pipe must have burst somewhere, because one of bedroom floors had caved in slightly at one end, and a musty swamp sat stagnant in the depression. Kobi found another room containing a baby's crib. The curtains were closed. Wallpaper, where it wasn't peeled away, showed an illustrated alphabet. *C*, he noted, was *cat*. Just a normal cat. Apparently people used to keep them as pets! He found himself doubting if such an animal ever really existed. Cute and cuddly, with a fluffy tail. It seemed ridiculous.

"What were those things?" said the smaller girl. She was shaking a little.

"Chokerplants," said Kobi. "Haven't you seen them before?"

She shook her head.

"Fionn?" said the tall girl. She was clutching the boy's jaw in her hand, trying to keep his head from flopping. "Fionn, snap out of it."

"I think Guardian Krenner got away," said the dark-skinned girl.

The other shook her head, looking desolate. "Even if he did— he left us, Niki." She took a deep breath, then looked hard at Kobi. "We can't stay here."

Kobi had so many questions. Who were they? Did they have a base somewhere nearby? He didn't think the grown-ups could be their parents—they looked more like soldiers. And the girl had just called one a Guardian, whatever that meant. But the questions would have to wait. "We can't go back into the street," he said. "Chokers can sense any movement. I've never seen so many in one place. If we—"

The curtains stirred, and the boy sucked in a gasp. Kobi grabbed him quickly and slid a hand over his mouth.

The tip of a Chokerplant eased silently into the room.

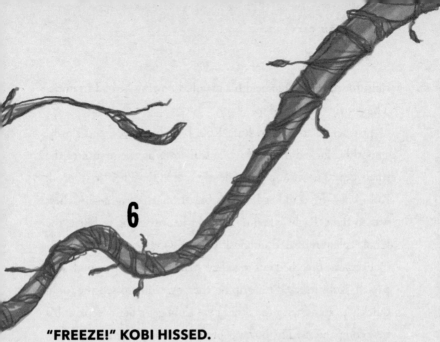

6

"FREEZE!" KOBI HISSED.

The others obeyed, backs pressed against the wall and eyes wide to the whites, as the tendril tested the air. Across its length, Kobi saw the rows of tiny serrated thorns, like teeth. It jerked suddenly, rearing higher, and the boy in front of Kobi tensed. Kobi's own skin was covered in sweat from the rush up the stairs. He just hoped that Chokers couldn't taste fear too. The boy in front of him was trembling, but everyone else's limbs were perfectly still. Kobi could see the tall girl's eyes moving toward the door.

Don't do it, he thought. *You'll never make it.*

The Chokerplant swayed back and forth, bumped into the crib, then rose. As it slipped through the window, Kobi saw it was a good foot across at the root. Easily thick enough to crush any one of them if it latched on. The tip reached the door, paused, then doubled back, clinging to the wall. Kobi realized it was coming right for his head. He held his breath, knowing he had to move. The deadly vine closed in.

Just before it reached him, Kobi bent his knees, and slowly, smoothly, ducked his head while still covering the mouth of the small boy. The vine passed silently over him. Then it stopped. Kobi knew he couldn't hold his breath much longer—his chest was so tight. Right when he thought he was going to burst, the Chokerplant retreated sinuously out the window again.

Everyone breathed out together. After a few more seconds had passed, Kobi released his grip on the boy, who crossed the room quickly to stand with the other two. Kobi got a better look at his new companions. The boy was probably about eleven, really pale, with freckles and sandy hair, but the two girls were older. The shorter, olive-skinned girl had a bob haircut, stark green-brown eyes set in a fierce expression, and a scattering of pimples across her jawbone. The tall girl was actually quite gangly, her brown skin gleaming with sweat. Her black eyes pointed slightly upward at the outer corners, and she had sharp cheekbones, with long glossy black hair. Adrenaline drained from Kobi's body, making him shaky, and, unexpectedly, his voice seemed to die in his throat.

"Do you think they're gone?" the girl with the bob whispered. *Niki, was that what her friend had called her?*

Kobi wasn't sure if she was speaking to him or not. The older girl nodded.

The boy—*Fionn*, Kobi remembered—started to cry softly.

"The other Guardians . . . ," said Niki.

"They're dead," said the other girl, clenching her jaw.

"But maybe we should—"

"They're *dead*."

Kobi watched them argue in wonder, hardly able to believe he was actually sharing the room with other people and hearing them speak. Real kids, not much different from himself. After so long thinking he and his dad were alone. What would his dad think of it?

"Who *are* you?" Kobi said, finding his voice finally.

The oldest girl flashed a look at the other two. He wasn't sure what the look meant. "My name's Asha," she said, then cocked her head toward the boy at her side. "This is Fionn."

"Niki," said the younger girl. "And you?"

"I'm . . ." Kobi hesitated. This was too weird. He'd never had to introduce himself before. Never thought he'd ever have to. "I'm Kobi," he managed. "What were you doing out there?"

Asha glanced at the others. "Looking for you."

Kobi's heart soared. That could only mean one thing. "You've found my dad?"

Asha frowned. "Your *dad*? Sorry, but I don't know anything about that. The Guardians got wind of potential survivors in the city, that's all. They brought us out here to help track them down. But you're the only one we've found."

Kobi's hopes died again. He tried to process what the girl was saying. *Outside the city. That's where they must be from.* It seemed crazy. "And the Guardians were the grown-ups with you?" asked Kobi. *Not their parents, then . . .* "The ones who . . ."

"How are we going to get back to Healhome if they're dead?" said Niki. She started to go toward the window, but Kobi pushed out an arm to stop her.

"Hey! Don't!" he cried, panicked.

She turned on him, shoving him back. As she touched his chest, Kobi felt a shock of electricity that threw him back against the wall. Blue sparks crackled between Niki's fingers. He stared. *How is that possible?* "Keep your hands to yourself," she hissed.

"Okay!" he said, raising his arms. "Just be careful by the window."

He couldn't take his eyes off her hands, and he wondered what his father would make of it. He was about to ask what Healhome was, but Asha spoke first. "I guess we need to get back to the transport. Krenner went that way."

"He left us," said Niki. "He just ran away."

The boy called Fionn hadn't spoken yet. He didn't look great at all. His eyes seemed sunken, and he looked like he needed a good meal. Kobi wondered what rations they had—the other two looked healthy.

"I doubt he made it," said Kobi.

Niki glared again, like he'd said something offensive.

"We should go to the transport," Asha repeated. "Even if Guardian Krenner didn't reach it, there must be a way to contact Healhome from the cockpit. They'll send a rescue party."

Kobi had no idea what a transport was, or Healhome. Was he

supposed to know? It sounded like some kind of medical place. But *home* sounded safe.

"We need to stay put," said Kobi. "Four people out there—it's too dangerous at night."

They all looked at him as if waiting for him to continue, to give them some instruction or offer an explanation for what was happening to them. "You weren't even being careful," he said. "What were you thinking, just walking about like that?"

"Some thanks we get," said Niki.

Kobi didn't understand. *I was the one who helped them!*

"The transport's the only way out," said Niki. "We can't just wait around here."

Out of where? thought Kobi.

Asha took a deep breath. "We hadn't walked far before we found him," she said. "I think I remember the way."

"Right," said Niki. "Let's go."

Kobi was so busy watching them talk that they were already out the door by the time he realized exactly what they were saying. He hurried after them. Did they not realize the dangers? He could picture his father screaming at him that traveling around at night in the central district was suicide. But maybe it was worth the risk to find this transport. If there were more adults from this Healhome base, they could help him find his dad.

"There'll be a back door," he said. "Less Chokers maybe."

Asha nodded grimly, then the boy groaned, clutching his

stomach. Asha ran to him. "Fionn?"

Fionn looked at her, eyes tinged with desperation.

"It's the Waste," Asha explained, an arm around Fionn's shoulder. "He suffers worse than us. The Guardians were carrying extra shots—there might be some still on the transport."

The boy was clearly ill, so there didn't seem to be a choice. Kobi wondered what their "shots" contained. And if they had a vehicle, they might have other useful tech too.

"Lead the way," said Niki.

They took the stairs, Kobi up front, with Asha and Fionn behind, and Niki at the rear. The silent boy seemed to have recovered enough to walk, but every so often he'd grimace in pain. Was he mute? Or just scared? Kobi had so many questions, but they could wait.

They reached the rear exit on the ground floor and stopped in front of it. The door was plastic, covered in mold. Thick ivy on the other side of the glass blocked any view out. Kobi thought the other kids looked unsure now.

"How often have you traveled outside?" Kobi asked.

Asha looked around at the others, and Niki glared back silently. "Never before today," said the tall girl.

"We don't need to go outside," said Niki. "Why would we want to?"

Kobi was momentarily shocked. *They've never been outside?* "Okay, I'm going to give you a crash course, then," he said. "We need to keep spaced out, single file, at least ten yards apart. Move one at a time and signal to each other when you see it's clear. Look up, down, all around you. Look again. Always be looking. Use all your senses, too. Trust your instincts." It felt odd explaining all this stuff. He was usually the one being lectured. "If in doubt, don't move. Stay as still as you can. But if a predator appears, run like you've never run in your life. Head for the nearest place you can barricade yourself in, and if there's nowhere to hide, then climb the nearest tree and wait it out. Unless it's a cougar. They can climb trees. Then, well . . ." He trailed off. Niki chewed her lip, agitated. Asha was staring at Kobi. The young boy nodded at him. He seemed the least afraid. "Stay beneath the canopy where you can," Kobi added. "Snatchers have infrared vision and heat detection. They work better at night."

"Let's just go," snapped Niki.

Kobi pulled open the door. It led into an alleyway that ran behind the apartment building. Trash cans were moss-covered lumps, and trees crossed above them, growing in and out of walls. But there were no Chokerplants.

Kobi held up his hand. "Okay, go. Now." They scurried up to the next intersection, then took turns to dart across the road to where an old railway overpass crossed. It had collapsed in the center, crushing cars beneath it. The soft undergrowth cushioned their steps.

Asha paused beside a leaning row of vine-coated streetlights, frowning as she looked up and down the road. "Which way?" she whispered to Niki.

The girl pointed south. "Up there . . . I think."

Kobi's eyes searched the trees. The sun was just beginning to come up, a faint pale haze through the canopy. Some predators preferred to hunt at dawn, so it wasn't much of a relief. With so many in the party, anything could go wrong. *Too many variables. Too many risks.*

Asha gave a signal with her hand and then began to move again. Kobi followed.

The vehicle they called the transport was sitting right in the middle of the street—it was about the size of one of the Bill Gates school buses, but it looked a lot more high-tech. Shaped like a squat bullet, it had two stubby wings extending from each side.

"That thing flies?" whispered Kobi, amazed. He wondered how anyone could have built it. Or was it scavenged from some kind of military base?

Asha went to the door and pulled at the handle. It didn't open. She pulled again.

"No, no, no!" she said.

"It's palm print–activated," exclaimed Niki in a loud exasperated voice. "What did you expect?"

"Shhh!" hissed Kobi.

"Great," said Niki. "What now?"

Fionn looked on, his eyes wide.

"Let me try," said Kobi, moving up to the door.

"It's locked," said Asha. "The Guardians are the only ones who can open it. I guess Krenner didn't make it after all."

Kobi took hold of the handle, gripping tightly.

"It's *locked*," repeated Niki.

Kobi tugged on the handle. He felt his sinews cracking as he tried to pull the door open. The metal dug into his palm, but he gritted his teeth and strained harder. *Come on. . . .*

With a shriek of metal, the handle broke away, and he fell backward into Asha.

"Well, aren't you strong!" she said. "Is that the Waste?"

"I guess so," said Kobi. He couldn't tell if she was impressed or not.

"Good for him," said Niki. "But now we're never getting inside."

Kobi had to admit she was right. He felt stupid, annoyed with himself.

"We have to wait," said Niki.

"But for how long?" said Asha. "We weren't due back for hours. By the time they realize we're in trouble and scramble another transport, then get here . . ." She trailed off, eyes flicking toward Fionn. Kobi recognized the waxy look to the pale boy's skin and the sheen of sweat. Waste exposure. His dad had looked the same way in the early stages of contamination, when the cleansers were wearing off. Fionn didn't seem afraid, though, staring around at the Waste wilderness with wonder. He'd seemed the most natural at moving through the undergrowth, and Kobi had often lost sight of him scurrying ahead. The young boy raised his hand in the air. A giant butterfly with multicolored patterns on its wings landed on his sleeve.

"Whoa," said Niki, backing away. Fionn suddenly doubled over in a fit of coughing, and the insect flapped away.

Kobi took a deep breath, thinking over the options. It really wasn't safe to linger in the city much longer, especially considering none of the others were trained to survive out there and one of the team was already suffering. He felt reluctant to leave, though. He could push on to his dad's labs—they were only a couple of hours away. But Fionn's condition would only worsen, and Kobi wanted to keep these people on his side, if they could help him find his dad. "I have anti-Waste cleansers back at my base."

"Where's that?" asked Asha.

"West of the city," said Kobi. "A few hours from here." He glanced at Fionn. The boy wouldn't be able to travel all that fast, he realized. "Depending on how quick we can move."

"No way," said Niki. "I'm staying right here and waiting for the Guardians."

Asha stepped up closer to her. "Nik, we have to stick together. Fionn might not last until the Guardians get here."

Kobi saw the other girl's jaw tighten. *She's just scared too.*

"How do we even know we can trust him?" she said, cocking her head toward Kobi.

Kobi felt a flash of annoyance. "Hey! I'm right here!" he said.

Doesn't she get it? I'd rather be looking for my dad than looking after them!

"We don't have a choice," said Asha. "Fionn needs a boost. And we can't just wait out here in the open."

Niki made a grunting noise, which Kobi understood to mean "Fine."

Asha turned to him. "Lead the way, Kobi."

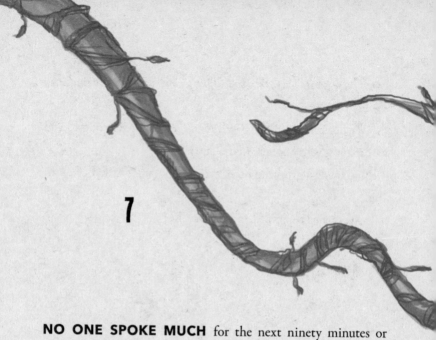

7

NO ONE SPOKE MUCH for the next ninety minutes or so, communicating only with hand signals and occasional mutterings. *This way. Stop. Go. Watch the angles.* In some ways, Kobi found it easier than using words. At least he knew he wasn't missing anything in the others' tones, or glances, or the hundred other ways the three friends could understand one another that he seemed separated from.

Sometimes Fionn would drop back behind the others, worrying Asha. But he soon reappeared, like a pale ghost in the foliage. They reached the bridge just as the sun was drifting above the giant sycamores. With every thirty feet of progress, Kobi began to calm. *We're going to make it. We're nearly home.*

By the time they made it to the other side, he felt relaxed enough to speak properly. With Asha sticking close to Fionn, he dropped back until he was next to Niki.

"You said you were looking for survivors," he said. "Why?"

"How do I know?" she said. "Trust me, I wish I'd never agreed to come."

Asha must have heard because she edged nearer with Fionn. "All the Guardians told us is that there could be people in the city," she said before pausing. "They knew we could help find them." There seemed something left unsaid, but she didn't offer anything more.

"And you're from somewhere called Healhome?" continued Kobi. "So it isn't inside the city somewhere?"

Niki laughed, like he'd said something funny. "It isn't in a Seattle high school, if that's what you mean."

"No," said Asha, giving Niki a light shove. "It's a quarantined facility."

A facility. What did that mean? He pictured a compound protected with fences and guards in masks. Or was it a group of buildings, more like a town? "And you flew here in one of those transports?"

"No, we took the bus!" said Niki. Kobi was taken aback.

"Niki, he's just curious," said Asha.

"I know, but let's save the questions. Seriously, how much farther is this base of yours?"

"Not far," said Kobi. He didn't want to irritate Niki, but he couldn't help asking, "The Guardians—if they're not your parents, who are they?"

Niki puffed out her cheeks. Asha shot her a look. "Scientists mostly," Asha said. "Some teachers. They're looking for a cure."

"And have they found one?"

"Not yet," said Asha sadly. Then she smiled. "But they will!"

Kobi smiled back. He couldn't believe it, and neither would his dad. There were others working to fight the Waste! After so long, thinking they were alone. Who knew what new breakthroughs might be just around the corner? "How many of you are there?"

"Kids?" said Asha. "Thirteen, ranging from eleven to sixteen. Guardians—I don't know—maybe ten times that."

"And you all live in Healhome? What about outside?"

"There is no outside," said Niki impatiently. "Well, there is, but it's all like this." She jerked her chin at the view, wearing a look of disgust.

"They don't let us out," said Asha. "The risk of contagion is too great."

Kobi remembered the strange disparity between the suited adults and the kids. "But you're here now, breathing the air, touching things. You must get infected."

"We're already infected," said Asha matter-of-factly. "For some reason we're noncontagious, though. The Guardians think it's because we were exposed while our mothers were pregnant. Maybe that's what happened to you too?"

Kobi nodded. "Yes! That's what my dad thinks."

"So where do you think he is now?"

Kobi paused a moment before answering. They'd reached the place where the Chokers had nearly pulled him underground after his stupid attempt at a long-jump record. "I don't know," he said.

"He went to visit his lab in the city to do tests. He's looking for a cure too."

"For himself?"

"Yes," said Kobi. "He's managed to take some of my antibodies and synthesize them to create medication. It's not one hundred percent, but it helps him. I guess he always hoped there'd be others too."

Asha seemed to be thinking hard for a moment. "You've been living out here in the Wastelands all your life? Just you and your dad?"

Kobi nodded.

"He sounds like a cool guy," Asha continued.

Kobi felt a flush of pride. "Yeah, he is. *Cool.*"

They took the longer route to bypass the Choker chasm, and soon they were passing through the trees, toward the school. Fresh plants had already sprouted from the roots and plants he'd cut away. As they went, Kobi felt his steps quicken a little and realized that he was letting a new hope creep into his head. *What if my dad's made it back while I was away?* He forced himself to slow. And as they broke through the tree line in front of the overgrown front steps, Kobi saw the padlocks were still in place on the outside of the door. His heart sank. *It was a silly thought anyway.*

"This is it?" said Niki, sounding distinctly unimpressed as Kobi stooped to unfasten the lower lock. From the corner of his eye, he saw Asha shove her and mouth something. He felt himself liking the tall girl more and more.

He twisted the key in the second padlock, then peeled away the tape. "Stay close to me," he said. "There are traps inside."

Fionn doubled up with a gasp. "We need to hurry," said Asha.

Kobi opened the door and the other two half carried the sick boy inside. Kobi hurriedly completed the door-sealing and decontaminating protocols. Asha turned and watched him with a concerned frown. Niki sighed loudly. "Really?" she said.

Kobi ignored her. He finished in a few moments, and they passed along the corridor to the fridges in the science rooms. Despite the circumstances, it felt good to be back. He noticed Niki casting her gaze about the place, but Kobi couldn't read her expression.

Kobi passed a length of rubber tubing to Asha. "Extend his right arm and tie this above his elbow." He'd administered his dad's shots a hundred times—a training precaution in case his father was ever incapable. He knew what he was doing. Asha laid out Fionn's arm and tied the ligature while Kobi went to the fridge and took out a vial of Waste cleanser, then unwrapped a syringe from a sterile package. He suctioned up the clear liquid, then pressed the excess air out. Fionn's eyes were rolling back in his head.

"Hurry!" said Asha.

"Are you sure this will work?" asked Niki suspiciously.

"I hope so," said Kobi. He located a blue vein and concentrated, with his tongue between his teeth. Fionn didn't react as the needle pierced his skin. Kobi pressed home the syringe's plunger.

The effect was almost instantaneous. Fionn blinked rapidly and sat up with a deep breath. His eyes were alert, and color rushed into his cheeks. He seemed a little unsure where he was at first but offered a shy smile when his eyes landed on Asha. Kobi smiled and felt a small pang of jealousy. Fionn and Asha seemed almost like brother and sister. Niki nodded with a kind of begrudging satisfaction.

"You did it!" said Asha.

Kobi breathed a long sigh of relief. But his dad's voice kicked in almost at once.

"Follow the protocols, Kobi. No slacking."

"We need to decontaminate before we head out again," he said. "We'll all be carrying Waste spores on our clothes. We can refuel and have a bit of a rest."

Fionn stood up a little shakily.

"Where's the decon chamber?" said Niki.

"School showers are fourth door down on the left, in the changing rooms," said Kobi.

"And the girls?" said Asha.

Kobi frowned, confused.

"The girls' changing rooms?" said Niki.

"Oh, I never . . . erm . . ."

"We'll find them," said Asha. "Don't worry."

Niki rolled her eyes.

"I'll get some bags to seal your clothes for the laundry," said Kobi, trying not to get angry. "There's all kinds of stuff in the lost and found. Something will fit."

"Great!" said Niki, sounding like she couldn't have meant it less.

As he showered, Kobi couldn't help his thoughts carrying him away. *Survivors.* His dad had always told him the chances of ever coming into contact with any, even if they walked a thousand miles, or crossed the ocean, were close to zero, but here they were. Flesh and blood. At least, he thought they were. After his strange dream in the hospital, what if this was just his mind playing tricks as well? Maybe he'd wake up and be back in the empty school. It felt a bit dumb, but he closed his eyes and said to himself, *Wake up.*

Nope. Still here. Still real.

And they weren't any old survivors. Not just desperate people toughing it out like him and his dad. They seemed organized. Comfortable, by the sounds of it. They had technology and transports, medical care and proper research in this place they called Healhome. Surely they could help him track down his father. And what then? Life would change completely, without a doubt. Food, safety, medicine for his dad. Asha seemed nice, and Fionn too, even if he didn't speak. Niki wasn't very friendly, but two out of three wasn't bad. And anyway, she was probably just scared, her first time away from the quarantine facility.

Kobi dried himself, changed into clean clothes, and was waiting in the corridor as the others emerged. Asha had managed to find a Bill Gates sports uniform of blue shorts and a white T-shirt, plus some tennis shoes, while Fionn had gone for cargo shorts and a shirt that hung practically down to his knees. He wore high-tops with the laces hanging out. Of the three of them, Niki seemed to have done best—with a pair of jeans, a cheerleading jacket, and sneakers.

"You hungry?" he asked them.

"Sure!" said Asha.

"Then follow me," said Kobi.

The newcomers gazed around in wonder as he led them through the school, past the huge cafeteria, the music rooms, and the library. He guessed they'd never been in one before. He and his dad had always slept in the old gym—they'd moved some beds from the nurse's office, and there were two comfy couches to relax on and a camping stove for cooking. Old mats were spread across the floor, providing some insulation.

The cabinets were pretty empty—especially after his last aborted forage. He thought about more Barkz, but he could just imagine Niki's face, so instead he went to the special-occasion cabinet, taking out two large cans of sausages and baked beans. He figured that soon food wouldn't be an issue anyway. Healhome—wherever it was—must have enough food to support all the kids and adults there. Asha and Niki didn't look malnourished.

"Take a seat," he said as he poured the cans into a pan on the camp stove. He lit the gas with a flint and steel, and soon mouthwatering smells filled the room. Fionn nudged Kobi, smiling. The young boy raised his hands and made a shape with them. On the back wall of the gym a shadow butterfly fluttered in the glow from the gas fire.

Kobi grinned. "That's nothing." He raised his own hands, making the shape of a lynx, forming the creature's long ears by extending his thumbs.

"No one's impressed," said Niki. She turned away, and as she did so, Fionn caught Kobi's eye, placing his palms together, the fingers forming a snout, and the space underneath the thumb making an eye. A wolf. Fionn made the shadow wolf bite down on Niki's head. Asha and Kobi stifled laughs.

Niki turned around, frowning. "Honestly, you guys are such babies, laughing at shadow puppets."

"Hey, do you mind if we look around?" asked Asha.

Kobi frowned. "Of course. Help yourselves. Just don't touch any of the window or door seals."

Niki remained flopped on the sofa, but Fionn went straight to a set of shelves that Kobi used for his books and old comics. He started taking them out and staring at the pages in wonder.

"Don't you have books at your place?" Kobi asked Asha, who was looking at one of the medical posters still tacked to the wall.

"Not many," she said.

"There's a whole library here," said Kobi as he stirred the beans.

"Shame we won't be staying long enough to enjoy it," muttered Niki. "Do you have any sort of radio transmitter? We need to get in touch with the Guardians."

"Just a receiver," said Kobi. They'd used it to pick up

electromagnetic disturbance emitted by Snatchers rather than any distress calls. He stirred the beans again, ignoring Niki as she rolled her eyes and made a huffing sound. It did make Kobi wonder: Why hadn't his dad ever tried to contact anyone with some kind of radio? If they could receive radio frequencies, why couldn't they send them out? Who knows, Kobi and his dad might have met up with these Guardians years ago. He pushed the thought from his mind. What was done was done. "We shouldn't leave it more than an hour before we head back to the transport. There are tools we could use to break open the door."

"Go out there again?" said Niki. "No way. The Guardians will find us here. We can create a smoke signal or something. Anyway, I'm exhausted. I've been up all night."

"A smoke signal wouldn't be a good idea," said Kobi.

"They'll be out there looking for us soon," said Asha. "We need to stay near the transport."

Kobi spooned out the beans and sausages onto four plates and handed them out with forks.

"Thank you," said Asha.

Fionn nodded and smiled, and began to eat at once, gasping as he shoveled the food into his mouth.

"Careful!" said Kobi. "They're hot."

Niki looked at the plate doubtfully. "What is it?" she said.

"Just eat it, Nik," said Asha. "Or I will!"

Kobi forced himself to take his time, savoring every mouthful, but it was still over far too soon.

"I have some hot chocolate too," he said.

"What's chocolate?" asked Asha.

Kobi stared at her in disbelief. "Seriously? You've never had chocolate?"

Asha shook her head.

"So what do you eat in Healhome?" asked Kobi.

"We're self-sufficient," cut in Niki. 'The Guardians take care of our diet with a mixture of synthetic protein and vitamins, supplements, plus vegetables grown at the facility."

"Right," said Kobi. "Well, wait until you try Chocoholic."

As he waited for the water to boil to mix the drinks, he tried to find out more about the place they called Healhome. Apparently it was built in an old military skyscraper, with many floors dedicated to a different aspect of survival in the Wastelands—Waste research, living quarters, food production, technology, transport.

"Healhome is totally quarantined," Niki finished explaining. "*Totally.*" Her gaze swept slowly around the hall. "There are decontaminated chambers with vacuum suction pipes, herbicide baths for haz suits, guards who protect us twenty-four-seven, computerized perimeter guns, all that kind of stuff. Guess it's what you'd expect from scientists and ex-military." She squinted as she inspected the school gym, as if she might suddenly uncover a secret platoon of guards or robotic sentry guns that she'd missed. "This place must be *teeming* with Waste."

Kobi was too absorbed by Niki's description of Healhome to rise to her obvious goading. "We have our protocols," Kobi said.

"We tape the doors, and the vents. We shower—"

"Oh yes, the showers!" said Niki. "That's totally foolproof."

Kobi's hand tensed on the kettle and water spilled over the side of one of the cups. He put down the kettle.

"I risked my life to save you from the Chokers," he said. "I invited you back here to look after Fionn when I needed to go find my dad. The least you could do is be nice."

Asha tensed, Fionn looked alarmed, but Niki just glared for a moment. Then her eyes softened.

"I'm sorry," she said, as if suddenly tired. "This is strange for us. The mission was just to locate survivors. We never expected any of"—she waved her hand around the room—"any of this."

Kobi wiped up the spilled water. "It's okay," he said. "It's weird for me too. My dad and I thought it would always just be us. I guess he didn't want to give us false hope." He handed around the steaming mugs. "But I don't get it. Why bring *you* out here to find us? No offense, but you're just kids."

"No offense taken," said Niki. "But we're not normal kids. And you're not either. We saw what you did to the handle of the transport door. What else can you do?"

"What do you mean?" asked Kobi.

"What other abilities do you have?" asked Asha. She sipped the hot chocolate. "This stuff is amazing, by the way!"

Kobi shrugged, a little embarrassed. "I can jump long distances, run fast. I heal quickly. I bench press four hun—"

"I mean besides strength and enhanced regeneration," said

Asha. "Those are baseline abilities. We all have those, at least to some degree. Maybe not as much as you, but do you have any specialty?"

"Oh," said Kobi. "I don't know. That's it, I guess." He recalled the shock Niki had given him. "The thing with the electricity—is that a specialty? Because of the Waste?"

Niki nodded, then reached across toward Fionn. She wiggled her fingers, and Fionn's hair fluttered up to stand on end. The young boy giggled. "I can create and pick up electrical signals," said Niki. "The Waste changed my nerve endings. The Guardians thought that if survivors were using an electrical device, I'd be able to sense it."

"What about Fionn?" Kobi asked Asha.

"He's a Projector," replied the tall girl, taking a sip of her drink. "Seriously, we need to tell the Guardians to get some of this stuff."

"They'll never go for it," said Niki.

"Fionn's able to transmit his brain waves to other organisms that have been affected by Waste contamination," said Asha. "If the connection's good, he can communicate. Manipulate, even. We thought he might be able to talk to survivors from a distance."

Kobi stared at the young boy, who smiled back. If he was trying to communicate now, Kobi couldn't sense it. Then he remembered the voice he'd heard in his dream at the medical center—a boy's voice. In all the terror, it had been the one comforting sound. Could that have been Fionn? He thought of the odd, prickling headache he felt as he woke. Recently, he'd been having other headaches like that. Maybe that was Fionn trying to contact him from afar . . .

"And you?" he asked Asha.

"I'm a Receptor," said the older girl. "A sort of empath. I can sense the presence of organisms that have been contaminated with Waste. It means I can kind of understand Fionn, because he sends his thoughts to me."

"She's a mind reader!" said Niki.

"Not really," Asha protested. "Most of the time, it's more like getting vague emotions."

Kobi grinned. "Can you tell what I'm thinking now?"

Asha cocked her head. "I don't need to. You're thinking you'd like to be able to do this too. But trust me—it's not that great."

"And the Guardians thought you could find me?" said Kobi.

"I did find you," said Asha. "That's why we were in the vicinity."

A thought leaped into Kobi's head. "So you could use your powers to sense my dad too!"

"I could," said Asha. "But I didn't pick anything up when we were in the city."

"Oh," said Kobi.

"That doesn't mean he's not there," added Asha quickly. "I sense all Waste-infected organic material, flora and fauna, so sometimes it's confusing."

Kobi tried to put on a smile. He knew that with every moment that went by, his father would be growing weaker. But with the four of them, and maybe the Guardians too, they had a great chance of tracking his dad.

"So have the other kids all got powers too?"

"The ones who survived," said Niki, her tone blank.

Kobi felt the mood in the room darkening. Asha spoke quietly. "We came to Healhome over a period of about three years, all babies. All Waste-infected and potentially contagious. They give us the cleansers to try to wipe the Waste from our bodies, but they aren't completely effective." Kobi noticed Asha called the drugs used by the Guardians cleansers—just like Kobi and his dad. *Must be a coincidence.* "Some died pretty quickly," Asha continued. "The rest of us are still alive, but our conditions are getting worse. The cleansers don't completely destroy Waste from our systems, and nothing can heal the damage Waste does each time." Her eyes took on a sorrowful sheen, and Kobi realized what she was saying.

They're all living under a death sentence. That's why the Guardians keep them so tightly quarantined. And why they only get fed healthy food.

"I have plenty of Waste cleansers here," he said. "They last six days max on my dad, depending on how exposed he is to Waste, but if you're already resistant, they'll probably work even better for you."

"Thank you," said Asha. Fionn jerked his head. "Fionn says he feels better than ever, by the way. Your dad is obviously an amazing scientist."

Kobi blushed. "He is." He wondered if any of his visitors knew anything about their parents, but he guessed not, if they'd been at Healhome since they were babies.

"You said the drugs would *probably* work better for us," said Niki. "Does that mean they do for you?"

"I don't take them," said Kobi. "I'm immune."

Their faces all jerked toward him.

"Very funny," said Niki.

"I'm serious," said Kobi.

"Completely?" said Asha. "So you don't take any medication?"

Kobi nodded. "Only some vitamin pills because our diet's not great. Dad's paranoid about me getting sick. But I stopped taking those not long after he left. Seemed pointless."

"But how is that possible?" said Niki. "No one's immune."

Kobi shrugged. "That's why my dad goes to his labs. He runs tests on my blood samples, looking for a cure."

"I guess that explains why the Guardians' dart didn't bring you down," said Asha. She pointed to the rifle leaning up against a wall. "The compound reacts with Waste-contaminated cells in the nervous system. They only had it on the lowest setting, D-One, but it should have been enough to bring down a person."

"But you *must* be infected," said Niki. "Your enhanced strength and speed . . ."

"Dad says my mom became infected while she was pregnant with me, that's all. She had me just in time, before she . . . well, y'know."

"I'm sorry," said Asha, lowering her gaze.

"It's okay," said Kobi. "I never knew her. It was harder for him, I think."

"We need to get you back to the Guardians," said Asha. "They're going to go nuts when they hear about this."

"I need to find my dad, though," he said.

"So you keep saying," said Niki. "How do you even know he's still alive?"

"Nik!" cried Asha, shocked. She turned to Kobi and smiled. "With the Guardians' help, we'll track him down in no time," she said.

"I'm not moving," said Niki. "They'll find us here eventually. We'll find a way to make a signal. Anyway, we can't go outside. You saw what those plants did."

"I know how to avoid the Chokers," added Kobi.

Asha nodded. "And we'll be prepared this time." She picked up the rifle and cracked out the magazine. "Seven rounds left."

"Can I see?" asked Kobi.

Asha paused, shared a glance with Kobi, then said, "Sure."

She flicked the safety and handed the weapon over. Kobi's dad had sometimes carried a hunting rifle, but he didn't like to use it because of the noise. "We normally just use crossbows," he muttered. The dart rifle looked like much more advanced tech—it was made of some sort of hard resin rather than metal, lightweight and sleek. There was a dimmed digital display on the back. It was only as he turned it over to hand it back that he noticed raised letters on the stock, black as well, and almost invisible. He almost dropped it, blood draining from his face.

The letters, in a familiar font, read *CLAWS*.

"What's the matter?" asked Asha.

Kobi stood up, backing toward the door. That didn't make any sense. CLAWS—just like the Snatcher.

"Hey, give that back!" said Niki, climbing off the couch menacingly.

Kobi fiddled, fingers awkward, and took off the safety, pointing the gun at the younger girl.

"Whoa!" said Asha. "Kobi, what are you doing?"

"Who are you?" he asked.

8

"WE TOLD YOU," SAID Asha. She moved, but only to position herself in front of Fionn, who was trembling. "We're from Healhome."

"You're from CLAWS!" said Kobi.

"Just put it down!" Niki shouted.

Kobi stood in the doorframe, trying to think. If they wanted to take him, they could have done it at any time. But why did their gun have the same manufacturer as the Snatchers? Looking at the stock, he saw there was some sort of dial, ranging from one to nine. It must control the dose of the toxin.

"Please, Kobi," said Asha. "We're on your side."

Kobi wasn't sure of anything, but he believed Asha was telling the truth. He lowered the gun.

"What's your problem?" said Niki, breathing a sigh.

Kobi turned the stock around and ran his finger along the

raised print. "CLAWS," he said. "They're the ones who made the Snatchers. We thought they were long gone."

"What are these Snatchers?" asked Asha.

Did she really not know? Seeing the confusion in her eyes, and the fear on the faces of the others, he felt suddenly foolish brandishing a gun at them. They weren't Waste cougars. They were people. Kids, like him. They were all just trying to survive.

He turned. "Follow me," he said.

In the woodwork room, they stood in front of the hunched metal creature. "*That's* a Snatcher," he said.

Niki took a step back, and Fionn even scurried behind Asha.

"They patrol the sky over the city," Kobi continued. "They're kill drones, taking any Waste-infected creatures for extermination. My dad deactivated this one."

Asha approached closer, inspecting the letters on the Snatcher's carapace. There was no doubt—even the lettering was the same as on the gun. "Who told you that?" she asked.

"I've *seen* it happen," said Kobi. "Yesterday, one took an infected wolf right in front of me."

Asha circled the drone. "And you saw it kill the wolf?"

"Well, no," said Kobi. She didn't sound at all convinced. "But . . ."

"So how do you know that's what it's for?" said Niki. "It's probably just designed to pick up organic material for testing."

Kobi paused, suddenly feeling like a little kid. Did she have to be so condescending? The blood was rising in his cheeks. "My dad told me. He was terrified of them." He walked over to the Snatcher and lifted up the end of one of its legs. It was hooked in a vicious steel claw, razor-sharp. "Doesn't look so friendly to me. Oh, and there's their sting too." From underneath the carapace he pulled out an extendable metal rod, which ended in a long needle the size of Kobi's forearm. "I've seen it use this. The animals look pretty dead afterward."

Silence fell for a few seconds. Kobi's grip was sweaty on the gun.

"How come we didn't know about these things?" Asha asked Fionn and Niki. Fionn's face was grim, and he looked at Asha, and Kobi wondered if he'd sent her a message telepathically. She looked unsure.

"Oh, come on," said Niki. "So what if the Guardians don't tell us stuff. We're just kids. We need to focus on getting healthy."

Asha looked at Fionn again, and he was shaking his head slowly. "I don't know what they're for," said Asha, "but CLAWS isn't evil. They're not killers. It's the opposite. I think your dad might have been wrong."

Kobi shook his head. *Dad is never wrong, about anything. He can't afford to be.*

. . . Except about there being survivors close by.

Doubt began to creep into Kobi's mind. But no, he had to trust his dad over these kids. The Guardians had shot at him with their dart guns, when Kobi had only been trying to talk with them. He was just glad he hadn't been captured. He'd probably be a prisoner in this Healhome place now as well.

"Can't you see he's brainwashed?" said Niki. "We'd be safer out there!"

"Shut up!" said Kobi. Without really thinking, he jerked the rifle toward her.

"Hey!" said Asha. "Be careful, Kobi."

He realized, whatever the truth was, that he shouldn't be acting like this. They hadn't tried to hurt him once, even though they'd had plenty of opportunity. He pointed the gun at the floor instead.

"Psycho," muttered Niki.

"CLAWS is just the developer of the tech or something," said Asha, though she didn't sound all that certain. "They *run* Healhome. It's nothing sinister."

"But . . ."

"They're good people, Kobi. They look after us." Although she'd directed what she said at Kobi, her gaze was locked on Fionn. The young boy's expression was stony. Kobi got the impression that Fionn didn't have such a high opinion of the Guardians as the others.

"My money says these Snatchers are our ticket out of here," said Niki. "I mean, they're probably linked up to Healhome, right?" She moved closer to the metal contraption. "I bet these eyes are cameras. . . ."

"Please, don't touch it," said Kobi a little desperately. "It's deactivated, but . . ."

"It's just a drone," said Niki. "There's no need to wet your pants."

"Niki, give him a break," said Asha.

Niki sighed and backed off. "It's a miracle he's survived this long," she said. "I'm just trying to get us home alive."

"This *is* my home," said Kobi. "I was raised here. It was always just me and my dad. I can't leave, not until I find him. And I don't think I want the Guardians' help anymore. Look, I appreciate you looking for me, but I never asked for any of it. You say this Healhome place is safe, but . . . at least here we can do what we want. And we *are* safe. We have protocols! And I've only just met you." He backed away, overwhelmed by it all. "I can help you get back to the transport, but I'm not turning myself in."

Niki was staring at him with something close to contempt, but Asha offered a small sympathetic smile. "Fionn, can you show him?" she asked.

"Show me what?" said Kobi.

"Healhome," said Asha. "You don't have to take our word for it."

The boy hesitated a moment, as though afraid.

"It won't hurt," urged Asha.

Kobi placed the gun on a table, and Fionn approached. His face had paled, the freckles standing out over his thin cheeks. He turned and looked at Asha again, and she said, "You can do it, Fionn. Show him." He put out a hand toward Kobi's head.

"Close your eyes," said Asha. "It might feel a bit weird."

Kobi was lost. He didn't know who to trust or what to believe. But he couldn't see how this small, scared boy could possibly be planning to harm him. Asha smiled again, reassuringly. Kobi let his eyelids drop. Then he felt Fionn's fingers touch his temple. No one had really touched him like that, so deliberately, before.

Slowly lights began to intrude from the perimeter of his vision. Then the scene cleared, and he saw what looked like a game taking place, with kids and grown-ups—twenty or more—tossing a Frisbee between them. It was in some sort of hall. All the kids wore the same gray uniforms, and the adults were dressed in a variety of different color tunics. He saw Asha leaping up and snatching the Frisbee from the air, heard cheering. He noticed Niki too, looking bored, chatting to another boy, tall and lean like a rock climber, with hair falling over one side of his face. Kobi was amazed at what he was seeing. And then he saw Fionn himself, waiting in a corner by the sidelines. He looked isolated. The shouts of the players dimmed, and Kobi could sense an emotion building. One of fear, anger. And then the Fionn in the vision looked up and seemed to meet Kobi's eye. The vision faded.

Kobi opened his eyes and saw Fionn had retracted his hand.

"That was . . . amazing," he said.

"Fionn's powers are unique," said Asha. But the young boy didn't seem to hear. He turned away.

Kobi stared after him. "I was talking about that place. Was it Healhome?"

Asha nodded.

"And those people—they were the Guardians?"

"We told you—they look after us," said Niki.

Kobi had a dull pain emanating right from the spot Fionn had touched, and massaged it. His brow felt hot, and the edges of his head felt like they were prickling with static. It must have been Fionn's emotions he had felt in the vision. Why was the boy angry and scared? Was he trying to tell Kobi something in the vision?

"What's wrong?" said Asha.

"I've got a headache," said Kobi. "I think it's from the telepathy. I've been having pain in my head since Dad left. I think it might have been Fionn trying to contact me."

"I've never heard of anyone getting a headache from telepathic messaging," said Asha. "And your dad left awhile ago, right? We only got dropped in yesterday."

"Oh," said Kobi.

Niki crossed to the other corner of the room, where a fire door led out to the school grounds. She started tearing at the sealant tape.

"Hey, what are you doing?" called Kobi, rushing after her. The others followed more slowly.

Niki shoved the door's bar open, and light spilled into the classroom. Light, and millions of invisible Waste spores. Kobi could almost see them flooding inside, filling every corner of the room as quickly as the despair filling him. Years of care and caution literally out the window.

"I'm going home!" she said. "I don't care if you want to stay. Can't you see—those things, the 'Snatchers' or whatever you call them, they're our ticket out of here." She stepped outside, waving her arms and shouting at the sky, "Hey, come and get me!"

Kobi seized one of her arms and tugged. "Don't! Get inside!"

Niki tried to struggle free, but Kobi was stronger. He manhandled her back into the classroom. "You're going to get us all killed!" he said.

They both fell onto the floor, just inside the open door. All Kobi could think of was the Waste taking hold, breaking through the school's defenses like an unstoppable army.

"Let me go!" screamed Niki.

The next moment, Kobi felt a painful jolt down his left side, making him spasm. He rolled away, crying out. At first he couldn't tell what had happened—he just knew he couldn't move at all. His muscles weren't listening. Then he saw the sparks across Niki's fingers. Asha knelt at his side. "Are you okay, Kobi?"

"Close the door," mumbled Kobi weakly. "Please . . ."

Niki stood up, scowling. "He's crazy," she said.

"Let's all just calm down," said Asha. "Fionn, close the door."

The silent boy hurried over and pulled the door shut. Kobi wondered what level of contamination might already have occurred. He still felt woozy but managed to sit up.

"You don't understand," he said.

"And *you're* just being paranoid," said Niki. Kobi noticed she had tears in her eyes. "Not everything and everybody are out to get you. The Guardians . . ."

"Wait!" said Asha, head jerking up, hyperaware. "I sense some—"

A low growl cut her off.

"What was that?" said Niki.

Through the classroom blinds, Kobi could see a shadow—a *huge* shadow—moving alongside the window. Kobi gripped Asha's arm, and she helped him to stand. Adrenaline pounded through his body, giving a bit more life to his limp right side. He put his fingers to his lips, but the others didn't need telling. All their eyes were fixed on the creature prowling outside. Then the shadow vanished.

After a few seconds, Niki whispered, "I think it's gone."

With a crash, the door shook as something slammed into it from the other side. They all jumped.

Fionn backed away quickly.

"It's trying to get in," said Asha.

"We have to go," Kobi said. He stumbled with the others toward the classroom door.

SMASH! The fire door broke free of its upper hinges, and on the other side Kobi saw shaggy gray fur and a single yellow eye. "Wolf!" he shouted. "Go!"

Their shoes slapped and squeaked down the central hallway as they ran. Kobi was limping, his muscles along his left side stubbornly refusing to fire after Niki's shock. At the junction of corridors he looked back to see the wolf prowl from the classroom too. It paused, breathing labored, about a hundred feet away.

A crossbow bolt was jutting from his foreleg. It was the same creature Kobi had encountered in the city. *It must have tracked us here. And then Niki got its attention.*

"The dart gun's still in the classroom," whispered Asha.

The wolf's head hung low, tongue lolling. It took a short pace toward them.

Kobi glanced right. "There are more weapons in the front office," he said. But even if they ran that way, they didn't stand a chance. The crossbows and hunting daggers were in a cupboard. The wolf would easily close the distance before they could get prepared. If they took a left, he knew they could at least get to the main hall—maybe barricade the doors with a table. *Buy some time.*

"Fionn, stop!" hissed Niki.

Kobi's heart almost stopped as he saw that the young boy, against all logic, was edging slowly past him. Not away from the wolf, but toward it.

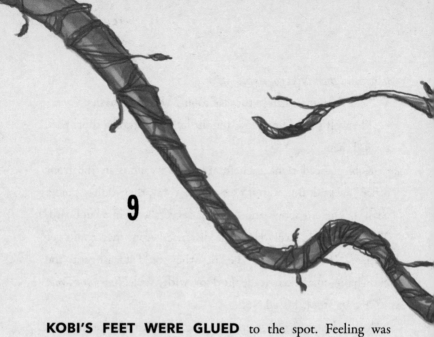

9

KOBI'S FEET WERE GLUED to the spot. Feeling was returning in spiky tingles to his arm and leg. Fionn, he saw, was visibly trembling as he crept along the corridor. *What's he doing? He's going to be ripped apart.*

"Come back, Fionn," said Niki, her voice choked with terror.

Fionn either didn't hear or did and ignored the advice. The wolf's lips curled back, and it snarled again, eyes narrowing.

It's going to pounce, thought Kobi. *It's going to kill him.*

He looked back toward the office. If he went now, while the wolf was distracted, he could probably get a weapon in time to save the others.

"Wait," said Asha, eyes glued to her friend. "Fionn knows what he's doing."

Does he?

The distance between the boy and wolf was down to twenty

yards, then fifteen. Kobi's breath caught in his throat as the wolf moved too, closing the space between them further. He could hardly bear to look but couldn't look away either. At any moment, he expected the massive predator to launch and fasten its teeth onto Fionn's neck. But when they were ten yards apart, the wolf's ears rose from their flattened position, and its tail drooped.

"It's in pain," said Asha, frowning. "It's scared too. I can sense it."

Fionn stopped, looking tiny in the middle of the corridor. His legs were still shaking. The wolf padded right up to him, lifted its muzzle, and sniffed at the boy's face. Fionn flinched, then lifted a pale hand and laid it gently on the side of the wolf's head. Kobi couldn't believe what he was seeing.

"He's projecting a soothing emotion," said Asha quietly. "Telling the wolf we're not a threat—that we can help."

"This is crazy," whispered Niki.

For once, Kobi agreed with her. It was *insane.*

But it was really happening. The wolf yawned, revealing rows of jagged teeth, then its hind legs folded underneath it and it lay down in front of Fionn.

"No sudden moves," said Asha. "Fionn's calming it down. He's telling it we have food." She threw Kobi a sideways look. "You do have some food, don't you?"

Kobi nodded. He knew exactly what they could use. "Wait here."

Walking as steadily as he could, he headed back toward the

kitchen and fished out several cans of Barkz, emptying two into a large dish. He grabbed some antiseptic spray too, then rushed back. When he arrived, Asha and Niki were closer to the wolf, though still not as close as Fionn, who was sitting on the floor, right beside it. Practically *leaning* on it! Kobi slowed his steps, and walked over. *If they can do it, so can I . . .*

Asha smiled. "Can you take out the arrow?" she asked.

Kobi laid down the dog food beside the wolf's head, and it began to eat at once, gulping everything down in a matter of seconds. He inspected the arrow. The shaft was barbed, he knew, but if he twisted the rear end, the barbs would retract and he could pull it out easily.

Which was all fine, *in theory.*.

With his instincts screaming at him not to, he reached for the bolt. As soon as his fingers touched it, the wolf's head jerked around and growled at him, releasing a blast of terrible, fetid breath. Kobi backed off.

"It's all right," he said, wondering if the creature could understand. "Good doggy," he tried.

Fionn stroked the wolf's ears, and it seemed to relax again. The quiet boy was looking at Asha meaningfully.

"Go on," said the older girl. "He's telling the wolf you're a friend."

Friends with a Waste-infected wolf . . . , thought Kobi. His dad would never believe it possible.

He touched the shaft again, holding it firmly in his left hand.

This time the wolf didn't move, though it kept one yellow eye fixed warily on him. Kobi twisted the end of the bolt with his right hand, then applied force as gently as he could, easing the arrow from the flesh. Thankfully it came out without too much pressure. He handed it back to Niki, then sprayed plenty of the antiseptic over the wound.

The wolf laid out a paw and nudged the food bowl.

"He wants more," said Asha.

Kobi nodded and began to open another can.

"It can't stay here," said Niki. "What if it brings others, or decides it's still hungry? Put the food outside."

Good idea.

Kobi picked up the bowl and held it out toward the wolf. "Come on. Follow me?"

It seemed to understand, and rose to its full height on four paws. Kobi went back into the classroom and crossed to the broken door. Quickly checking the coast was clear, he carried the bowl outside, and laid it on the asphalt basketball court, well away from the school buildings. The wolf actually waited patiently while he emptied two more cans, then lumbered forward, shouldering Kobi aside with its bulk. As it fell to eating, Kobi jogged back toward the classroom.

"We should block the door," he said. "Niki, the janitor's closet is three doors down the hall. There's a drill and a toolbox. Bring it here."

Niki didn't object and hurried off. While he and Asha lifted the door back into place, he watched the wolf finishing up. It might not be a threat now, but that didn't mean it wouldn't turn on them later. They couldn't afford to have it roaming the school—aside from the obvious danger, its fur was probably covered in Waste spores.

Niki soon returned, and, between them, they nailed the door upright, then reinforced it with a board fixed across the base, and another farther up. If the wolf really wanted to break in again, it might be able to, but hopefully it would just move on.

When they were done, Kobi led the others out, gathering the Waste-cleanser syringes from the fridge. They'd last for several days out of cold storage. Asha took the dart rifle and looped the strap over her shoulder.

"Just to be on the safe side," she said.

Kobi closed the classroom door, then applied lots of sealing tape to the frame. The classroom itself was lost, and he already dreaded the battle to keep the rest of the school Waste-free. Fionn was watching the whole thing unfold, staring wide-eyed.

"Fionn, that was incredibly brave," Asha said, hugging the boy close.

"Yeah, and incredibly dumb!" said Niki, but she was grinning.

Kobi wanted to join the moment of triumph. In the end, he couldn't work out quite what to do, and then it was too late. "You saved all of our lives," he said. "Thank you."

Fionn himself could barely look at them. There were tears in his eyes, and he looked younger than ever, and lost, like the boy Kobi had seen in the vision. *Maybe he was scared after all*, Kobi thought. But it was more than that. If anything, he seemed ashamed.

"So what now?" asked Niki.

Kobi looked at the seal on the door again. When his dad did get back, he wouldn't be impressed. "I've got some work to do. We have security protocols to follow. You could help if you want."

"Sure," said Asha.

"What about getting back to the Guardians?" asked Niki.

"Because your last plan worked so well," muttered Asha.

"There must be a way to get a message out somehow," said Niki.

Kobi shook his head. "Look, I need to find my dad," he said. "At noon, I'm going out." He gave Niki a hard stare. "I can help you get to the Guardians, but I'm not coming with them." He looked at Asha, who nodded briskly. "There are blankets down in the nurse's office," he said, "Make yourselves at home and try to get an hour's sleep—it might be a while before we can get any more, and Dad thinks it helps recharge my abilities, so I'm guessing it's the same for you. One hour. Then we go."

"Kobi, help me!"

His dad's voice.

Kobi was running through the city, jumping roots and swinging under branches with ease. His feet almost seemed to float over the foliage, and nothing could slow him down. He wasn't even worried about predators or Snatchers. He just had to find his dad.

"Help!"

Ahead he saw a split in the road. A crack. He slowed his gliding steps and crept toward the edge. There was something there—a single shoe. Dad's shoe.

Kneeling, he picked it up, fear clouding his heart and making his head pound. What did it mean? Had his dad fallen in? He took the flashlight from his backpack and shined it over the edge. His dad stood on a ledge about seven feet down. He looked unhurt. He looked healthy, and in the back of his mind Kobi knew that was impossible. Not after nearly three weeks of being out in the city, alone, without his medication.

"Kobi, thank goodness. Get me out of here!"

Kobi lay on his stomach and reached over the edge. His dad clawed up, and their fingers met, locking onto each other. Their gazes connected. Kobi smiled. Started to lift.

Two things happened at once. Beyond his father, in the depths of broken asphalt and earth, something moved. At the same time, his dad's eyes widened in horror. Kobi saw the barbed tendril of a Choker looping around his waist. Suddenly his dad was twice as heavy.

"Kobi, pull!" said his dad.

Kobi heaved, arm straining. Shoulder straining. His dad's face became a grimace.

"No," he said, voice strangled. "No, Kobi!"

Their hands slipped a fraction, sweat loosening their grips.

"Hold on!" he cried.

His dad's face twisted with fear. "Don't let me go, Son. Please. Don't let me go."

But Kobi knew he couldn't hold on. Their fingers slowly, surely slid apart, and Kobi felt his hope turn to despair with every inch of grip he lost, as the weight on his arm grew, and grew, and...

... and then it was gone. His dad didn't say a word as he plummeted into the abyss.

Kobi screamed into the darkness.

He woke, bolting upright, drenched in sweat, and beside him a shadow sat up too.

"Kobi?" said Asha.

Kobi's chest was heaving. "Dad..." he mumbled.

"It's all right. You're safe," said Asha. Kobi couldn't make out her features in the dim light, but she reached out and touched his shoulder. His breathing slowly calmed.

"It was just a bad dream," continued Asha. "If your dad's survived this long, he'd never get caught by one of those plants."

Kobi frowned. "How could you know that?"

Asha let go of his shoulder. "I told you—I'm a Receptor. Sleep thoughts are more emotionally charged than waking ones. Less interference."

Kobi wasn't sure he liked the idea of her looking so deeply into his thoughts. He had a headache again.

Asha shrugged. "Sorry," she said. "It's not deliberate. I can't control it completely."

They were quiet for a few moments. Fionn and Niki were both curled up, at opposite ends of the couch. Kobi checked his watch and saw it was almost time to leave. Noon was the hottest time of the day and the most uncomfortable to move around in—as it was for all the other animals. It was the safest time to travel. He lay back down, sweat cooling on his skin.

"That Waste cleanser you gave Fionn is better than anything we have at Healhome," said Asha. "He's the sickest of all of us, you know. The Guardians try to keep on top of it, but they can't. Every month he gets weaker."

Kobi thought that he heard the beginnings of tears in Asha's voice. He knew exactly what she was getting at. *Fionn hasn't got long . . .*

"My dad has more of the medicine at his lab," he said. "He might be able to help Fionn."

Asha sniffed. "Do you really think he's there?" she asked.

He could hardly bear the look of desperation in her face, and the strange feeling it caused in his gut. *No one's ever depended on me before.* But he couldn't lie to her. The window of survival was shrinking by the hour, if it was even still open at all. "I hope so," he said, looking away.

For what seemed an eternity, she didn't answer, and when she did, it was only quiet. "I hope so too. I really do."

He glanced across at her again and saw she was staring at the ceiling.

"I never knew my parents," she said at last. "None of us did."

Kobi knew she was waiting for a response, but he wasn't sure what to say or do. She'd said something about her mother being infected but nothing about her own father. Had he died before she was born? Dad always said every cloud had a silver lining, but if she was an orphan, the cloud looked pretty dark all over.

"But you have the Guardians," he managed.

"Some of them are nice . . . ," said Asha.

Kobi sensed she wanted to say more. "But not all?"

"There's one—Melanie. She's in charge. Niki adores her. But the others—they're not really encouraged to form close bonds with the patients. You know, in case the worst happens."

Kobi nodded, not sure what to say.

"Fionn doesn't like them. He hasn't since . . ." She trailed off. "We only have each other, I suppose," said Asha.

"Like brother and sister," said Kobi.

"Exactly," said Asha.

On the sofa, Niki suddenly stirred. "What time is it?" she asked.

"Almost time to head out," said Kobi.

"Where?" said Niki, suddenly more awake. "Forgive me for doubting you, but I really think it would be better just to wait here." Her eyes shone with genuine fear. Kobi was starting to understand that the girl put up a hard exterior, but really she was just afraid, confused, and out of her comfort zone. "I mean, at least it's safe here," she pleaded.

"No," said Kobi. He didn't want to sound harsh, but they couldn't waste any more time.

"Nik . . . ," said Asha.

Fionn woke too now, and was looking from one to the other, eyes startled.

"She can stay here if she really wants," said Kobi, even though he hadn't wanted to offer, "but there are rules."

"No, we go together," said Asha.

"You can't make me," said Niki, hitching her chin defiantly.

Asha breathed a sigh through her nose.

Kobi didn't have the words, or the time, to argue, and began his preparations for leaving. He went to work resetting all the traps and checking all the doors around the school, just like he and his dad had always done together.

He headed toward the science rooms, tugging on his dad's homemade pump-action disinfectant equipment, and wearing a face mask and goggles. It was high concentration, enough to kill just about any regular plants on contact, and to seriously slow down the spread of Waste spores. But before he even reached the science rooms, he got a nasty surprise. The takeover had already begun, and it was worse than he expected. There were patches of creepers on the ceiling and walls. *That's not right*, he thought dimly. *It shouldn't be* that *bad.* Still, it might not be permanent. Repeated treatments with the disinfectant might do the job. . . .

He followed the path of vegetation back toward the outbreak location, his heart sinking as it grew more dense. More worrying. He began to doubt even his dad's concoction would be enough. Then, as he rounded the corner, his sinking heart plummeted into despair when he saw the reason for the incredible growth.

The classroom door was wide-open.

Someone had peeled away the sealing tape he'd so diligently applied.

Kobi approached slowly, anger bubbling in his gut. *Niki. It has to be. But why?*

The woodwork lab was already overrun, with all the workbenches, the desks, and the walls completely covered in a layer of moss and wildflowers. The Snatcher in the corner was snared in thin tendrils of greenery too. But it was the rest of the school Kobi was worried about. Depending on how long the door had been open, the volume of Waste spores in the school could be catastrophic.

I was so stupid. I trusted them.

Kobi had turned away, determined to confront Niki, when he heard the softest of mechanical hums. He spun around, searching the room. He froze as his eyes met those of the Snatcher. Its visual sensors glowed red, fixating on him. And even though his body screamed at him to run, a tiny voice of logic was weighing the explanations and settling on the obvious.

Niki! She switched it on.

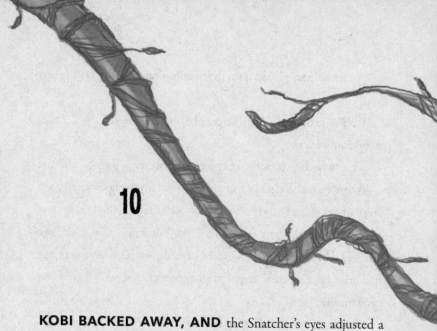

10

KOBI BACKED AWAY, AND the Snatcher's eyes adjusted a fraction to track him. Otherwise, it didn't move.

It can't, Kobi told himself. *It's malfunctioned.*

But could it still send signals back to its hub? If its positioning systems were online, it could report on its location, couldn't it? Niki must have used her electrical power to start it up.

Kobi ran from the room. His anger had melted, leaving only a deep dread. *How long have we got?*

He found Asha and Fionn sitting together in the library, both poring over the same book. "We have to go, now! Where's Niki?"

Asha shrugged. "Why—what's the matter?"

"She's betrayed us!" said Kobi.

Asha stood up sharply. "What?"

"She switched on the Snatcher," said Kobi. He slammed a hand down on the librarian's desk, splintering the wood. "They'll be coming for us. We need to get out."

Fionn stood up too. Though his eyes showed fear, his jaw was set. He nodded and stepped toward Kobi.

"Fionn . . . ," began Asha.

"Come on!" said Kobi.

"Wait," said Asha frowning. "Are you sure? Where is Niki now?"

Kobi was already running, trying to get his thoughts in some sort of order. His dad's voice came through clearly. *We trained for this, Son. You know what to do. The base is compromised. Emergency evac.* He needed to grab all the weapons and supplies he could carry. There were several ways out of the school, but if the Snatchers were coming from the city, they'd be running straight into their path.

Niki emerged from the school gym ahead, not looking guilty in the slightest. She was actually *smiling*.

"Why did you do it?" shouted Kobi, though he knew exactly.

Niki looked taken aback at his furious tone. "What are you talking about?"

"I trusted you," said Kobi, practically spitting with disgust. Asha and Fionn arrived behind him. Asha was carrying the dart rifle, not that it could help in the slightest against a robotic enemy. At that moment, Kobi's ears picked up sounds. A mechanical whirring sound that meant only one thing. More Snatchers. *Already?*

"They're here!" he said, looking up at the ceiling.

"Who's here?" cried Niki.

I can't believe she's still keeping up the act.

"Snatchers," Kobi said, "as if you didn't know."

Several thuds hit the roof above their heads, and a moment later the sound of smashing glass from several directions.

Kobi didn't know which way to run. *How many are there?*

There was no way to get to his regular supplies.

"There's a secret way out," he said to the others. "Follow me."

He set off at a run toward the reception area, but stopped after a few steps as the front doors of the school crashed inward. Smoke spilled inside, followed by two Snatchers on foot, their metal legs arching up and down as they skittered into the corridor.

One of the Snatchers advanced quickly, and Niki slipped backward, landing on the floor. "We're from Healhome!" she shouted. "Please, don't—" The metal spider reared up in front her and the young girl screamed as two forelegs clamped around her middle and lifted her into the air. A long flexible metal arm wound out sickeningly from under the Snatcher's carapace, like the tail of a scorpion but on its underside. The "sting" reared up and jabbed Niki in the neck. The girl's body went instantly limp and the Snatcher retreated with its prey.

Kobi grabbed Fionn's arm and tugged him the other way. His mind ran over the possibilities, the ways out.

"Kobi, wait!" shouted Asha.

He didn't. Niki was lost—probably dead already—but he couldn't process that now. He couldn't think about anything except getting away. He and Fionn skidded around a corner and a moment later Asha came too. Her lips were trembling. "Niki . . . ," she said.

A Snatcher's feet rattled after them. "Come on!" yelled Kobi. They ran. At the woodwork room, Kobi dodged quickly inside and went to the cabinet at the back. *Please be where I remember.*

The grenades were tucked at the back, two of them. By the time he emerged into the corridor again, the Snatcher was rounding the bend. It stalked toward them with calm menace.

"Go!" Kobi yelled to the others, and as they fled, he paused with his finger on the pin. His dad had run through the drill a hundred times with a disarmed one. This was real. He tugged the pin loose, stooped, and rolled the grenade as the Snatcher approached, then ducked back into the classroom.

The boom was deafening, shattering the glass panel in the door, and shrapnel tore across the work desks. Kobi peered out and saw the Snatcher on its side, three remaining legs scrabbling. He didn't stick around and ran in the other direction. Asha and Fionn were beside an old water fountain.

"Niki . . . ," said Asha. "We should go back."

Kobi paid no attention. Niki could pay for her own mistakes for all he cared. There were more thuds, coming from the other direction. He put an arm around Fionn's shoulder and led him a few feet up, to a door that read "Janitor."

He shouldered it open and pulled Fionn into the room on the other side.

Follow the emergency protocol. No mistakes.

Asha entered too, and Kobi pushed the door closed, and locked it from the inside. Complete darkness.

You know what to do.

"Stay close," he said.

With one hand still on Fionn, Kobi took six strides along the wall, reached the end, and followed it at ninety degrees. His toes bumped the crate on the floor. Crouching, he eased it aside, then scrabbled on the ground until his fingers found the metal ring. It lifted easily, opening the hatch.

"There are stairs here," he said. "Asha, you guys go first—I need to close the hatch behind us."

He wondered if a Snatcher could even fit down here but didn't want to wait to find out.

The other two shuffled past blindly. Kobi could hear heavy breathing and feel the heat of their bodies. After they passed, he swung the hatch closed and followed. The air down there was musty and cool.

"Where are we going?" asked Asha.

"Just keep walking," said Kobi. "It's an old service tunnel linked to a storm shelter. There's a wheel lock on a door a hundred and forty-three paces away."

He let his own fingers trail along the wall, walking briskly until they reached the end. He bumped into one of the others, then reached left for the alcove he knew was there and grabbed the canvas sack—his emergency provisions. Then, off the hooks below, the crossbow and sheathed machete on a belt. Kobi placed a foot on the rung of a metal ladder and reached for the ceiling, taking hold of the cold metal wheel. With a few squeaking turns it opened inward, and he climbed up, pausing for a moment to check the interior of the abandoned storage shed, which teemed with plant life. He could just about make out the shapes of old sports equipment—helmets, pads, hurdles—beneath the vegetation. There was a flashlight in the sack, he knew, but he didn't want to risk drawing any attention from the Snatchers at the school. Behind him, Asha and Fionn clambered out as well.

"Are we safe?" asked Asha.

Kobi put his fingers to his lips. "We're at the perimeter of the school grounds," he whispered. "Not clear yet."

In a crouch, he headed to the shed's wooden door, locked from the inside with a rusty key. He turned it slowly, then eased the door open a fraction, eye to the crack. He could see the long grass flatten and swirl from the wind from the Snatcher's thrusters as they flew around lazily; he counted at least five. Kobi knew the long grass didn't obscure their extensive sensor array.

"I don't understand," said Asha, shaking her head. "If those things belong to CLAWS . . ."

Fionn touched her arm, his face questioning.

"I don't, Fi," said Asha. Her bottom lip trembled. "I really don't."

Kobi remembered the younger girl's terrified scream as the Snatcher seized her, and the way she slumped when the sting jabbed into her. There was nothing to make him think Niki could possibly be alive.

So much for their *Guardians*.

He watched the school. Snatchers were scurrying in and out of doors and windows like wasps entering their hive. *I'm never going back there . . ,* he realized. Everything was ruined, and it was all because he'd taken in the three strangers. He'd been too nice. Too trusting. Not anymore.

"We can't stay," he said. "Are you coming with me or not?"

Asha looked at Fionn, clearly making up her mind. Not for the first time, Kobi found himself puzzling at their strange connection. Fionn stepped toward Kobi. He held up his hands, placing the thumbs together and spreading the palms. Kobi realized he was making the shape of the butterfly shadow puppet. Fionn made the hand animal flutter away.

Asha looked at Fionn and then turned to Kobi. "We're with you."

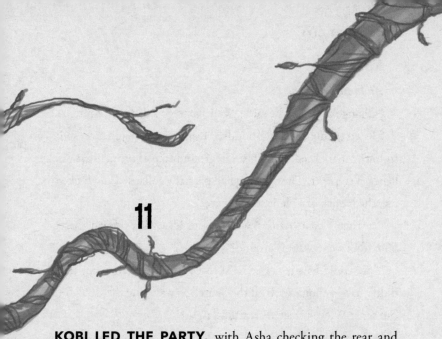

11

KOBI LED THE PARTY, with Asha checking the rear and Fionn between them. Kobi went as fast as he dared, and he sensed Asha's occasional impatience as he held them back for a few more minutes here and there. *She's never had to do this before. She doesn't know how easy it would be to make a mistake.*

"They're at the school," she said as they paused under the shelter of a towering oak. "They won't find us out here."

"We can't take risks," said Kobi. And how he wished he'd never taken any! From the moment he met them, he'd thrown all his caution aside. *And look where it got me. . . .*

It was three hours before they reached the bridge. As much as Kobi was on edge he felt glad to be heading for the lab, in search of his dad. But when he saw the sky ahead he groaned. Across the cityscape were more Snatchers than he'd ever laid eyes on. Maybe thirty, crisscrossing over and among the skyscrapers.

All hunting for us. . . .

"Change of plans," he said. "We have to go a different route."

He led them back three hundred feet, to where a junction split from the main road, into an underground transit tunnel that ran beneath the river. The opening had partially collapsed and looked like the mouth of a plant-strewn cave.

"In there?" said Asha. "We have no idea what's down there! Shouldn't we stay aboveground?"

Kobi could hardly say he relished the thought either, but they didn't have a choice with all the Snatchers prowling the sky. "You can sense Waste-infected creatures, right?"

Asha nodded. "Yes, but—"

"Okay, so you can warn us if there's anything nearby," said Kobi.

Asha smiled uncertainly. "I can *warn* you, but it might be too late by then."

Fionn touched her arm. Kobi was beginning to understand now. The physical connection helped them communicate. "I know that," said Asha, sounding a bit exasperated. "But that was one wolf, Fionn. We have no idea what lives"—she glanced at the tunnel entrance—"down there."

Fionn looked at Kobi, then back at Asha, who drew a deep breath. "Fionn says you know what you're doing."

"I know if we stand around talking much longer, we're asking for trouble," said Kobi. "We can't waste time. We need to keep moving." He began to walk down the ramp toward several concrete slabs ten feet tall, which lay across the entrance. Dad had said they tried to close some of the roads when the infection took hold, to quarantine the city. Way too late, of course—the airborne spores of the Waste didn't care about roadblocks. He jumped and gripped the lip, then hauled himself onto the top. The other two followed reluctantly. Kobi reached down and helped them over.

As they dropped to the other side, Kobi took out his flashlight. The view picked out in the flashlight's beam wasn't inviting. Giant shrubs with ghostlike branches and thorns spanned the tunnel, growing in and through cracks in the walls. Bulbous yellow fungus sprouted from abandoned cars. Everything gleamed with a slimy moist sheen. Kobi wondered if his dad had ever come this way and what he would have made of it. No—he would never have done anything so stupid. Then again, he never had dozens of Snatchers on his trail.

But we can't turn back. It's the only route out of the Snatchers' view.

"Stay focused and we'll get through this," he said, trying to sound confident. He took out his crossbow and handed it to Fionn. The young boy held it without much conviction. *He's more likely to shoot himself in the foot than anything else.* Kobi nodded to the dart gun hanging around Asha's waist. "Is that set high?"

"D-Nine," said Asha. "Lethal dose. I don't know how many shots it will give though."

Kobi began to walk, picking a path between the cars. It looked like there'd been crashes down here, because among the vegetation in the cars sat raggedy skeletons, still coated in fragments of clothing. Strange tropical-looking flowers sprouted from eye sockets and crumbling skulls. Kobi heard Fionn's and Asha's steps falter whenever the flashlight beam fell on another horrible sight.

"It's all right," said Asha. "They can't hurt us."

Kobi kept the flashlight moving. He wondered how acute Asha's telepathic senses were. She'd picked up on the Chokerplants a moment before the ambush near the hospital, but there could be plenty of other things lurking down here. Things Kobi couldn't even imagine. After all the years of careful planning and execution, all the lessons his dad had drilled into him about being cautious, here he was breaking every rule in the book. Rushing headlong into the unknown.

Up ahead, the center of the tunnel had collapsed, with plants growing at strange angles as the ground dipped. Kobi crept toward the lip.

"There's definitely something down there," said Asha. "I feel it."

The only way across the hole was the trunk of a tree lying over the center. It was wide enough to climb over, and Kobi thought it would take their weight easily, even if they all crossed together. Still, the idea of walking over the abyss was risky. If there were Chokerplants lurking below—they'd be sitting ducks during the crossing.

Kobi shined his flashlight over the edge. Below was another road, with the remains of a couple more vehicles. Something was moving at the dim edges of the flashlight's beam, but when he tried to pin it down it was gone. He shrugged off the backpack and took out the flare gun from inside. He had only three spare flares, so he had to be careful.

"Let's see, shall we?" he said.

He aimed the flare gun and fired into the abyss. The green light spilled over the debris of the car and the knotted plants. From several places at once, cockroaches the size of cats swarmed to get out of the brightness. They scuttled off into holes and gaps and grates.

Asha jerked back, letting out a short hiss of breath. "It's all right," said Kobi. "They're ugly, but they're harmless." He took the crossbow back from Fionn and handed him a Taser from his belt instead. "This is better at close range. If anything comes near you, just point and shoot."

They crossed the trunk to the far side without incident. Kobi took out the city map from the emergency bag. It wasn't as detailed as the map back at the school, but at least it had all the city's roads. He traced their tunnel into the city—where it branched off in several directions. "We can cover a lot of ground down here," he said. "I don't think the Snatchers will be able to follow us."

They continued through the abandoned tunnel, flashlight beam playing over the eerie swamplike growths. The plants down here were less vibrant than above, the air slightly rotten. Even Waste-infected plants did better in the sunlight.

Kobi measured their progress roughly in his head, picking markers every one hundred feet or so. Soon he was sure they must have reached the other side of the river, and as the tunnel branched, he took the leftmost junction.

"Wait!" whispered Asha. She closed her eyes for a moment. "I sense more Chokerplants. I think they're up ahead." She raised the rifle.

They slowed down, and Kobi drew his machete. "Let's check it out."

Neither of the other kids argued, but Kobi sensed them a fraction behind him as they crept farther, rounding a bend. Asha was right. Two hundred feet up the tunnel was almost entirely blocked with a monstrous explosion of pale roots, some more than three feet thick. They grew from the floor and into the tunnel roof, where the concrete was broken apart. Kobi's flashlight beam played over the tangled branches. There was a way through to the other side, but it would involve clambering between the knotted limbs. At any point, the Chokerplants might stir to life and wrap around them like constrictors crushing the life from their prey.

"I think we have to double back," Asha said.

Kobi realized she was right. He checked the map again and saw there was another way. A much longer route. *We just have to hope it's not blocked too.*

They'd taken a few steps when Asha stopped again. "Oh no. Something's coming."

Kobi heard it too, and his heart pumped harder. Something mechanical—the hum of hydraulics. *Snatchers.* "They've found us," he said. He began to move back toward the Chokerplants.

"Wait!" said Asha. "We can't."

Kobi's dad had always had a theory about Chokerplants. Time to test it. Kobi crouched and picked up a lump of shattered concrete from the floor. Drawing back his arm, he hurled the block as hard as he could. It thumped into the pale limbs, then rattled down to the ground.

The Chokerplant didn't move an inch.

"Perhaps we *can* make it through," he said.

"Are you insane?" said Asha.

"My dad always said Chokers were most sensitive to vibrations toward the tips of the vines," he said. "The roots not so much. If we're careful, I think we can make it."

"You think?"

"Trust me," said Kobi.

Fionn nodded his pinched face bravely, and Asha let out a grunt of frustration but came as well.

The clanking of the Snatchers was echoing closer. Kobi imagined them flooding over the car wrecks—sensors scanning the darkness for signs of human life. Once they locked on, that was it. There'd be no hesitation. *We don't have long.*

Kobi tried not to let his fear show as they approached the gargantuan root system. He shined his flashlight to show the others the way, and hopped over a horizontal twisting trunk. Asha helped Fionn scramble onto the top, and Kobi lifted him over the other side, then followed. The rest of the structure didn't move at all. Asha was trembling. "I can *feel* it," she whispered. "It's all around us."

They had to crouch under a looping branch, then squeeze between more of the thicket. Kobi couldn't help feeling they were entering the stomach of some massive beast, which wasn't far from the truth. But as he shined his flashlight through the shadows and coils, he could see the other side, maybe seventy-five feet away. *Not far.*

Suddenly more light trickled through the roots around them. Kobi glanced back and saw a Snatcher rounding the bend of the tunnel. It picked up its pace, scurrying toward the Chokerplant roots.

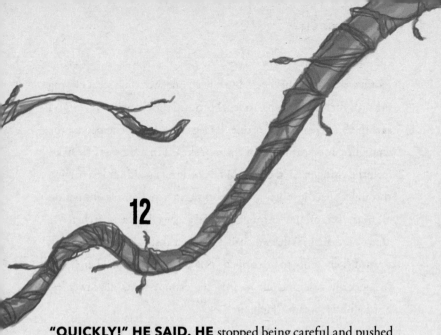

12

"QUICKLY!" HE SAID. HE stopped being careful and pushed further into the morass of branches. Asha and Fionn pressed close behind. As he jumped between a forked trunk, the lights from the Snatcher intensified. He didn't need his flashlight anymore.

"It's coming this way fast!" cried Asha.

Kobi looked back and saw the metal contraption picking its way through behind them. Its shell bashed into the Choker roots with brute force, and Kobi heard one of them snap. At the same moment, horror gripped his chest as the branches around them stirred to life. The thick roots squirmed and flexed like the tentacles of some giant squid. Kobi ducked as one swept overhead. *It's searching for prey.*

The Snatcher continued after them, knocked this way and that by the snaking roots but coming on relentlessly. Shafts of blinding light cut across Kobi's path as he struggled on, checking Asha and

Fionn were still on his heels. He'd head one way, then see it closing off, only for another gap to open. He heard the crunch of metal and saw the Snatcher tip to its side. Its legs were being trapped by the strangling roots, and one of them broke off in a shower of sparks. Still the thing pressed on. Kobi reached the far side at last, diving through a space just before the roots tightened. Fionn came out on all fours, scrambling through to safety as well. The Snatcher was almost on them. Asha was still a few feet inside. She tried to run toward them, only to be tripped. The flash of the Snatcher closed in suddenly, reaching out an arm that clamped over her lower leg. She let out a scream. "Help me!"

Kobi reached in and found her arm, but when he tugged, she didn't move. "Fionn, grab on too," shouted Kobi. At any moment, he expected the roots to seize on Asha. If they did, it was over.

Fionn took Asha's other arm, grimacing. The rifle was just visible, but Kobi couldn't see a way to reach it. And still the Snatcher wasn't letting go. The tendrils of Chokerplant were lashing across its carapace, and as each did, Kobi saw them tighten with immense power, denting the metal as they squeezed. The contraption was trying to move but could only shift a little—its sensor arrays jerking this way and that as its robot mind tried to work out what was happening. It made Kobi think of a fly trapped in a web, when every move only worsened its fate.

Kobi's grip began to slip on Asha's arm, and he knew he was seconds from losing her. The terror etched on her features told him she knew exactly the same. *Please . . . ,* he thought. *Not like this. . . .*

Then Fionn let go. Asha screamed, but Fionn thrust his arm deep into the roots, gritting his teeth. A moment later the vines jerked and recoiled, and suddenly Kobi was falling back, crying out with a mighty heave. Asha slid free. They hauled her together out of the writhing plant and didn't stop dragging until they were well clear. A single metal arm reached out after them, before a terrible crunching of metal and fizzing of sparks. The arm flopped, and the rest of the Snatcher disappeared completely in the constricting Choker branches.

For a moment they all breathed heavily, in shock. Then Kobi realized what must have happened. Fionn had managed to pull the rifle's trigger, discharging a dart into the Chokerplant. Not enough to kill an organism so huge, but enough to slow it down for just long enough.

"You saved her!" he said, and Fionn, pale and sweating, nodded grimly.

Kobi stood up, regaining his senses. With any luck, and he thought they were due some, the Chokerplant would stop any more Snatchers from coming through from that direction, so they'd bought themselves some time at least.

"Yes, I'm fine," Asha was saying as Fionn looked at her leg. Apart from a tear in her blue shorts, she looked unhurt.

Kobi turned his attention farther down the tunnel—and felt

his heart sink into despair. It was completely blocked by another massive Chokerplant. It looked like the roof had collapsed as well, mixing with blocks of masonry and tangled rusting vehicles.

"We're trapped," he said simply.

They walked slowly toward the looming mountain of roots and debris. Kobi stared at it helplessly. Even with his strength, there was no way they could even begin to shift enough to find a way through. *We're going to die down here.*

"What is it, Fionn?" asked Asha.

Kobi saw the boy had drifted off toward the edge of the tunnel and was peering at a swathe of lianas. He shined the flashlight that way and saw that the vines were actually half covering the mouth of a side tunnel. Fionn scooped some aside with his hands. The opening was a flattened circle about four feet across and three feet tall. From the rough gouges in the solid layers of concrete, it looked like it had been chipped away rather than bored mechanically. Whoever had dug it had left the jagged ends of pipework and wiring frayed at the edges.

Kobi shined his flashlight inside, and saw the tunnel led slightly downward, roughly straight. Looking at his map, he couldn't figure out where it could possibly go.

"We have no idea what's down there," he said.

"We didn't let that stop us before," Asha reminded him. "Besides, we have no choice. I'll go first."

She took the flashlight from Kobi's hand and climbed in,

shuffling down feetfirst. Fionn went next, with Kobi following at the rear. The passageway had a few smaller branches at odd angles, but they stuck to the main route. *No way people made this,* thought Kobi. *They wouldn't even fit down some of those offshoots.* He pushed the anxieties aside. The concrete of the walls gave way to bare earth, with occasional fragments of what looked like beams of timber. It was hard to judge the distance in the tunnels, but Kobi guessed they'd gone about a hundred feet when the way ahead opened up, and they found themselves huddled in a room with collapsed shelves along the wall and what looked like a filthy pane of glass opposite. There were only a few small patches of plant life—almost nothing.

Asha shined the flashlight across the glass, where back-to-front letters read "Candy's Haberdashery." Wasn't that an old word for some sort of store?

There was a door, slightly ajar, and they walked through it, all speechless. Kobi's frown deepened. There were paving slabs beneath their feet, and they were standing in an actual street, with brick arches and walls, and a row of small storefronts like some sort of old-fashioned shopping mall. It made no sense, because the roof was supported by a mixture of brickwork, metal stanchions, and beams.

"Where in the world are we?" said Asha.

They walked on. The remains of furniture sat in some of the rooms they passed. Kobi spotted counters, walls of decorated tiles.

A few signs remained. "Mr. Bunting's Confectioners," "Black's Ironmonger," a funeral home with a coffin still sitting on a bier. Mostly, though, the place was empty and abandoned.

After a while, Kobi realized his feet were crossing timber floorboards. They climbed three steps onto an elevated walkway.

"It's like a buried town," said Asha.

Her words snagged at a thread of memory—and a moment later Kobi placed it. A book he'd read in the school library.

"This is the old Seattle Underground!" he said, trying to recall. "In the past, maybe the nineteenth century, it was at ground level. There was a fire or something and it all got built over."

His flashlight flickered a little, and Kobi realized right away the one thing he was missing. Spare batteries.

In one of the abandoned stores across the way—a butcher's shop judging by the old model of a pig—were a few bundles of more-modern clothing. Kobi's skin prickled. Did that mean someone else had come down here? More survivors, maybe. He found it hard to believe people could be living down here anymore. But then, anything seemed possible now. He entered the shop, which Kobi could tell at once wasn't quarantined. There were moldy camping mats and rolled-up sleeping bags. A stove and some empty cans of food lay on the ground, but spiderwebs covered most of them. Not promising.

But someone had been sleeping here, at some point.

It was the same story in the next room, and Kobi was about to leave when his flashlight beam fell on something bright. Bile rose into his throat as he realized it was an arm bone, with skeletal fingers still attached, sticking out from under a blanket.

"Don't let Fionn in here," he called. He didn't want the younger boy getting scared.

"What is it?" answered Asha from outside.

"Just give me a minute."

Kobi moved the sleeping bag with his foot and saw the rest of the skeleton was small and clothed in a dress. One hand still clutched a teddy bear. His stomach lurched, and he turned away and left quickly.

"I don't think we're going to find anyone alive down here," he told Asha and Fionn. "People must have been trying to escape the Waste, but it didn't work."

"Do you think they made that tunnel we came down?" Asha asked doubtfully.

Kobi shrugged. "Maybe." He breathed a heavy sigh, scanning about. His eyes fell on a backpack. "We might be able to scavenge some supplies, though. You want to take a look around and meet back at the haberdashery in a few minutes?"

"Sure," said Asha. "I'll shout if we run into any trouble."

Fionn went with her, and Kobi opened up the backpack. Not much—lighter fluid and matches, an old paperback book, a pack of playing cards, a water canteen, a sweater. He took the fire-lighting stuff and left the rest. He thought about taking one of the sleeping bags as well, but it felt a bit wrong. Aside from the one small skeleton, he didn't come across any other human remains.

They might have moved on before they died, of course, but from the back of his mind a more worrying option surfaced. If they'd tried to change camp, why hadn't they taken anything with them?

What if something took them?

He told himself he was being paranoid. Apart from the spiderwebs, there was no sign of any other living thing down here.

He found some candy bars in a drawer, along with some bottles of soda. They might still be okay.

When he emerged and returned to the meeting spot, Fionn and Asha were waiting. Asha proudly held up a small hatchet in one hand and a flashlight in the other. But the ax didn't look all that sharp, and when Kobi tried the flashlight it was dead. When theirs failed, the darkness down there would be absolute. Fionn had an old smartphone in his hands, inspecting it.

"Dad said everyone had one of those," said Kobi. "Or watches or glasses or even chips inside their bodies." They looked at him blankly, and Kobi guessed that they had been told less about what life was like before Waste than he had. He passed out the candy bars.

Fionn looked at his suspiciously.

Kobi almost laughed. Candy was one of the main foods that didn't perish, and over the years he'd eaten a lot. "Something tells me you're going to like it," he said.

Fionn tore his open and took a tentative bite, but soon he was grinning from ear to ear.

Kobi's flashlight flickered. "Uh-oh," he said.

"Do you have any more batteries?" asked Asha.

He shook his head. "Here, hold this." He handed her the flashlight, stood up, and went back into one of the stores. The sweater would do. He tried not to panic—whenever the generator had packed up at the school, throwing them into blackness, his dad had said the dark was nothing to be afraid of. But down here it felt almost physical, a pure suffocating barrier. They might never find their way out again. He took a length of broken timber, wrapping the sweater tightly around one end, then doused it in lighter fluid to make a torch. When he lit it, the rich yellow glow of firelight spread through the eerie abandoned streets. At the same time, his heart rate began to slow.

He felt a flush of pride as he imagined his dad congratulating him on his quick thinking. The flashlight gave out completely a couple of seconds later. Fionn and Asha looked relieved too. They ate another candy bar each.

"Fionn says it's peaceful here," said Asha, her face bronze in the flame's light.

"He doesn't seem to mind being up on the surface, either," said Kobi.

"Yeah . . . ," said Asha, looking worriedly at Fionn. "I wouldn't have guessed he would take to the outside so easily. Personally, I'm a fan of anywhere where there are fewer things trying to kill us."

Kobi nodded. He knew where the Waste was concerned that the situation could change in an instant. Survival was about being ready for those changes. *Never rest on your laurels*, Dad used to say. *"There's always work to be done."*

"We need to make some spare torches," he said. "I don't know how long this will last."

Leaving Fionn with another candy bar, they went back to fetch more materials. Once they were out of earshot, sifting through the old clothes in the butcher's shop, Kobi whispered to Asha.

"What's up with him anyway? Why can't he talk?"

Asha tossed aside a paperback book. "He could once. Something bad happened when he was younger. At Healhome."

Kobi remembered the feeling of anger, fear, and loneliness he'd felt emanating from Fionn during the vision of Healhome. He remembered what Niki had said about some kids not being as physically resistant as others. He peered out at Fionn, who was still quietly eating. Poor kid had probably seen more than one of his friends die. And if Asha was right about his condition, he was on borrowed time too. Kobi was starting to suspect that Fionn wanted to spend his last days free of Healhome: a place where kids slipped into death without ever having truly lived.

They finished fashioning the torches, and Kobi told Asha he was going to look for exits leading to the surface. He made his way past Fionn. The younger boy was holding up his hands in the flickering light, making a wolf silhouette against the wall. "That's great, Fionn," said Kobi. *That kid really can't get enough of shadow puppets.* Kobi carried on along the passageway. The torchlight gradually petered out the farther he went, and it was as he reached the limits of its illumination that he saw something in the roof ahead. The faintish green glow of natural light. He walked directly underneath and realized it was a skylight, crisscrossed with a metal frame. Greenery coated its upper side, but Kobi understood he must be looking at the overground city, and it was dawn.

He was about to go back and tell the others when they came rushing up to him, firelight playing over their frightened features.

"Kobi—something's coming!" said Asha, gripping the dart rifle.

13

"MORE SNATCHERS?" SAID KOBI.

Asha was breathing hard. "No. Something Waste-infected."
She threw a glance back the way they'd come. "It's getting close."

Kobi heard a noise. A screeching, chittering sound, growing by
the second. He couldn't tell where it was coming from, but Asha's
attention seemed fixed in one direction. And as he stared too, fear
eating at his heart, he saw in the torchlight the floor was coming
alive with a mass of furred flesh. *Rats.* Some the size of small dogs,
others perhaps a foot long. It was hard to make out their individual
bodies as they clambered over one another in a seething torrent.
Dozens of them. Asha fired a dart, but they kept coming.

"Run!" said Kobi.

Bumping into one another, stumbling over uneven ground,
they turned and fled, but they'd gone just a few paces when Asha
pulled them back. "More," she said.

And she was right. Another stream of rodents were closing from the other direction. *Surrounded.* Kobi's skin crawled as he saw the full horror of the swarm. The Waste hadn't only made these creatures bigger, it had malformed them too. Some were bald or covered in glistening sores. Others had two heads or hobbled lopsidedly on stunted legs. Others had overgrown teeth growing through their faces like miniature tusks.

"Fionn, do something!" said Asha.

The boy closed his eyes and thrust out both hands on either side like he was trying to hold back two invisible walls. Kobi felt a prickle through his body, like he could pick up the strange signals Fionn was sending out. And the rats *did* slow, as if momentarily stunned. But the effect was short-lived, and they scurried on in frantic waves.

"Over here!" said Kobi, then took out the remains of the lighter fluid. He poured it in two lines on either side of them, fifteen feet apart, then held the torch to the ground. Flames licked across the floor, but only a few inches high. He drew his machete, and Asha took the ax. Fionn snatched the Taser.

Now we know what took the survivors' remains. . . .

The rats reached the boundaries of the fire and paused, tumbling over one another. But almost at once, one of the leaders landed in the fire with a terrible squeal, rolling around in panic. The fire was extinguished in seconds.

The remainder of the rats streamed over their dying kin. A scrawny, jagged-clawed thing threw itself at Kobi, who hacked it aside midair. He kicked another, before a smaller one latched on to his jeans and began to claw its way up. A shriek came from behind Kobi as one rolled past with the Taser prongs jutting from his neck. Kobi grabbed the rat from his waist and hurled it as hard as he could at a wall. It hit with a dull splat. Asha was spinning, trying to use the stock of the rifle to bash rats aside, but there were two fighting up her back, unreachable. Kobi sent them tumbling with a prod of the torch.

The creatures flooded around Kobi's ankles, and he felt the sharp sting of claws and teeth. He kicked and stamped as best he could, but for every rodent he killed or tossed clear, more swarmed after it. Asha tried to climb, using the ledge of a wall, but the rats simply piled over one another and jumped to reach her, and she fell back down into the melee. She swiped the ax, over and over in wide arcs, driving them back. Kobi ignored the ones on his own body, wading through with the torch at ground level, kicking and stamping. Some caught alight and charged blindly, setting fire to more. The bitter smell of burnt rodent flesh was all around.

Then, inside his head, he heard the jolt of a barked command. *"Look above you!"*

Kobi looked up and saw a two-headed rat with a wizened hind leg scurrying directly above, along a roof beam. It dropped toward him, and Kobi gave an upward swipe. The machete blade cut the creature in two and covered him in gobbets of blood and gore.

"Fionn!" roared Asha. Kobi saw the boy had fallen to one knee and dropped the Taser. A rat had sunk its teeth into his forearm, and though he shook it violently, the thing wasn't letting go. More were crawling up his legs and lower body. He shot a desperate look to Kobi. Kobi's scalp tingled in a burst of pins and needles. Though Fionn didn't say a word, the young boy's voice echoed inside Kobi's head, like in a tunnel. *"Help me!"*

In the same moment, a powerful, strange kind of fear gripped Kobi's stomach. He realized, somehow, that it was not his own. He was *feeling* Fionn's terror.

He dropped the torch and tried to stagger across to help the young boy. Asha was coming from the other side. Dead and dying rats squelched and squirmed underfoot, and Kobi tripped, collapsing headlong into the morass. He felt rats covering him almost at once. He tried to stand, and through his panic, he saw Asha reach Fionn's side and begin to rip off the marauding rodents. At the same time, she herself was swamped.

We can't win! thought Kobi. *They're going to eat us alive.*

A loud crash made him twist around. The skylight showered in shards of glass and something massive tumbled into the tunnel from above. *What now?*

The creature landed, shaking more debris from its fur, then raised its head in a growl. Kobi took a heartbeat to understand what he was seeing. *The wolf! From the school!*

It made no sense—it must have followed them for miles.

The gray-furred predator set into the rats at once, crushing them beneath its paws and snatching them up with its teeth— two, three at a time. With vicious shakes of its head, it broke bones and tore at flesh. Kobi managed to stand, and attacked with his machete again, slashing until his arm ached. It felt like he'd been fighting for hours, but it must have been only a minute or so before hundreds of dead rats were gathered at their feet and against the blood-spattered walls. The remainder turned and fled as quickly as they had swept in, and their chattering died away into the darkness.

It took a second or two before Kobi could even think, then he saw Asha was cradling Fionn in her lap. She looked up through tear-filled eyes. "He's really badly hurt, Kobi."

Kobi struggled over, trying to ignore the pain across his body. The wolf shambled over too and lowered its enormous head to nuzzle at Fionn. Despite their grave situation, Kobi couldn't help but wonder how the wolf had found them, and why it had come to their aid. *It must have followed Fionn, and it realized he was in trouble.*

The boy was breathing shallowly, and his eyes were half-open, the whites a worrying shade of yellow. A sheen of sweat covered his forehead. His hands and forearms were badly bitten, and there were patches of blood across his torso too. But it didn't look like any arteries had been severed. He just looked desperately weak, like he could lose consciousness any minute.

"The rats have contaminated him with more Waste," said Asha.

He hasn't got long, thought Kobi, with sudden awful clarity. *He needs cleansers.* Kobi hadn't been able to grab any before they left the school. *We need to get him to the lab, fast.*

"Don't worry, Fi," he said. "We'll get you out of here."

His eyes met Asha's. "How?" she mouthed.

Kobi looked around in desperation, then pointed at the hole in the roof, where the wolf had burst through into the derelict street. The smoke from the fizzling torch was spilling out into the dawn of the city.

"The lab can't be far, but we have to get up into the city to see where we are."

Kobi stood and went to the skylight. The street was about twelve feet up. Kobi's first attempt to make the jump fell well short. The wolf cocked its head, then padded over.

"It wants to help," said Asha.

Kobi swallowed. "Are you sure?"

The wolf pushed him out of the way, then lowered itself to the ground.

"Go ahead, get on," said Asha.

Kobi shot her a wary glance. *Easy for you to say.*

Taking a deep breath, he sank his hands into the thick fur and hoisted himself over the wolf's back. It lurched to its feet sharply, almost throwing him off. But Kobi was closer to the ceiling and managed to loop his hands over the lip, pulling himself up to street level. Gusting sea air and a gray dawn greeted him. The skylight opened onto one of the streets a block back from the bay, under a tree-coated flyover beside the old docks. The harbor wall had been overwhelmed in places, undermined by the onslaught of virulent plant life. What remained leading to the water was a huge swamp of seaweed. The Great Wheel loomed a couple of blocks north. Dad said it had once been an amusement park ride, but now it listed to one side, coated with vines and the occasional tangle of a bird's nest in its old cars.

Below, Asha was tying a rope around Fionn's armpits. She pulled it tight, then tossed the other end up. Kobi caught it. Bracing his feet on either side of the skylight, he gritted his teeth and then hoisted Fionn up. The injured boy groaned softly.

Asha came next, leaving the wolf below. As she clambered into the open, she gazed around in astonishment at the windswept harbor, then began to unfasten the rope from Fionn.

"Do you think the wolf can make it?" asked Kobi. He wasn't sure he even *wanted* it to. There was enough to think about already.

The wolf growled, bunched its hind legs, and sprang upward. Its plate-size front paws gripped the sidewalk, and for a moment its lower body scrabbled before it heaved itself up beside them. "Nice jump!" said Asha, stroking its manelike ruff. The wolf licked her hand with its thick slab of a tongue. Kobi couldn't even imagine what his dad would have said.

Asha stroked Fionn's head. "How far to the lab?" she asked.

Kobi took out the map from his back pocket. "About thirty blocks," he said.

The wolf lowered its head again, toward Fionn.

"It wants to carry him," said Asha. Kobi scooped up the boy and laid him carefully across the wolf's broad back.

They set off toward the waterfront, where the city's looming towers opened onto the expanse of gray blue. Asha kept a hand on Fionn to keep him steady, and Kobi held his crossbow ready, just in case. When they reached the road that ran alongside the sea, they turned north.

As they walked, Kobi kept his eyes peeled for any sign of movement. Occasionally he saw a Snatcher in the distance, but nothing came close. His head was throbbing dully.

"You were pretty awesome in that fight," said Asha.

"You too," said Kobi. "Remind me not to make you and your ax angry."

Asha chuckled.

Kobi rubbed his temples.

"You okay?" asked Asha.

"Just tired, I guess," said Kobi.

Asha was silent for a while, and for some reason Kobi sensed she was uncomfortable.

He heard other sounds—the shushing and slap of water on the dock, the whistle of wind.

He looked out to the sea, where white crests frilled the choppy waves. A giant ferry, like a small island, rested up against the other side of the bay, but really, from here, there was no sign of the Waste or its effects. He could almost have been looking out from the city as it was, before the virus hit.

"Kobi . . . ," Asha said slowly. "Your headaches. You said they started just after your dad left, right?"

He frowned at her. "Yeah."

"What changed when he left? Why do you think you started having them then?"

He didn't know what she meant. "Well, I was on my own. That was pretty different. Maybe stress?"

"But did any of your routines change? To do with your health." Her eyes were wide and focused as if she was seeing something obvious that he wasn't.

Kobi opened his mouth, confused, then closed it again as a sick feeling rose in his stomach. *She couldn't mean . . .* "My vitamins. You think my vitamins stopped my picking up telepathic signals." An icy stab rushed up through his chest. "They were vitamins! Why would my dad want to stop me from receiving anything telepathic? He didn't even know Waste could do that to people!" His voice was raised. "No." He shook his head. Asha just watched him.

"Think about it, Kobi," she said. "He didn't want telepaths being able to track you. He didn't want us to find you."

"No!" Kobi shouted it this time. "You're saying that Dad knew about you. About the Guardians. It's just coincidence that my headaches started when he left. Or maybe it was a side effect he didn't know about."

Asha curled down her bottom lip and nodded. "Yeah. Maybe. . . ."

Kobi said nothing. They continued on in uncomfortable silence. "Well, we can ask him soon," said Kobi, forging ahead, cheeks feeling hot. *No, she's wrong. My dad wouldn't lie to me. He would have wanted us to find other survivors. Unless he knew the Guardians were dangerous. . . .*

As they crossed each block, past the old cafés and restaurants and apartment buildings, the Space Needle occasionally appeared, piercing the sky. Snatchers docked and swarmed, more than he'd ever seen before, but as tiny as flies from this distance. He thought CLAWS must have sent more in. What kind of resources did these people have? Who were they?

Whoever they are, they won't stop looking for us, he thought.

He checked the map, looking for the quickest route, and spotted a set of narrow alleys a couple of blocks over called Pike Place Market. They could cut right through. He remembered his dad talking about it. Before the Waste came, it was a bustling place where you could buy fresh produce of all kinds. Fruit and vegetables just off the tree or out of the ground, not in a can ten years out of date. Kobi thought it sounded a bit weird, even though he'd read about such things and seen pictures. But his dad spoke about peeling an orange like it was the best thing in the universe. They turned inland.

The sign for Pike Place, which read simply "Public Market Center," had crashed down into the street, and they picked their way past its metal frame to the covered market itself. Old delivery trucks, spilling pallets and crates, had been left outside.

The entrance was dark, with a few shafts of light where the roof had collapsed. The wolf sniffed as they approached.

"You sense anything?" Kobi asked Asha.

"Hard to say," she replied. "Can't tell if I'm picking up the wolf or something else."

Still, they proceeded slowly. The inside of the market was like a dank cave—anything fresh had rotted away long ago. Fionn muttered occasionally, not words exactly but worried grunts and groans, like he was having some sort of nightmare. Each time, Asha reached over and touched him softly. At one point a helicopter definitely drew nearer, and they all stopped, holding their breath, as its shadow passed overhead.

"Maybe the Snatcher in the tunnel sent back some sort of signal," Asha said, sounding nervous. "They might be on our trail. We can't afford any delays. Fionn . . . I've never seen him this bad before."

Most of the clothes stores were swamped in vegetation, but in one Kobi spotted some coats still wrapped in polythene and untouched by any plant growth. He pulled them out.

"Wear this," he said, handing a duffer jacket to Asha. "They might help mask our heat signatures." He pulled one on himself and carefully draped the other over Fionn.

Anything to give us an advantage. When we get in the open again, we'll need it.

On the far side of the market, they paused at the doors.

The university where the lab was located was still a dozen blocks east and four south, the route uphill. In the daylight, most of the bigger predators would be asleep, but if a Snatcher or a CLAWS chopper flew overhead, they'd be in trouble. Fionn's skin was almost pearly white, his breathing wheezy. Kobi felt for the boy's pulse. It was racing.

They didn't have a choice. They had to press on.

The first part of the journey took them between towering green skyscrapers. Most of the flora in the streets consisted of wide-leaf giant ferns and exotic flowers sprouting from the former shop fronts. But as they climbed higher still, the buildings shrank and the way ahead grew more forested and wild. The squat buildings on either side of the road were almost entirely coated, like small green hillocks with only the flashes of steel or glass to show their true nature. It was so much farther than Kobi had ever come before. As they traveled, he counted off the blocks on his map.

Near the university campus, the wolf stopped by a stream that babbled across the road. It dipped its head to drink, then lifted its dripping muzzle.

"We're here," Kobi said, eyeing the complex of plant-covered buildings ahead. It didn't look at all promising, but his heart thundered. "Can you sense Dad?" he asked Asha.

She paused and looked around, and then sighed and shook her head. "No . . . But that doesn't mean he's not here. There's a lot of interference, and if I haven't met someone it's harder to recognize their electromagnetic brain signatures. That's what the Guardians told me."

"Let's split up. Call out if you find anything that looks like a lab."

Kobi turned to the wolf. Fionn lay draped over its back,

murmuring, his fingers clenching at the wolf's coarse fur, like a baby instinctively gripping its parent. Kobi strode over to the wolf, who looked up from the stream, its muzzle wet, tongue lolling from its mouth. Kobi pressed his foot into the wet earth in front of the wolf. He crouched over the print, pointed at it, then jabbed a finger to his chest. "Remember when you tracked me behind the tree stump? You found where I was hiding." He swept his finger over the building complex. "I need you to find someone hiding now." The wolf's yellow-stained eyes glinted with intelligence as it gazed down at the print, then at the surroundings. With a growl, it brushed past Kobi down the overgrown street, nose dipped to the ground. Kobi grinned at Asha, but she was watching Fionn being carried away. "Fionn will be safe with the wolf," Kobi said.

Asha nodded. "I know." She tapped her head. "I'll keep track of them anyway. I'll come and find you if I discover anything."

Kobi wanted to tell her to be careful, and go over his father's rules of traveling through built-up areas. But Asha was already treading carefully through what looked to have once been a parking lot. Kobi turned in the other direction, hurrying down a slight incline, to a wide sunken courtyard surrounded by steps. It looked a bit like the jungle-claimed ruins of the Aztec ziggurats that he'd seen in books from the school library. The Waste made everything, ancient and modern, look the same.

He had no idea how big the university complex was or where the lab might be. Now that they were there, the doubts he'd kept at bay set in and multiplied. If his dad had made it there, why on earth would he have stayed until now? He'd spent so long thinking about reaching the university, he hadn't even stopped to consider how big the complex might be, or where he'd even start. He'd thought, if his Dad *was* here, he'd somehow just know, as if they had an invisible connection or a telepathic link like Asha's.

He was beginning to lose hope when he heard a far-off cry. Asha was calling to him. He sprinted in her direction, and arrived just at the same time as Fionn and the wolf.

"I've found something," she said. "Look."

Under an archway, foliage had been cut away from a doorway, and there were engraved letters on a brass plaque beside the door: "GrowCycle Laboratories."

The same company that sponsored the football stadium. The ones behind the outbreak. Kobi's dad said they were a biotech company, but perhaps they had done some of their research here too.

"Think this could be it?" said Asha.

It couldn't be a coincidence that the door was partially cleared. Someone had used it. Recently.

"It has to be," said Kobi, trying to keep himself from getting carried away. He tried the door, and it was unlocked. No sign of anyone inside, and it was filled with plant life.

"Dad!" he called. "It's me—Kobi!" His shouts echoed along the deserted corridor.

"We need to help Fionn," said Asha. "Where's the cleanser?"

"I don't know," said Kobi. "Let's split up."

They wandered across the mossy, spongy corridor, checking the doors on either side. It seemed to be offices and the occasional classroom. A small kitchen area.

The wolf paused, sniffing at a set of vine-ensnared stairs. It swung its head toward them.

"It's found a scent," said Asha.

The wolf stood by Kobi and bent down so Kobi could lift Fionn off its back. Then the wolf began to climb the steps, nose lowered.

Asha hurried after it, and Kobi, carrying Fionn, followed. When they reached the top, his heart flipped. The wolf was waiting by a door a few feet up—a door sealed from the outside with tape, which could only mean one thing. "That's it!" he said. But at the same time, as he hurried toward the door, he felt a drag in his stomach as he realized what the tape on the outside meant. Whether he'd come and gone or never made it in the first place, his dad wasn't there.

Asha shoved through, tearing the tape, and they rushed into a room filled with signs of his father. A lab coat hanging on a peg, masks and gloves. A notebook with a pen resting on it. Vials and test tubes in racks. A board covered in his dad's handwriting. And there, in the corner, a working fridge, no doubt powered by solar panels on the roof. Kobi laid Fionn on the table, and went to it. Inside were several vials in a rack marked with a chemical formula in his dad's hand. Cleansers. They were dated, all within the last two months.

He grabbed one of the antibody dosages and a sterilized syringe pack.

"Quickly!" said Asha. "I think he's stopped breathing. Fi, hang on!"

Kobi tore open the pack with his teeth and loaded the syringe. Fionn was completely limp—he looked like a corpse already. Kobi tapped his arm a couple of times hard to get a vein up. No reaction. Holding his breath he plunged the syringe and eased the medicine into Fionn's arm.

"Please . . . Please . . . ," Asha mumbled. She clutched Fionn's hand, massaging the back. "Have you got any more? Give him more."

Kobi wanted to tell her that if this dose didn't work, there was no point injecting more, but he already suspected it might be too late. "Wait . . ." was all he could manage.

The seconds ticked on, and Fionn just lay there like a doll. Asha began to cry quietly.

Finally the wolf lay down too, whining with its head on its paws.

Like it already knew.

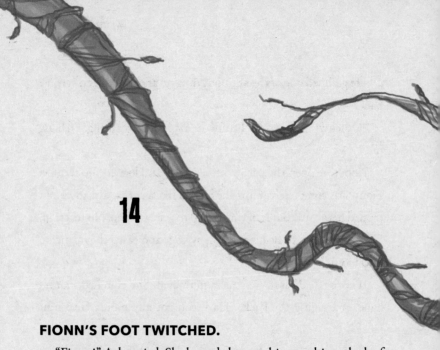

14

FIONN'S FOOT TWITCHED.

"Fionn!" Asha cried. She leaned closer to him, pushing a lock of hair from his brow. "Fionn, can you hear me?"

Then Fionn's lips parted and he let out a moan. A smile exploded across Asha's face. "Fionn, we're right here. Don't try to move."

But Fionn did anyway, opening his eyes and rolling onto his side. He half fell off the table, but Asha rescued him. "Stay put," she said.

Fionn was blinking, looking left and right, then focusing on Asha.

"Kobi saved you," she said.

"My dad saved you," said Kobi, smiling down. "We're at his lab at the university."

Fionn managed to sit, dangling his legs over the side of the table. He mimicked drinking.

Kobi fished his canteen out and handed it to Fionn, who drank deeply. Afterward, he wiped his mouth. He looked at them both. "Thank you," he said out loud, making Kobi pull back in surprise. Asha laughed. She grabbed him in a fierce hug. "I thought . . . I'd lost you."

Fionn grinned. He petted the wolf that was nuzzling him.

"Just rest up for a few minutes," said Kobi. "I've got to see if there are any clues about where my dad is." He spotted some sealing tape and tossed it to Asha. "Would you mind sealing the door?"

Asha nodded. "You think your dad made it here?"

"I hope so."

Kobi scanned the room—there was a notebook on the lab bench, with a pen beside it. Kobi opened it to look and skipped to the most recent page, hoping to find a date that might tell him when his dad was last here. Apart from a few scribbles of various chemical equations, and some complex molecular diagrams, there was nothing to help. The lab was adjoined by an office. The door was open, and inside was a desk, bookshelves, and a couch with a sleeping bag rolled at one end. The trash can held some empty cans of food, but it was hard to tell when they might have been eaten. Kobi imagined his dad at the desk, working as he ate. There was an empty syringe in the trash can too.

But it was the photo on the desk that drew his attention. His dad, looking so young, standing shoulder to shoulder with three others; one was an older man in a black gown, and the other two, along with Kobi's father, wore mortarboard hats and clutched rolled-up scrolls of paper. Graduation day. Maybe the old guy was a professor. Kobi picked the photo up carefully to look closer. It *had* to be pre-Waste. The four people in the image stood on the grassy shore of some lake or river, in front of a huge, modern, multistory mansion, surrounded by exotic flowers and trees. The photo had been taken from a jetty, just visible extending through the water in the foreground. The older professor was a large man with thick gray hair and a trimmed beard. He wore spectacles, and his head was drawn back in a hearty laugh. One of the students beside Kobi's dad was a tall and sallow-cheeked man with dark auburn hair. He had his arm over Kobi's dad's shoulder and smiled at the camera. Kobi's dad was looking sideways at the woman beside him. Kobi felt an odd prickle across his skin. His dad had never wanted to talk about Kobi's mother, clamming up at the first mention, and after a while Kobi had learned to stop asking. Could this be her? She had straight, black hair and delicate features. Kobi tried to see himself in them but couldn't. He put the frame back down, sadly. Trying to imagine life before the Waste was almost impossible. The picture looked fake, or like something taken on another planet.

Kobi sat down in the desk chair, taking the room in. On the wall opposite were two posters with the same GrowCycle lettering from the front door. One showed acres and acres of crops growing in neat rows. Some sort of harvesting vehicle was cutting through the center, spelling out the letters *GAIA*, and across the bottom of the poster were the words—*Nourishing Humanity*. The other poster showed the cover of a magazine called *TIME*. It was a picture of a bearded, smiling man. His face was etched with deep lines, and spectacles were balanced on his large nose. Kobi recognized him as the older man from the graduation photo. He wore a lab coat and held up an impossibly glossy apple as if about to sink his very white teeth into it. The headline in the corner read: "Professor Alan Apana, head of GrowCycle's GAIA program, reveals the hunger that drove him to solve the world's food shortage."

Kobi's father had known Alan Apana, the head of GrowCycle. The man who had destroyed the world. Kobi tried to focus his whirring thoughts. In some ways it made sense. His father had managed to survive because he had understood how to create the cleansers from Kobi's blood. He had always been reticent to talk about the past, about the Waste disaster. Was that because . . . he was involved in it? Had he worked at GrowCycle? He was young back then. He couldn't have been high up in the company. *No, you're reading too much into one photo. Apana was probably just his teacher.*

Kobi continued to search the room. He pulled out the desk drawers and ruffled through their contents. Apart from some stationery, there were reports of meetings, mostly dated in early 2031, which was hardly a surprise. In the bottom one, there was a bound set of pages. The cover simply read:

GAIA 1.3: New Findings (Restricted. For L3 Clearance Personnel Only)

I guess that includes me now, thought Kobi.

He scanned the opening paragraphs. It had been compiled offsite, at a location called the Park, and though Kobi was only skimming, certain words stood out: *preliminary findings . . . worrying trends in primary and secondary samples . . . unexpected side effects in organic samples . . . rapid growth combined with potent mutagenesis.*

Kobi looked up to check on Asha and Fionn. They were sitting together, stroking the wolf, which was lifting first one paw, then the other, as if obeying direct commands. Fionn was actually laughing.

Kobi returned to the report, forcing himself to read more slowly and take it all in. He didn't understand some of the language, but the meaning was quite clear. A scientific team—their signatures listed at the bottom of the report—was carrying out research into the GAIA program. Kobi scanned the signatures quickly but, thankfully, his father's name, Jon Hales, wasn't among them. Kobi found himself shaking his head in dismay at the reasoned scientific tone. It was like no one saw the catastrophe coming. There was evidence that the fertilizer was mutagenic, increasing its effectiveness but also bringing the risk of toxicity. A couple of scientists had already fallen ill after accidental exposure. The report ended with three recommendations.

The immediate suspension of GAIA 1.3 testing until further evaluations can be carried out.

Delay in testing at the Park site.

An urgent meeting with the PR and communications teams at GrowCycle.

A voice made him look up. Asha was standing in the door. He hadn't even heard her approach. "Sorry?"

"You were in another world. I said, 'Anything interesting?'"

I was in the past, thought Kobi.

Kobi closed the report.

"Did you find any leads on your dad?" asked Asha softly.

Kobi pushed himself to his feet. Looking at the cans in the trash, and then the rolled-up sleeping bag, he felt a sharp stab of emptiness. It was almost a month now, and he hadn't come across a single clue his dad was alive. "No."

He heard a sudden growl from the other room and a man's voice, then Fionn yelped. Asha turned on her heel and they both rushed in. Kobi looked around in confusion, searching for the source of the voice, heart thudding in expectation. But all he saw was the wolf, hackles up and snarling. Fionn was pressed against the wall.

There was a disembodied head sitting on the workbench, being projected from a shoe-size black box. It flickered in and out of resolution, and though it was talking, the words were sporadic, and out of time with the movement of its lips.

"... careful, Jon ... No, we shouldn't. ... onto us. We're supposed to be scientists, right?" Kobi edged nearer. He had no idea who the man was. "You have to send more, Jon. Test subjects' reactions are remarkable. . . . If it turns out to be . . . we've won! Please, as soon as you can. . . . It was all worth it."

The face came into sharper focus, and then Kobi froze. He had seen it in the other room. The head belonged to the gangly graduate standing beside his father, only now the man was much older, with salt-and-pepper hair and a gaunt look.

So many thoughts and feelings tangled in his mind, such deep confusion, but the foremost was betrayal. The man in the hologram was talking to his father. He was calling him Jon. And that meant one thing.

Dad's been lying to me. He said there was no one else, and he knew it wasn't true.

"It's all right," said Asha to Fionn. "You haven't done anything wrong." She glanced at Kobi.

"Who is that man?"

Kobi couldn't produce words. He stared at the flickering projection. The man's face was frozen in urgency—in the middle of sharing something with Kobi's father that Kobi had been excluded from.

It's a coincidence, he tried to tell himself. *The drone is old. It could be a recording. Jon could be anyone.*

But Kobi's brain was too rational, too well-trained to take stock, add up the probabilities, and draw logical conclusions for him to believe it.

"There has to be a reason," Kobi murmured.

"Jon's your dad, right?" said Asha. She didn't seem to get the significance of what she was saying.

"Jon's my dad." Kobi echoed, hoping it might give him some form of comfort, but he just sounded desperate. Memories flashed through his mind. All the times his dad could have told him the truth. All the times he'd lied instead. *The secret trips to the lab. He told me I was too young to come, but that wasn't the reason he left me behind. He didn't want me to see this. Asha is probably right about the vitamin pills too. He didn't want me to sense other people.*

It all seemed to fill Kobi up, too overwhelming to contain. He fell into a seat at the desk, heart vibrating so much he felt his body might shatter.

He didn't trust me. . . . Is that it? Because I'm just a kid.

Kobi wanted to believe that was the reason. His father had just wanted to protect him, not give him false hope. But Kobi looked up at Asha and Fionn, their faces cast with pity, and thought about the times he had asked his father about other survivors like them. Kobi had *longed* to find others. He'd suggested over and over that they search, improve the radio receiver, build a smoke fire somewhere they could hide from Snatchers. And always, his dad had refused.

"It's just us, Kobi. It's me and you. Focus on that."

"How did you make it play the message, Fionn?" Kobi tried to speak slowly, calmly, but the words wavered. "I want to hear the whole thing."

Fionn stepped forward tentatively and passed a hand over the device.

The head scrambled and reset. It played back with the same interference.

". . . in trouble . . . an intelligence leak . . . change locations, just to be . . . don't know . . . be careful, Jon. . . . No, we shouldn't. . . . onto us. We're supposed to be scientists, right?"

Kobi let it play, listening intently, hoping to glean some further clues. The holo-message went on to describe a new batch of anti-Waste drugs that Kobi's dad was sending out. Kobi thought back to the vials of Waste cleansers in the fridge back at the school. His dad had developed them from samples of Kobi's blood. But where was he sending them? If Kobi had just *known,* he would have been happy to help. It didn't make sense. *Why didn't he tell me the truth? What possible reason did he have to lie?*

And what did this message have to do with his disappearing?

"Maybe your dad was in touch with CLAWS," said Asha hopefully. "This guy says he's a scientist, and it sounds like they were working on a Waste cure."

Kobi listened a third time. *Test subjects?* Dad was sending vials of his Waste cleanser to some sort of test site. Somewhere a drone could get to. But it sounded like something underhanded. They were worried about getting caught. In among the shock, the hurt, Kobi wondered what exactly his dad was involved in.

Kobi noticed a folder resting on the table near the drone and recognized his father's handwriting. The title of the folder was 2.0, written in bold, typed font. At the top of the folder his dad had scrawled: *Other Testing. Full Cure, Part Two. Send to Alex.* The familiar handwriting made Kobi's father's deceit feel more real, more personal. A well of emotion rose suddenly, threatening to drown Kobi from the inside. *How could he have done this to me?*

"I need some time to think," he said quietly to Asha.

No one answered, and as Kobi stood and turned, he heard the now-familiar pneumatic hiss of the dart gun. He felt a thump in his midriff and saw the dart protruding from his clothes.

"What?"

Asha was standing there, lowering the weapon.

"Sorry, Kobi," she said.

And it sounded like she truly meant it.

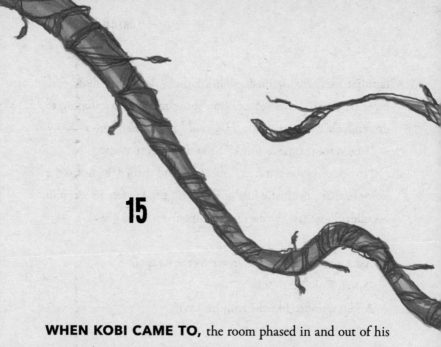

15

WHEN KOBI CAME TO, the room phased in and out of his vision. There were two Ashas, both standing by the window. Strips of sealing tape lay on the floor.

"What are you doing?" said Kobi, his voice slurred. He tried to stand, but his feet skidded out from beneath him and he crumpled. It made no sense.

Fionn was wailing, pawing at Asha in distress. The wolf was pacing behind them, growling, hackles raised.

"It has to be done, Fionn," she said.

"No!" the boy replied.

Kobi grabbed at her leg, angry but weak. She easily pulled her foot away, then pointed the dart rifle at him again. "It's done, Kobi. They're coming. Now back off. You've taken a D-Three. Another might kill you."

Fionn placed himself in between them, holding out his arms. "No!" he said again.

A flicker of doubt crossed Asha's face, but she hardened her jaw. "I know he helped us," she said. "But that doesn't change anything."

Kobi felt so fuzzy. He managed to stand but toppled back as if the floor itself was rearing up. "Why?" was all he could say, but as he asked the question, the answer formed in his mind. "It was you, wasn't it, who reactivated the Snatcher? Not Niki. You want CLAWS to come and get us."

"I had to," said Asha. "Your dad's research can save lives."

Fionn rushed at her again, grabbing for the gun, but she sidestepped and shoved him in the back. He crashed into the wolf, which growled, and moved away.

"Don't you see?" said Asha. "Those cleansers aren't like ours, Fi! They might lead to a real cure."

Kobi's confusion burned away in a flare of anger. He thought his head might actually be clearing. "You have no right!" he said. "I trusted you—I saved your lives!"

"And we're saving yours," said Asha. "You just can't see it yet."

"By attacking me?" said Kobi. Yes, the dose was definitely wearing off. The room concentrated into tight focus. *Should have gone D-Four if you wanted to keep me down*, he thought triumphantly. He wondered if he could get the gun away from her. Maybe not worth the risk.

"By calling the Guardians," said Asha. "They'll see the flare and come for us."

Flare. He saw that the window to the room was smashed. She'd fired the flare gun from Kobi's supply bag into the sky, where it could be seen from miles and miles around. How long did they have before the Snatchers came?

"You can't survive out here on your own," said Asha, meeting Kobi's furious glare.

"I'm not on my own!" shouted Kobi. "When I find my dad . . ."

Asha sighed. "Kobi, he's gone," she said softly. "Accept it. You're better off with us now."

Fionn sobbed, shaking his head. He stared at Asha like he hardly knew her. "No," he said. "Don't take me back."

"Go to hell," Kobi said, then pretended to stumble back before turning and running for the door.

"Stop!" snapped Asha.

Kobi didn't look back, charging out into the corridor. He'd almost made it to the stairs when he heard the thudding of helicopter rotors directly outside, then the thundering of boots on the floor below. *They're here already!* Of course they were. They've been looking for us since the school. They were just waiting for the signal. Asha must have briefed them through the Snatcher's comms in the woodwork room. She had this plan all along. She knew if the Snatchers came, it would force Kobi out and she could follow him to his dad's base and his research. He felt almost bad for Niki, that he had blamed her. He'd been such an idiot.

The first of the guards was coming up the stairs, masked and wearing protective gear. He raised a gun at Kobi. "Freeze!"

Kobi jumped, feetfirst, and slammed into the guard, sending him tumbling back down the steps. He clambered over, only to see half a dozen more guards waiting below. The two leaders knelt and fired, and Kobi felt another dart pierce his shoulder. He pulled it out and kept on running, throwing himself into their midst. Hands tried to grab him, but Kobi lashed out wildly, raining punches and kicks wherever he could. *They won't take me!* And then he was free, sprinting back toward the door into the outside world. If he could reach it, maybe he had a chance to slip away.

A Snatcher blocked the doorway, lumbering through and filling the corridor. Instead of slowing, Kobi pumped his legs harder, drawing his machete and charging. *Just have to get past.* As he neared, he dropped into a slide, skidding across the ground under the massive metal legs. He swung the machete at the same time, and the blade crunched right through one of the leg joints. He fetched up on the other side, leaving the Snatcher skittering clumsily for balance as sparks crackled over its severed foot. Kobi felt a little woozy already. They'd upped their doses too. How long did he have?

The CLAWS guards were shouting at him to stop, and a sharp sting told him another dart had hit the back of his leg. The Snatcher reached out, and a single claw caught in Kobi's shirt, yanking him back down onto the floor. The Snatcher reared over him. Kobi threw up his arms, then saw the creature jolt under a heavy impact. The air was filled with a fierce guttural snarling as furred flesh met with metal. Kobi scrambled away. The wolf was on top of the Snatcher, paws wrapped over its carapace and tearing with its teeth. Frayed wires and loose hydraulic cables spilled free as the huge predator savaged the robot. Behind Kobi saw the CLAWS guards holding back a screaming Fionn. Three Snatchers crashed down on top of the wolf, pinning it to the ground. Stingers extended from their metal underbellies, pumping a tranquilizer into the wolf's body. Kobi watched, frozen in horror, as the creature's strength drained away.

He stumbled on through the door and into the street. The tree line was just a few feet away. Just a few more steps and—

He saw the shadow coming, and before he could look up, metal legs closed around his middle and hoisted him off the ground on blasting jets. Kobi twisted and rammed the hilt of the machete into another Snatcher's "face." The metal dented, and something inside made a fizzing sound. The Snatcher lurched sideways, like a giant lazy bee struggling to take off. Kobi smashed it with another blow, and the grip around his waist loosened a fraction. He slipped through, and his legs slammed into the ground, leaving him gasping for breath. He tried to move, but his limbs felt numb. The Snatcher rose away, leaning sideways at an odd angle, and then careered into the side of a building, exploding on impact.

He managed to get onto his knees, then one foot. Clumsily he began to half hobble, half crawl toward the trees. Another dart hit him beneath the armpit. He didn't have the strength to pull it out.

The guards' voices were distant, like he was underwater, and the trees ahead became a green smear, shadowy at the edges. Kobi's own breath came like a wheeze.

One of his hands gave way beneath him, and his face hit the ground hard. He tasted earth. Rolling over with a groan, he saw feet all around, then guns; bio suits; and blank, masked faces. His field of vision was shrinking fast.

Then Asha's face appeared, anxious. She leaned closer.

"It's going to be all right," she said. "Stop fighting."

Kobi didn't believe her, but he didn't have a choice. Though his mind told him to get up, to punch and kick and scream, his body was impossibly heavy. The black shadows closed in completely.

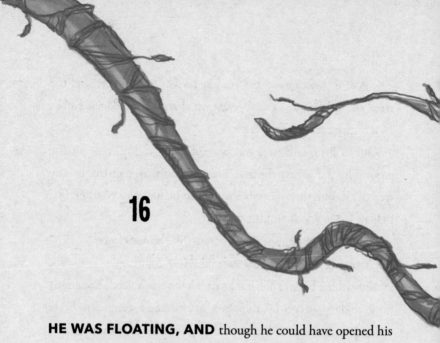

16

HE WAS FLOATING, AND though he could have opened his eyes, he didn't want to. Better just to enjoy the sensation of being at rest, in the dark, every muscle relaxed and cushioned. There were voices—his ears took in the sound—and he kept them at the reaches of his brain, an incomprehensible murmuring.

But slowly, Kobi's consciousness took over. His limbs reported, via nerve endings, and neurons fired across his mind. *I'm lying in a bed. The comfiest bed I've ever felt.*

". . . abnormal readings. The tranquilizer is wearing off fast." A man's voice. "It should've kept him under for hours—it was a level five dosage. The girl wasn't lying about this kid."

Then a woman, deep and commanding and a little irritated: "Why would she? Take more blood while he's still under."

Kobi felt a cold hand on his elbow, then the prick of a needle. He tugged his arm away. There was a gasp, and the rattle of metal on metal, then he opened his eyes into blinding light.

"He's waking up!"

Kobi threw off a sheet, rolled sideways. His bare feet hit the floor. He blinked until he could see clearly. A sterile-looking room, with a normal bed against one wall. Monitors and a table of instruments. Two middle-aged men in lab coats, one poised with a syringe. Another man in a more military-looking uniform, his hand on a holstered gun. A single door, closed, and a large glass viewing panel beside it, with several men and women in pale uniforms, all marked across the chest with the CLAWS logo.

Kobi realized he was in his underwear and nothing else.

"Where am I?" said Kobi.

The doctors looked at each other, then toward Kobi. No, behind him. He spun around to see a woman in a dark suit and white blouse watching him from an armchair. She had gray hair cut short, and pixieish sharp features. Her pale blue eyes, wide-spaced, seemed familiar.

"Welcome to Healhome, Kobi."

She climbed smoothly from the confines of the chair.

Kobi remembered what had happened at his dad's lab, and his terror spiked. They'd caught him. Brought him here. He saw a tray with a scalpel on the table and made a grab.

"Hey, no!" shouted one of the doctors.

But Kobi had it in his hand. He seized the woman's arm and pulled her in front of him, holding the scalpel at her throat. She was slight, her limbs birdlike.

"Let me out of here!" he said to anyone listening.

On the other side of the glass, a guard spoke into a walkie-talkie. In the treatment room, the one with the gun drew it and pointed it at Kobi's head.

The woman in front of Kobi held up a hand. "Stand down, Mr. Krenner," she said.

"I can take him out," said the guard, keeping the gun trained.

"I gave you an order," said the woman. Though her body felt weak, she spoke with calm authority.

He obeyed, but his eyes didn't move from Kobi's, and his lip curled in a snarl.

"Kobi," said his captor calmly. "There's really no need for this. We're the good guys."

"You kidnapped me," said Kobi. He backed away toward the door, keeping his eyes on the doctors. Both had raised their hands, staring at him in alarm.

"Kobi, let's just talk, all right?" said the woman.

Kobi gripped her firmly with one hand and tried the door. It was locked, but there was some sort of keypad: "How do I open this? What's the code?"

"We need to discuss some things first," said the woman.

Kobi knew he would never hurt her, but she didn't need to know that.

"I'll kill you," he said.

"If you do, we'll all be stuck in here," she said. "Only I have the code. This is my facility. My name is Melanie Garcia."

Kobi's hand was shaking. Asha had talked about a head Guardian—Niki seemed to like her. Though Niki liking someone didn't count for much . . .

"Kobi, we've been searching for you for a long time. Please, believe me, we're your friends. Put this thing down."

"I don't trust you," he said. "Where's Fionn? And Asha?"

"Fionn is being looked after in a quarantine environment," she said. "He's not in such robust health as you and Asha—he needs close monitoring. But all signs show whatever drug you gave him worked remarkably well. Asha's right here."

Kobi heard a knocking at the glass and turned to see Asha on the other side. She'd changed into clean clothes—a gray one-piece jumpsuit.

"I'm here, Kobi," she said, her voice muffled by the glass.

She betrayed me. She brought them to the school first, then Dad's lab. Still, just the sight of her in this strange place gave him a shot of relief. A face, even hers, softened his panic. It was all too confusing.

"You lied to me all along," said Kobi.

"Not all along," she replied a little sadly. "I told you—our job was to find survivors. But, Kobi, don't you see—those cleansers your dad made are amazing. We need them. And we need *you*."

Kobi shoved Melanie off him. He wasn't sure what he was doing, but he put the scalpel to his own neck, right over his carotid artery.

Now Melanie looked a little alarmed. "Kobi, don't do anything stupid. We're on *your side*—"

"Then prove it," he interrupted desperately. "Just open the door."

Melanie straightened her skirt and nodded. "Very well, Kobi. But please, don't hurt anyone, least of all yourself."

He backed away as she approached. Kobi watched her tap in a six-digit code, and the door slid open. The guards on the other side bristled.

"Tell them to drop their guns," said Kobi.

Melanie hesitated, then nodded. The guards obeyed, laying their weapons gently on the ground.

"And back off, toward the wall!" said Kobi.

They did as he said, but Asha approached the door.

"Please, Kobi. Don't do this. The Guardians can help you."

Kobi couldn't tell if she was lying or not, but he needed time. He lunged at her, grabbing her arm, then wrapped his own around her. She struggled in his grip, but he squeezed tighter until she cried out.

"Ow—Kobi, that hurts!" she said.

"You're coming with me," he replied.

He dragged her out, then under an archway. The large room was surrounded by chambers just like the one he'd come from, glass-paneled but decorated with more individual pieces of furniture. Colored bedspreads and pictures on the walls. A foosball table, a dartboard, and something that looked like an old-fashioned jukebox. There were posters on the walls, and TVs. There were kids in the rooms, all wearing the same uniform as Asha. They all came to the glass to watch as he and Asha made their way past. There were double elevator doors at one end of the room, and several doors at the other.

"Which is the way out?" said Kobi in Asha's ear.

"Out where?" said Asha.

"I'm going back to Seattle," said Kobi. "Where are the transports?"

"They're on the hangar level—top floor. We're not allowed up there unaccompanied."

He pulled her toward the elevator doors, ignoring the staring kids. Some of them looked a little odd, but he didn't have time to focus. The Guardians emerged from the viewing room, following Melanie. "Kobi—this isn't a prison. It's a medical facility."

Kobi reached the elevator and stabbed the call button, which lit up. The doors slid open almost at once. He paused, suddenly afraid. It looked so small inside, like a cage. Melanie and the guards were moving closer, though. He backed in with Asha. One side was covered in buttons. He pressed the highest number, 182. The doors closed, sealing them in.

With a tiny bump, they began to rise from level 42. Kobi's stomach lurched with the sensation. He let Asha go, and she sagged against the wall, shaking her head.

"Kobi, please. You have to stop," said Asha.

Kobi didn't reply at first. He watched the numbers flash past as the elevator sped faster than Kobi would have thought possible.

Halfway between floors 153 and 154, the lift suddenly jolted to a stop. Kobi stabbed at the button, but nothing happened.

"What's going on?" he snapped.

"I guess they killed the circuits," said Asha. "They're not going to let you leave."

Kobi grabbed the doors on either side and heaved. They shuddered open, just a crack at first. Kobi braced himself and strained, forcing them farther apart. They were between floors, but he clambered out into a corridor. Red lights flashed across the ceiling and an alarm was sounding. Asha remained where she was.

"Kobi, come back!" she said.

Kobi ran to a door at the end and pushed through. Two adults were by a set of lockers and looked at him in astonishment. "You're not allowed up here," one said. Kobi ignored them and turned back the way he'd come. Asha was climbing out now as well. He reached another door. It was dark on the other side, but lights blinked on as he entered. He staggered, knees buckling—the room was filled with vats, stretching almost to the ceiling, and inside each he saw an animal suspended in clear liquid. A horse with a bulbous deformed body, a giant rabbit sliced in cross sections, a two-headed coyote. And so many more—all Waste-infected corpses. It was like a nightmare.

A voice sounded over internal speakers—Melanie Garcia's.

"We have an escaped patient. All personnel—if you see him, please apprehend."

Kobi walked between the vats, staring in horror at their

contents. Were all these creatures brought here by the Snatchers? So this was what the *research* looked like. . . .

He'd reached the far side of the room, and he was gazing at a giant dead bird, its wings splayed wide, extending the length of a bus. There was a door, and he went through it, finding himself in an unlit stairwell shaft, the walls bare concrete. He just had to get to the highest level. He had no idea if he could even fly a transport ship when he got there. If there was a Guardian, he could make them do it. He still had the scalpel.

Kobi heard a door slam open far below and looked over the balustrade. Guardians were swarming onto the stairs three floors down. Red tracer lights lanced through the darkness, and one flashed across his chest.

"He's up there! Alone!"

Kobi backed up as a dart chinked into the ceiling above and bounced off.

Kobi began to climb, leaping five or six steps at a time, his chest burning. His muscle endurance was five times the average, his dad had told Kobi. He pushed himself harder.

Eventually, he reached the top floor. A door led off the stairs, but it didn't budge from this side, and there was no handle. Kobi took a step back, then drove his foot into it. The door was steel and unmovable. Below, the guardians were closing—their shouts and the thump of their boots muffled. Kobi kicked again, and pain jarred up his knee.

The guardians were two floors down. At any moment he'd be

in the firing line. Taking a deep breath he threw himself shoulder-first into the door, bouncing off hopelessly.

The guardians' feet were tramping closer. Kobi launched his body against the door one last time, but he had no power left. Several tracers picked out points on the wall beside him, and he knew the game was up. Slowly, he lifted his hands, and turned to face them.

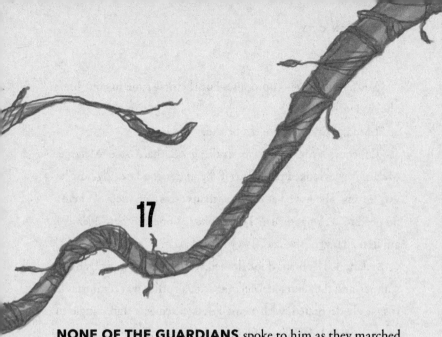

17

NONE OF THE GUARDIANS spoke to him as they marched him back to the elevator in formation. Four in front, four behind. Guns lowered, but close enough that they could reach out and touch each other. Even if Kobi could overpower one or two, the others would be ready. He didn't stand a chance.

The elevator was functioning again and descended back down to a different floor—88. Melanie was waiting for him. "Kobi, please, let me just explain everything to you, then, trust me, you won't want to run." She led him, escorted by the Guardians, through the bare corridor. Guardians in lab coats as well as plain clothes paced purposely through it.

"Let's go to my office," said Melanie, putting an arm on his shoulder. Kobi flinched involuntarily. He still wasn't used to being touched. Melanie seemed to mistake his gesture for fear.

"You're *safe*, Kobi—I promise. For the first time in your life." She smiled.

"I need to find my dad," Kobi said.

"Of course you do; we're working on that," said Melanie. Melanie's eyes looked pained, as if she understood exactly how he was feeling. She waved at the Guardians escorting them. "There's no need to accompany us." They looked at one another. "Please, I am in no danger," she said. They moved away.

Melanie led Kobi to a door, flashed a card from her waist against a scanner, and they entered. Melanie Garcia's office was comfortable if sparsely decorated, with a small desk tilted at a slight angle to show a large CLAWS logo, with touch buttons up the side in some sort of interactive display board. One wall was entirely given to a window, and Kobi gasped at the outlook. A carpet of green, as far as the eye could see. They were hundreds of feet up, above the tops of the tallest canopy. There were no buildings, no man-made structures of any sort. Asha was right—living on Healhome was like being marooned on an island in the middle of a vast ocean. He wondered how far they were from Seattle.

"Take a seat," said Melanie. She pressed a few buttons on the desk, then sat on the other side.

Kobi lowered himself into a comfortable leather chair. How are you feeling now?" she asked.

"Like a prisoner," said Kobi.

Melanie nodded thoughtfully. "I'm sorry things got out of

hand," she said. "You must understand, Kobi—bringing you here, *keeping* you here, it's all for your protection."

Kobi hardly needed to reply. He trusted his glare of contempt to do all the talking.

"You don't believe me," said Melanie. "And I don't blame you. The way we brought you in was . . . heavy-handed. We didn't know what we were dealing with, but we had to act fast, for your own safety."

"Stop saying that!" said Kobi. "I was fine out there."

"So far," said Melanie. He caught a flash of impatience in her eyes.

"So, what now?" he asked. "How long are you going to keep me here?"

"Until we can earn your trust," said Melanie.

Kobi almost laughed. *You may as well throw away the key, then.*

Melanie sighed. "I imagine it's a little odd, after so long alone."

"With my dad," Kobi corrected her.

He thought he saw Melanie flinch.

"I'm going to explain some things to you Kobi, some things you might not want to hear. Firstly, Asha told us about your headaches, and her theory about your father's vitamin pills."

"Did she . . . ?" said Kobi.

"She was correct," said Melanie. "We ran some tests on pills we found back at the school."

"Dad said I have to stay strong," said Kobi.

"They're not nutritional in the slightest," said the Healhome director. "They're neuropathic blockers that target the temporal lobe of your brain."

Kobi just shrugged. "And?" He didn't want to hear what she was going to say.

"They suppress your telepathic ability," said Melanie. "Jonathan was worried Projectors like Fionn would send you a message, or Receptors like Asha might sense you."

Kobi didn't say anything. He didn't want to believe it. The familiar way she'd said the name Jonathan chilled his blood. "You know my dad?"

Melanie hesitated. "This is going to be hard for you to hear, but I'll lay it out.

"The man you think is your father is a CLAWS scientist. Jonathan Hales kidnapped you, Kobi, and he took you to the only place we couldn't follow—the Wastelands. He—"

"Shut up," said Kobi. "You're lying. You—"

"No," said Melanie patiently. "*Dr. Hales* is the liar. He was one of us, here at CLAWS. And he was brilliant, Kobi, I'll admit it. He realized you were different from the others, and he took you because he wanted all the glory himself. He wanted to be the one to save the world."

"I don't believe you," said Kobi.

Melanie shrugged. "Why not? Ask yourself, Kobi—why did he never tell you about any of this?"

Kobi shook his head, searching for an answer, but he couldn't find one. He wasn't ready to accept it though.

Melanie tapped a few times on her desk screen. Then she rotated the display to face him. The page read "Personnel file C/HH/HalesJ," and showed a picture of his father looking a million miles from the man he'd last seen three weeks ago. But it was definitely the same person—a similar age to the photo from the lab, and Kobi's earliest memories. The file contained a list of specialisms, including *genetic sequencing*, *biotechnological engineering*, and *evolutionary biology*.

"Hales was a great mind," said Melanie, a little more brusquely, "but he always put himself first. I know it's hard to hear, but you have to forget about him."

Kobi smiled helplessly. *Forget about the man I've lived with all my life?* None of what she was telling him matched the person he knew. A good, caring, selfless man. "But he must have known he'd be exposing himself to Waste by leaving here," said Kobi.

"All the scientists were allocated a single orphan case," said Melanie. "You were his. He deleted all his notes before he disappeared, but we think he realized you were special and knew he could keep himself alive by synthesizing some of the compounds your body produces naturally. He should have lasted less than a week out there, but he managed almost thirteen years. He *used* you to stay alive." She paused and breathed out through her nose. "Like a parasite." She looked at the smiling face on the screen.

"You could have been here all this time," said Melanie. "You could have had friends. And we—CLAWS—might have found a cure years ago."

"That's all my dad wanted," said Kobi quietly. "I know it. He was using my blood to develop cleansers."

"The fact you still defend him does you credit," said Melanie. "It looks like Dr. Hales had an accomplice. Another renegade. We found the drone at the GrowCycle lab. We're running tests on the compounds we found in the lab as we speak."

At least that part of her story rang true. The face in the holographic message. But as for the rest of it . . . the stuff about his dad not being his real dad . . .

"He loved me," said Kobi, hugging himself. "I know he did."

Melanie placed a gentle hand on his wrist. "I think he probably did," she said. "In his own way. Kobi, Dr. Hales lost people to the Waste. His wife and child. We all lost . . . someone. He took you for the wrong reasons, for himself, but maybe he really did care for you as well."

Kobi closed his eyes, reeling, trying to shut out the world. But his mind rebelled, flashing up a jumble of memories. Riding his father's shoulders as a young boy, playing football in the gym, the candlelit meals filled with laughter, the sling when he'd broken his collarbone falling off a desk, the hundreds of stories they'd read together huddled under a blanket, the certificates and medal ceremonies when Kobi passed tests or achieved new feats of strength . . .

The *love*. What other word was there?

And yet, if Melanie Garcia was telling the truth, it was a lie too. An act that Dr. Hales had played from day one.

"Do you know how many kids we've lost here while Dr. Hales pursued his own fame?" Melanie said softly. Kobi waited. "Nineteen," she continued, her lip trembling. She tapped the screen several times and rows of images popped up—kids of every age. Some were in color—he saw Asha, Niki, and Fionn among them—but others were grayed out with the word *DECEASED* written beneath their portraits.

Kobi could hardly bear to look at their smiling faces. He leaned across and pressed the tab that closed the file, turning his gaze away as his eyes teared up.

"Look at me, Kobi," said Melanie.

He turned back to her.

"We can care for you here," she said. "And if Dr. Hales's secret research is confirmed, we may be closer than ever to a real cure." The director's eyes sparkled feverishly.

As he looked at Melanie, he realized he'd seen her before—the woman in the photo from the lab. Kobi had thought she might be his own mother. She looked so different now. But it was definitely her. More evidence that she was being straight with him.

"You were friends with him, weren't you?"

"Who? Jonathan? Yes. We were part of a group of highly able postgrad students that Alan Apana took under his wing. Apana— the man who engineered Waste—was once an emeritus professor of biochemistry at Seattle University. The 'minds of the future' he called us. Alex Mischik was another."

"That's who Dad—Hales—was communicating with. They were sending each other messages by drone."

Melanie sighed. "Yes, Mischik and Jonathan. They were always the most ambitious of all of us. Quite brilliant, both of them. No one could have predicted their plot to steal you. The arrogance is quite astounding. But then, they had the most arrogant of teachers. Anyway, that's enough about the past. Would you like to see him?"

"Who?" said Kobi.

Melanie looked grave. "I wanted to give you the full picture before I told you," she said. "We have Jonathan Hales in the infirmary, Kobi."

Kobi's blood chilled. Melanie tapped some buttons on the screen and it flicked to a camera feed showing Jonathan Hales lying on a bed. Kobi swallowed. His first reaction was relief, but it was soured by a bitter sickness in his stomach. Anger. That was what he felt. A pure, focused rage.

"He's in bad shape," Melanie said. "A retrieval drone picked him up about five days ago in the old city, and he was already unconscious. He couldn't tell us anything, so we knew we had to find you fast."

"So that's why you sent Asha and the others."

"They took an enormous risk," said Melanie. "For a long time, we'd doubted you and Dr. Hales could have even survived. When we found him, we found a picture of you in his wallet. To be honest, we couldn't believe it." Kobi nodded. He remembered the pictures well. Dad . . . Dr. Hales . . . had found an old Polaroid camera in a school cupboard. He took a shot of them both together every year in front of the same white board. He called it the yearbook photo.

"I don't want to see him," Kobi said.

Melanie frowned.

"I have nothing to say."

"We think it would be good for you to see him with your own eyes," said Melanie. "Of course, there is no rush. Though we think it would be cathartic for you, help you move on."

Kobi had already stood up and made his way to the wide window. He stared out across the panorama of the Wasteland. He shook his head and spoke softly. "I don't want to see him. My dad . . . my dad died out there."

18

KOBI WAS TAKEN BACK to the Healhome quarters. The kids were in their sectioned-off rooms still, but no one looked as relaxed as before. They huddled in groups, and when Kobi emerged with his armed escort, the looks he got were a mixture of naked disbelief and suspicion. He felt as though it was him behind the glass, being inspected like a zoo animal.

The guard called Krenner was there. Kobi remembered where he'd heard the name before. *He's the one who fled the Chokerplant attack. So he made it back.* He pressed a few buttons on a keypad by one of the glass walls. It slid upward, then he looked toward Kobi and gestured inside to an empty room. Kobi walked inside. The Guardians turned away, leaving only Krenner. He stared at Kobi with something close to hatred.

Melanie came from across the other side of the room, carrying a tablet and walking quickly, to stand beside the security guy. She muttered something to him, and he nodded, then turned and left, following his squad. Melanie focused on her tablet, swiping her finger a few times. The wall to Kobi's right folded open. Kobi found himself looking at the other kids he'd seen before, with nothing but air between them. There were about a dozen. There was a boy in the middle, tall with drooping hair, and a sinewy body like a rock climber. Kobi recognized him from Fionn's telepathic vision of the Frisbee game. He'd been speaking with Niki. Beside the rock climber boy was a girl with deep cracks across her skin, like bark. She swallowed, staring at Kobi. On the other side of the tall boy was another boy of a similar age, who looked Indian. He was short, with incredible yellow eyes. The others looked more or less normal. Kobi's periphery caught movement on a chair and a girl he hadn't even spotted peeled herself off sinuously and came to join the others. Her eyelids flickered. There was something weird about her hands. She grinned at him and waved her fingers, and Kobi saw that they were bulbous at the tips, like they were swollen.

No one else moved, and no one said anything, until Asha pushed to the front. She stood a yard in front of the others. "This is Kobi, everyone," she said quietly. "And Kobi, this is . . . everyone."

The tall rock climber kid in the center nodded. "Right."

The girl with the bulbous fingers whispered something in the yellow-eyed boy's ear.

"Why don't you ask him?" he replied.

"Is it true you lived outside?" she asked. "We don't believe Asha."

"Yes," Kobi said. He was very aware of his voice, with all these people listening, watching him. "We had a base in an old school. Me and my dad." He swallowed as he said the word. *Dad.* Kobi couldn't bear to tell the full truth right now. He was still trying to process it himself.

The kids all started talking at once, throwing questions at one another and him. The invisible barrier that seemed to hold them back before broke, and several edged toward him.

But in the chaos, Asha held back.

"Were there other kids?" asked a girl with ginger hair and freckles.

"What did you eat?" said a boy who looked painfully thin.

"Where's your dad now?" said the girl with bark skin, her long straight hair falling over her shoulders, almost down to her waist.

"Hey! Back off!" said the tall boy, holding out his arms. "Give the guy some space!" The bug-eyed boy approached, inspecting Kobi.

Through the viewing panels Kobi saw Melanie Garcia watching. She gave him a sympathetic smile, then left. That left only one Guardian, dressed in a lab coat and scribbling notes like he was documenting the meeting between the kids.

"Leon, he doesn't look like he's got a specialty," the bug-eyed boy said. "He's definitely not a blend." The boy's yellow eyes seemed to stare *through* Kobi, moving up and down. "And you know the weird thing? I can't see any Waste inside him. Maybe he's not one of us."

"He is," said Asha, moving forward, watching for Kobi's

reaction. Kobi didn't say anything.

The tall rock climber kid who must be Leon walked over. "Pleased to meet you anyway, Kobi," he said, and held out his hand. Kobi looked at it.

"He doesn't know you want to shake his hand!" said the girl with bulbous fingers, laughing. She leaped onto the glass screen and gripped hold with her fingers, splaying her body across the vertical wall like a gecko. Kobi gasped with astonishment.

"Stop it, Yaeko," said the bark-skinned girl. "Leon, don't . . ."

The gecko girl rolled her eyes and spoke wordlessly, bobbing her head, mimicking the other girl.

"What?" said Leon. "I'm just introducing myself, Jo. Come on, Kobi, just shake. That's what people do when they meet." Kobi found himself looking toward Asha, who nodded. Kobi took the other boy's hand and shook it slowly. It felt more than odd. Leon grinned at him, then Kobi felt his hand shudder violently. Suddenly his whole arm was vibrating. Kobi tried to pull away, but the boy gripped him tight.

"Hey!" Kobi tried to say, but his voice warbled. Everyone laughed. The boy let him go.

Asha said. "Leon's got fast-twitch muscles. Only they can keep on twitching in bursts like that."

Leon flexed his biceps. "Makes me *really* strong. Right, Rohan? They call me the Earthquake! Like the Flash mixed with the Thing but better! You like movies?"

"Shut up," said the yellow-eyed boy, shoving Leon jokingly. He turned to Kobi. "No one calls him the Earthquake. And, Leon, superhero movies suck."

Leon shrugged. "They're pretty much all we got." He grinned at Kobi. "I guess the Guardians think it's *aspirational* for us!"

"Leon's into Hollywood," said the girl with barklike skin. "He thinks he's an actor. You know what Hollywood was right?"

"Yeah," mumbled Kobi. "Me and . . . We had an old TV and hard drive at the school that we had working for a while."

"He's read books and seen movies," said Asha. "He's not a caveman."

"Caveman!" said Leon. "I like that. That can be your superhero name."

"He looks a bit tame to be a Caveman to me," said Yaeko. She was hanging from the ceiling now, her face upside down. "Cool, huh?" she said as Kobi stared.

Kobi was glad when Asha ushered him toward a sofa, where he took a seat. He felt totally overwhelmed.

"This must be weird for you, huh?" said Rohan as the other kids crowded around, sitting on other chairs and sofas, on beanbags, or lounging on the floor.

Yaeko was still hanging from the ceiling. "So, how'd you get here anyway?"

"It's kind of a long story," said Kobi.

Leon grinned and gestured to the room. "We're not going anywhere. You know about the whole apocalypse thing, right?"

Kobi talked. Mostly, they let him, and the only person who

didn't look rapt was Asha, but then she'd heard most of it before at the school. He sensed she wasn't so much listening to his words as watching him, reading the way he told his tale for the second time.

The interruptions he did get, every so often, were silly little things. About his lessons with his dad, about how they washed, and what the school looked like. When he talked about going outside, he saw only speechless faces. *They can't even imagine it*, he thought, and part of him felt almost guilty, as if he was boasting somehow for letting them know he'd entered a world they never could. As Kobi described his old life, he felt a pang of yearning, but it already seemed a million miles away.

And as he finished his story, the other kids told him theirs. It was the same tale for each—Healhome had been their home as long as any could remember. Not even Healhome—*this* very floor. Leon explained that the internal doors led to other rooms. He gave Kobi a tour. He showed him the tables and chairs in the canteen, served by a hatch in the wall, then the rows of doors to the individual dormitories and the washing facilities. There was a game room and a small gym, with weights, bikes, and treadmills. The biggest room was a huge hall with equipment inside that Leon called the training room. He seemed proud as he showed off the scope of their living space, but Kobi felt only a creeping sense of dread. *This is it?* Their world was safe, and clean, but it was tiny. He smiled and said nice things, all the time wondering how he was going to live here for the foreseeable future. Bill Gates was small, but at least he had the freedom to move around the classrooms. . . .

After a few hours, they sat down to eat in the canteen. Among all the deception, Asha had been telling the truth about one thing: the food. It was as bland as she'd said—cubes of slightly wobbly, squeaky stuff in a sauce that tasted artificially sweet. Rohan explained that the Guardians were hypervigilant about growing anything organic in case of infection, so all food was synthesized.

"It's safer," he said.

"It's disgusting," Kobi replied, smiling. Still, he was hungry enough to eat it all.

As they ate the dinner, he tried to remember all the kids' names. There was Johanna, Leon, Rohan, Yaeko. Reeta was the girl with red hair, he thought, but the others he found difficult to keep in his head. There was, maybe, a Heather, Sanjay, Paolo, and several others he went blank on. Did kids at school used to remember the names of everyone in their class?

After dinner, they went to the game room, which was spacious—about double the size of the lunch hall at Bill Gates. There were sofas and beanbags, a pool table and dart board, packs of playing cards of the kind he used to play with Dr. Hales, a selection of books a lot smaller than the school library's, and various board games. Some of the kids showed him gaming consoles, putting over their eyes goggles they called VR. Kobi tried the goggles on and jumped with fright when he found himself in a virtual world of a lava cave with some kind of giant dinosaur throwing shells at him. Jo said they had lessons with the Guardians every day, just like a normal school, though how she could know anything about what *normal* meant, Kobi didn't know.

They showed Kobi how to play a card game called last man standing, and he even won a few rounds. He pretended to be enjoying himself, but after a while he became bored. He felt annoyed at himself for feeling that way. *I'm safe. I have friends. I should be happy.* But the thought seemed ridiculous.

Leon hissed at Kobi. "Hey, dude, come in here." While the others continued with the card game, Kobi went with Asha, Rohan, and Leon into the training room. Kobi looked around it properly. It was like a gym mixed with a martial arts room mixed with a tech lab. Mats lay on the floor, a climbing wall reached one hundred feet up, and gymnastic equipment lay around the room, but there were also lots of scientific instruments and equipment near each apparatus. "This is where we test our powers, Caveman," said Leon. "We all have baseline abilities, but some of us have specialties that we try to develop. We're called blends."

A shape dropped down in front of him from above. It was Yaeko. "Boo."

"So I guess you can climb stuff," said Kobi.

"She's Gecko Girl!" said Leon.

"Don't call me that," said Yaeko.

Jo said, "Me, Yaeko, Rohan, Leon, Fionn, Asha, Niki, and a few others. We're blends. We're called that because the Guardians think that other organic DNA could have entered our bodies with the Waste, causing odd mutations. So we're kind of blended with other organisms from the natural world."

"You must be annoyed you don't have a specialty," said Yaeko to Kobi.

"I'm not," said Kobi, and the others laughed.

"Kobi may only have baseline abilities, but I told you, they're awesome," said Asha. "Show us, Kobi."

"Maybe later."

"Check this out," said Rohan. He made his way into a large area of the hall enclosed in a circular net that hung down from the ceiling. The netted area was about sixty-five feet in diameter. Near its perimeter stood tall cones with archery-type targets attached. Small machines carrying baseballs in a tub, with tubes at the front of them like large gun nozzles, were laid out around the net too. Rohan grabbed two baseball bats from a tub and stood in the middle of the net. He held one bat in each hand. "Draw!" he cried. Baseballs shot at him from all around. He spun and dodged, swinging the bats, often hitting multiple balls at once. The balls powered off, smashing down the targets.

"Rohan's specialty is his vision," said Leon, watching his friend proudly. "His spectral range has been increased on many levels. Or something sciencey like that. So, anyway, it's cool because he can process kinetic movement much faster. And he has night vision and can spot Waste inside people."

"That is pretty, er, *cool*," said Kobi.

"Why don't we do some group ability exercises?" said Jo.

"Go on!" said Yaeko, grinning. "Show us your powers, or we

might think you don't have any."

"I think I need some time on my own, actually," said Kobi. "I'm a bit tired." In truth he felt totally drained.

"Sure," said Asha. "You must be exhausted, and these guys can be hard work. Come with me." She led him to a spare dormitory and left him to get some rest. Kobi lay back on the thick mattress. It felt too soft, like he couldn't move, and the thick material made him sweat. He stared up at the ceiling. Luminescent stickers of stars mapped out the constellations. *Nothing like the real thing.* He felt overwhelmed, like someone drowning, kicking for the surface, but gradually giving in to the weight of water. The realization was dawning on him that he would be here forever. This was his home now.

He heard someone enter without knocking. It was Niki. Kobi sat up. The girl had a bandage across her forehead, but otherwise she looked fine. *The Snatcher didn't kill her. It brought her here.*

"You're okay," he said.

"Of course I am," she said blithely. "I just came from a physical. We do them a lot. Whatever, you'll get to know about things around here."

Kobi nodded. "It's good we made it back here. All of us. I'm sorry—you know—about blaming you for turning on the Snatcher."

"Yeah, you'll see how great it is here," said Niki, ignoring his apology. "We trust the Guardians. We're one big family. Sounds cheesy. But you'll get it soon. Just watch out for Yaeko. She's a real firebrand. That's why we get along so well." She gave a shy smile and left.

Kobi didn't know how long he slept. There was no natural light in Healhome, but the lights dimmed and brightened on a twenty-four-hour time cycle. When he woke, he stumbled out into the communal room, and from the dimmers it seemed like late evening, so he couldn't have been out too long. He felt on edge, restless, and guilty for being asleep; he felt like he needed to go through security protocols. *That's all in the past.* Surprisingly the thought made him feel sad. He got himself a glass of water from the canteen. He walked along the row of dorms until he came to one with a sign hanging on it, written in pen. "Fionn's Room." The door was slightly ajar, and he could see the young boy on his bed, reading. Kobi knocked and entered. Fionn looked up, putting down his book when he saw Kobi. "How are you feeling?" Kobi asked.

The pale, freckled boy shrugged. In the room, there was animal-themed decor everywhere—polar bears on a bed lamp, lionesses stalking the rug. The duvet was covered in a design of flying tropical birds, their colors gaudy and bright. Kobi noticed that there were no posters though, like in the rest of Healhome. Instead, pale rectangles stood out on the wall, where, Kobi guessed, posters used to be stuck, and there were remains of old stickers ripped from the chest of drawers. Only one remained: a picture of a howling gray wolf.

Kobi sat down next to Fionn on the bed, leaning against the

wall with feet dangling over the side. Kobi pointed to the sticker of the wolf. "What happened to our friend?" Fionn pointed up at the ceiling, then gripped some imaginary bars.

"They've got him up there? In a cage?"

Fionn nodded, then stared through the opposite wall, eyes glazed. He barely seemed present, as if his mind was still out in the Wastelands. The part of him that was here appeared utterly miserable. Kobi wanted to comfort him.

"Well, you guys were right about the Snatchers," Kobi said. "They don't kill things with their stings. And I'm sure they'll release the wolf, you know, back to its home. They probably just want to run some tests or something." Fionn didn't reply. "You're like me, aren't you?" Kobi said. "You find this place weird." Fionn met Kobi's gaze. "I feel like I'm surrounded by people, but I'm the loneliest I've ever been. You know?" Fionn looked down to his lap. He seemed as closed up as Kobi had ever known him. "I'm finding it pretty weird, if I'm honest," Kobi continued. "I reckon I could live here fine, though. And if I can, you can, right? We'll be friends."

There were tears in the boy's eyes. Kobi edged closer. "What's wrong, Fionn?" he said. "Why do you hate being here so much? The others seem to like it."

Fionn wiped his eyes. Then he gazed at Kobi, and Kobi felt his scalp prickling. Fionn was trying to send him something telepathically. Kobi reached for Fionn's hand and placed it on his temple. Fionn's look hardened, then he closed his eyes and Kobi did so too. The prickling sensation strengthened.

In the darkness, Kobi heard sounds first of all. A voice through a speaker: "We are bringing in the specimen now." There was a blaring sound and something like metal grating on metal. Sterile white light invaded Kobi's vision, and he found himself in a chamber at Healhome. Scientists looked on from behind a glass screen with clipboards, and some held strange metal devices like mini radars. Melanie was there. She nodded encouragingly through the glass at a young boy standing nearby to Kobi.

It was Fionn.

He looked no older than seven. There were wires taped all around his head, which was clean-shaven. The wires trailed down to some kind of machine attached to his belt. Kobi could see the green tracks of veins through the papery white skin on Fionn's scalp. The young boy stared at a door, which slid open. Three CLAWS guards entered, escorting a large industrial-type vehicle, with caterpillar tracks and a forklift at the front. In the vehicle's prongs rested a six-foot-square metal cage, with a pane of thick, semitransparent glass at the front. Muffled growls and scratching noises could be heard from inside it. They made Kobi's skin crawl. Sounded like a mammal. Big.

"Beginning Communicative Telepathy Experiment 13.2, date tenth of September 2049," said a bland male voice through the speaker. "Test Case Healhome Patient S591."

Fionn was shaking on the spot, squeezing his fists by his side.

What are they going to do to him? Kobi thought.

Melanie's voice took over the speaker. "You can do this, Fionn," she said. "Please, Fionn, you can; do this for me. You've shown that you can. This is no different from before." Melanie's tone—meant to be warm and encouraging—just sounded cold and robotic through the sound-channeling system.

"I don't think I can," said Fionn, in a squeaky voice. "I don't want to."

"Fionn," said Melanie, more sternly. "You must try. Remember what I said. You are helping to save the world. We need to understand the Waste. We need to understand what you can do."

"Okay," said Fionn. But he sounded terrified, confused. The cage slowly lowered to the floor on the forklift. The animal inside it began to thrash and roar, shaking the cage and denting the metal sides. Kobi drew back instinctively, even though he knew he was only a spectator to the vision. Through the frosted glass at the front, Kobi caught sight of a flash of long, furred limbs and a dark snout. Yellow eyes.

"Okay, please prepare, Fionn," said Melanie.

Fionn closed his eyes and screwed up his face. Little lights connected to the wires on his head began to light up. The forklift truck reversed, leaving the cage on the ground, and the guards backed away with it, toward the door. Fionn was sweating now, the dome of his head shining in the wan glow of the strip lighting. *No, they can't . . . ,* thought Kobi.

Fionn opened his eyes and began to sob. "No, don't leave it here."

"Focus, Fionn!" said Melanie. The lights along the wires connected to Fionn's head flashed brighter and quicker. "Hurry up and get out of there, Guard—"

A loud bang made Kobi jump. Spider cracks fissured over the cage's frosted glass like splitting ice. "Control it, Fionn!" urged Melanie from behind the glass. "You're transferring to it your distressed emotions. It's aggravating the animal! Happy thoughts, Fionn, remember! Think of happy things!"

Fionn opened his mouth "I—"

Smash.

The glass at the front of the cage shattered. Shouts echoed through the speaker. Some kind of mutated black bear, with elongated, spidery limbs and a snout more like a canine's squeezed through the broken glass. Kobi wanted to run to Fionn, to help him.

Fionn backed away. "No, it's out; I can't make it stop," he said, his voice a high-pitched croak. His back hit the wall, and he slid down it, burying his head in his knees.

"*No, Fionn!*" shouted Melanie's voice. "Guardians, get out of there!"

The bear padded toward Fionn. Kobi thought the creature would maul him any second, but the hum of the truck speeding away made the creature's head swing around with a snarl. The retreating guards fled, feet pounding on the white enamel floor. The bear's eyes glared yellow, maddened. Saliva whipped from its red gums. It bounded for the nearest Guardian.

"Evacuate!"

An alarm sounded.

The Guardian raised his gun, but the bear was on him in a mound of muscle and fur. Blood sprayed the glass screen, and behind it scientists screamed. *"Close the door!"* yelled Melanie. The steel-and-glass door began to slide shut.

The bear looked up to where the two other guards ran toward the exit. The guard in the truck jumped out and followed. It took a second for the bear to hunt them down. It bounded after them, pawing at one man, who had short blond hair. Screams ripped through the room. The bear turned on another guard, a dark-skinned woman with wide oval eyes. "Help me!" she screamed, pounding on the closed door. "Open the—" The bear's jaws closed on her neck and Kobi looked away.

The final guard was hiding behind the truck. The man—elderly with gray hair and a goatee—gazed imploringly at Fionn. "Do something, boy, please. Save me." The bear leaped onto the truck, which tipped, crushing the man, before the muscular creature set upon his exposed head. The man's legs—visible sticking out from the bear's body—shuddered briefly before going limp. A pool of red seeped around his boots. Fionn was sobbing in the corner.

The bear charged at the door, trying to escape. But the barrier was closed. The bear rebounded off. Enraged, it turned toward Fionn. It padded toward the small boy. Blood covered the creature's fur, matted and dark around the muzzle. It growled softly. It stopped in front of Fionn, bending over him. Fionn met the creature's eyes. The bear padded its feet on the spot, sniffed at Fionn, then pushed him with its snout. It snapped its jaws, then, at once, it seemed to calm, bowing its head. The lights on Fionn's head sensors twinkled. "Hold it there, Fionn!" said Melanie. "You're doing it!"

Streams of guards stormed into the room. Their semiautomatic weapons pulsed, and the bear roared as bullets exploded into its body. It tried to charge at the guards but fell. Its feet slipped from under it as it tried to stand again, and more bullets smashed into its side, making it shudder. It collapsed in a pool of blood. Kobi looked over at Fionn. The boy wasn't crying. His eyes were like marbles: hard, shining, empty of expression. His face and bald head were speckled with blood, and his gray suit was smeared with crimson where the bear had nuzzled him. Kobi stared in shock as the edges of the room dimmed, collapsing into the center. The vision faded.

Kobi's chest heaved with nausea. He gasped in a breath as he found himself in Fionn's bedroom. Next to him, Fionn was shaking, chest heaving.

"That was horrible," Kobi said. "I can't believe they did that to you."

"It's been a long road for him," said a quiet voice, and Kobi turned to see Asha walk slowly into the bedroom. "What happened with Fionn was terrible. It shouldn't have been allowed to happen."

"Asha . . . ," said Kobi quietly. "This place is making him worse again. He was starting to speak again before we left Seattle. And he seemed happy."

Asha looked upset. "I know . . . but . . . But here he will be cured. We all will. Thanks to you!"

"I didn't do anything," said Kobi, turning away. He shook his head. "It's not right."

"They need to understand the Wa—"

"I've already heard it all," snapped Kobi. "Don't you think it seems strange, though? That the Guardians don't tell you anything? That they make you do these *tests*? What were they even doing in that experiment with Fionn? It didn't look like it would help find a cure."

Asha was quiet. "We don't understand everything about what the Guardians do."

Kobi was about to reply when a Guardian entered the room. He spoke quickly. "Kobi. You need to come with us."

"Why?" said Kobi.

"It's Dr. Hales. His condition has worsened."

Kobi shivered, a dull weight in his chest. "What do you mean?"

"He doesn't have long. If you want to see him, I suggest you do so immediately."

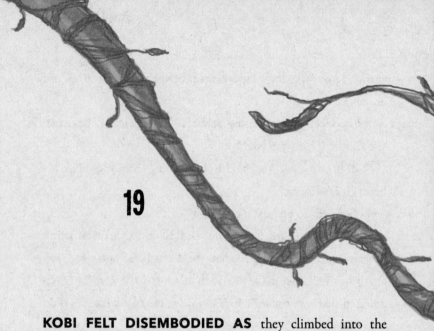

19

KOBI FELT DISEMBODIED AS they climbed into the elevator, like he was a ghost. The guard called Krenner was watching him with barely concealed hostility. Melanie was beside him, tapping something in a tablet. Asha was there too. She had insisted on coming.

The elevator climbed, and Kobi tried to clear his head. He wasn't sure what to think. Even *how* to think. In the space of a day, the world had tipped upside down and every time he thought he might have found some equilibrium, another earthquake shook him off his feet.

The elevator arrived, and the doors opened. "Are you ready, Kobi?" asked Melanie.

He nodded.

Level 108 was completely sterile—the walls bright white, with airlocks and keypad doorways. Wards on either side had glass viewing windows, and contained empty beds and large arrays of medical equipment. In one, a scientist in a hazmat suit was spraying some sort of chemical into the air.

A doctor in a lab coat sat at a desk making notes on a screen.

He looked up, eyeing Kobi quizzically.

"How's Dr. Hales doing?" asked Melanie.

"As we expected," said the doctor. "The prognosis hasn't changed."

"Is there no way to make him better?" asked Kobi.

The doctor glanced at Melanie, then said, "The Waste has been cleared from his system. We're keeping the quarantine as a precaution only. But the patient carried the toxic chemical on and off for almost thirteen years."

Melanie put her arm on Kobi's shoulder, softly. "The anti-Waste drugs he formulated knocked the contagion back, but each time, the damage was already done. It was always going to be a losing battle—"

"But he's cured. This guy just said so. The Waste's nullified."

"I'm sorry, but this time he won't pull through," said Melanie. "His organs are shutting down. We're making him comfortable, but that's all we can do."

"Where is he?" said Kobi.

"Room six—the last room on the left," said the doctor before turning to Melanie.

"Come this way, Kobi," said Melanie. Kobi set off, a step behind the director, followed by Asha.

At room six, Kobi looked through the glass. Waves of emotion almost floored him, buckling his legs and making his face crumple involuntarily.

The body on the bed looked more like a corpse than a living thing. Hales's face was gaunt—with sharp cheekbones under paper-thin gray skin. His eyes were closed, the ridges of the sockets pronounced. A blanket had been pulled up to his chest, which was covered in various wired pads, and his bare, bony arms were free, with drips feeding into each. His mouth, ventilator inserted, hung open, and only a few strands of hair remained. He looked a hundred years old. On a table in the room, a Polaroid was propped up against a vase of plastic flowers—the photo CLAWS must have found with Hales. Unlike the other "yearbook" photos, Hales was in this one, wrestling Kobi as the camera timer went off. Two laughing faces. How things used to be.

Kobi put his hands to the glass. Despite everything he'd learned—all the deception and lies—all he wanted to do was be with the man who had raised him.

As well as the IV stands, there were several wheeled monitors beside the bed, and some sort of pumping mechanism.

Kobi realized he was crying, but he didn't care. "Dad," he said, fingers pressed to the glass. *No—Jonathan . . .*

"I'll leave you to it," said Melanie. "Take as long as you need." She left the room.

"Do you want me to leave too?" asked Asha.

"No, you can stay here." Kobi paused. "I want you to."

He sat by Hales's bedside for he didn't know how long. He couldn't decide whether he was angry. As soon as a wave of fury crashed over him at the sheer scale of the lies, it passed, leaving his emotions awash in a confusion of memory and self-pity. He thought how utterly different life would be if he had been raised here, and he kept returning to just how precarious and deadly an existence it had been at the school, yet how normal it had felt at the time. Compared to the sanitized spaces of Healhome, they'd been living in the Stone Age. Scraping by, always hungry, or scared, or worried about the future, or whatever new menace they might come across. But Kobi missed it.

Kobi reached out and took the Polaroid from the table. He placed it in the pocket of his jumpsuit. He didn't know why he wanted to keep it. He only knew that it was the last remaining object from his old life, and the idea of it being thrown in the trash didn't seem right. For good or bad, Kobi couldn't entirely erase his past. But he could move on from it. He had to. Eventually, Kobi raised up a hand and placed it on Hales's arm. It felt skeletal. Tears dripped down Kobi's cheeks. "Goodbye, Jonathan."

Whether it was coincidence or whether the man on the bed had actually felt Kobi's touch, Jonathan Hales's eyelids fluttered, and his skull-like head turned sideways. The eyes that locked on his and widened were brown, without a hint of yellow. As they did, the patient jerked in bed, and the heart-rate monitor began to spike. An alarm beeped, flashing red on one of the monitors.

"What's wrong!" said Kobi. "Help him!"

A moment later, the doctor came running back, zipping up a hazmat suit. Behind Kobi, Asha edged closer too. The doctor tapped in a code and the airlock opened. Inside, he pulled on the helmet, then entered the room.

Jonathan Hales was convulsing on the bed, and one of his drips tore free. His leg almost toppled an IV stand.

The doctor worked quickly, grabbing a syringe and injecting Hales's shoulder. Slowly, Hales's spasms ceased, but as they did, he was reaching for the ventilator tube, as if trying to pull it free. The doctor gripped his arm and straightened it. In a few more seconds, the patient's eyes fluttered closed again.

"Come on, we should leave," said Asha.

She gave Kobi's arm a tug, and after a moment more—when the heart monitor dropped again to a regular beat—Kobi let himself be led away. He knew it would be the last time he would ever see his father—the man he'd *thought* was his father—alive again.

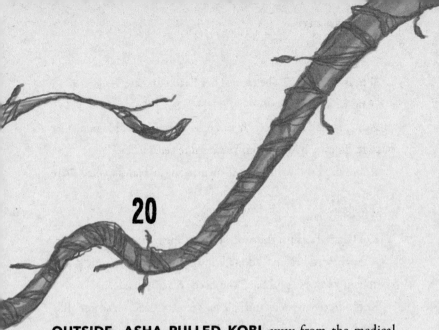

20

OUTSIDE, ASHA PULLED KOBI away from the medical rooms. Some Guardians stepped after her, but she said, "Give him a minute! Where are the restrooms?"

They pointed, and she pulled him through a door into a corridor and into a cubicle.

"What are you—" Kobi began, but she placed a finger to her lips. Her face was filled with urgency, eyes wide.

She made sure the door was clicked shut, then whispered, "I need to talk to you." She peered up at him, her eyes filled with confusion. "Kobi, something's going on, and I don't understand."

"Go on."

She seemed full of nervous energy. "You know I can read the thoughts of people who have been contaminated with Waste, right? Well, when I saw that man down there in the infirmary . . ."

"Dr. Hales?"

"I heard his voice." She tapped her head. "In here."

"And what did he say?"

Asha lowered her voice. "It was really clear, Kobi. He said, 'Get outside. They're lying to you. You need to see outside.'"

Kobi heard the words in his own head, in Hales's voice. "Are you sure?"

Asha nodded.

Kobi leaned against the wall. "He's telling us we need to escape."

Asha chewed her lip. "I don't know. It was very clear. He didn't say to run away. He said 'see.' You need to 'see' outside."

Kobi didn't understand. "I've seen outside. It's just like everywhere else—a wilderness. Haven't you been in Melanie's office?"

"No, of course not—we're not allowed."

"I have. I looked through the window. It's just miles and miles of—"

"She's got a window?" said Asha.

"Uh-huh," said Kobi.

Asha was frowning. "So why don't we? They said it was because of the Waste—that walls were safer."

Kobi shrugged. "But you've been in the transports—couldn't you see out of those?"

Asha shook her head. "Same excuse. Avoiding any risk of contagion."

Kobi had to admit—it was a bit weird. Still, he wasn't inclined to listen to anything Dr. Hales had to say.

He didn't say it, though, did he? He thought it. And why would he lie to himself?

"Is there a way to get outside?" he asked Asha. She nodded.

They hurried out of the restroom, along the corridor, until they reached the elevator, but Asha went past and pushed through a pair of double doors with a fire escape sign above it. The door opened onto concrete stairs. Kobi peered up. "No cameras. Hangar's top floor, right? One-eighty-two."

Asha nodded. "We're on one-fifty-one. That's a lot of climbing."

Kobi began to jog up the first flight. "Come on, then!"

Twenty floors later, enhanced strength and stamina or not, Kobi was tiring. Asha was flagging badly, and Kobi had to help her, then stop after each flight for a rest. They'd passed an internal door on every floor, and much as Kobi had wanted to look, it wasn't worth the risk. If there were alarms, or cameras, they'd be found out in seconds.

As Kobi waited on a floor toward the top, the lactic acid draining from his thighs, he wondered again if this was a waste of time. Asha seemed so convinced of what Hales had said, but the man on the bed had hardly been in a fit state to communicate anything. Plus, Kobi had seen what was outside, and it was exactly like everywhere else—completely overrun.

"I don't think I can go on," said Asha, sitting on a step.

"We're almost there," said Kobi. "Four more flights."

"You go—if there's something there, you can—"

An alarm started wailing, startling them both, and red lights along the ceiling flashed.

"They're on to us!" said Kobi. He hoisted Asha up to her feet as Melanie Garcia's voice said urgently over the speaker, "We have a code four. Two missing patients. All personnel respond."

The frantic siren seemed to give Asha a jolt of strength, and they set off again, Asha hauling herself with the bannister as Kobi took two steps at a time. Doors banged farther below, and he saw flashlight beams in arcs whipping up and down the stairwell. Then the thud of boots many floors down.

He grabbed Asha's arm to help her.

When they had two more floors to go, a door slammed not far below, and Kobi saw three Guardians emerge. They saw him too.

"Contact! Contact!" one shouted. "They're heading to the roof."

Kobi tugged Asha roughly up one more flight, then reached a door with the number *181*. *That's not right. There should be one more.* For a brief second he feared it might be locked, but as he felt the handle it turned. It pulled open, and they bundled through. Asha gasped and Kobi stopped dead, heels squeaking on the polished concrete floor.

Facing him were row upon row of crouching Snatchers, perhaps a hundred altogether.

Kobi held his breath, but the Snatchers did not move. *Deactivated.* There were two transports on the far side of the hangar space, one flush against a wall, the other a few yards away. There was no obvious way out.

Kobi knew they didn't have long. He ran, darting among the stationary Snatchers, with Asha trailing.

As they made their way to the closest transport, Kobi almost tripped on a ridge in the ground. He stopped, looking around. It was a circular section of flooring, maybe thirty feet across, slightly detached. Looking up, the ceiling seemed to be made of some sort of sliding hatch, with a cantilevered arm mechanism folded up. On the wall beside them was a panel of buttons.

It's a takeoff pad. . . .

"Stand back," he said, and he hit the green button. Straightaway, the circle of ground juddered and began to rise. At the same time, the ceiling hatches slid back to reveal a growing patch of black night sky.

"Freeze!" yelled a voice.

Guards spilled out from the stairwell and red lasers flashed all around him.

"Wait for me!" cried Asha.

Pfft. Pfft.

Darts ricocheted off the Snatchers' metal shells.

Asha reached up, and Kobi took her arms, lifting her onto the raising platform. They both crouched behind a Snatcher, using it for cover. *I wonder what dose their weapons are set to now. Probably enough to floor me right away.*

"Stop them!"

Melanie's voice. And as Kobi turned he saw her emerging from the elevator with Krenner and three other guards at her side.

Pfft. Pfft. Pfft. The darts all missed.

As the platform rose, Kobi and Asha stayed low to avoid being hit. He was ready to run in whatever direction seemed most promising. Maybe across the rooftops—there might be trees he could climb down, slipping into the foliage.

But then, as the night revealed itself, he couldn't move at all.

Kobi felt dizzy, his muscles utterly drained.

"No . . . ," said Asha at his side.

All he saw was gleaming metal and twinkling glass. Skyscrapers rising like gleaming spires toward the sky. Cars, sleek as bullets, zipping through the air. A train on a suspended track looping between buildings, tunneling into their sides like a caterpillar. Giant holographic images flashing, showing people, and clothes, and food, and faces. Kobi turned on the spot, reeling.

It stretched for miles in every direction.

Not a leaf in sight. Not a speck of green.

A perfect, Waste-free city.

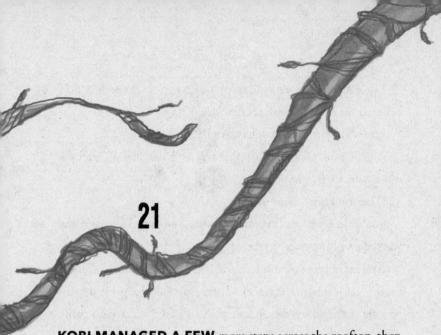

21

KOBI MANAGED A FEW more steps across the rooftop, then dropped to his knees, eyes drinking in the vista. A breeze chilled his skin. He could see people in the streets below—hundreds of them—walking across clean sidewalks, crossing the roads under flashing stop signs, as cars with impossibly reflective skins threaded almost soundlessly around bends, occasionally rising over one another, or climbing into the air and joining the other flying traffic looking like sparkling mirrors.

It can't be . . . I must be seeing things. They've done something to me.

Kobi was aware of the landing pad descending behind him, and the shouts of the Guardians, but he didn't have any inclination to move. He touched the asphalt of the roof with his fingertips. If this was a dream, it felt very real. He could feel the breeze on his face, and hear a thousand tiny noises coming from the city below.

Every second of every day of his conscious existence he'd believed the Waste was all there was.

Everything he had thought was a lie.

A glance at Asha told him this was no hallucination, and she was as surprised as he was.

"Did you know about this?"

She didn't answer. Her mouth was hanging open, and she walked past him, closer to the edge.

And as the sense of wonder throbbed through him, he felt like a fool. Because, really, the clues had been there all along. He'd spent so long petrified by the Snatchers, he'd never stopped to think how *strange* they were—how otherworldly—their technology way in advance of any of the detritus left within the Waste-ravaged city. The CLAWS weapons, their transport—all of it several years ahead of anything he'd come across in the ruins. It should have been clear—the world outside his green bubble had moved on.

He felt a piece of fabric being draped over him and a hand rest softly between his shoulder blades. Two Guardians ran forward and took hold of Asha's arms. She didn't protest. Her expression was one of pure bewilderment.

"It must be . . . a shock," said Melanie Garcia. Kobi turned to look up at her. She too was staring across the cityscape, the gust catching a few stray strands of hair.

Kobi stood up slowly. He had on some sort of robe and pulled it tighter around him. The remainder of the Guardians had stopped back near the hatch, their weapons lowered. The man called

Krenner stood slightly forward, his arms folded and a fierce look on his face.

"Welcome to New Seattle," replied Melanie.

"*New* Seattle?"

Melanie pointed off the rooftop, to their left. "The old city is that way, about two hundred miles. It's surrounded by a quarantine zone twenty miles wide—they dropped so many nukes, nothing will grow there for half a million years."

Kobi shook his head to try to clear it. "So the Waste is contained in the old Seattle?"

Melanie laughed bitterly. "I'm afraid not. The Waste is everywhere—every continent. It's a war on a thousand fronts that we can never win. But we have our enclaves, like this one. Places built by the survivors. And even if we can't win, we don't have to lose!"

Asha began to pull away from the Guardians, her focus sharpened on Melanie. "You lied to us!" Though she struggled, they held her firmly. "Let me go!" she said. "I'm going to tell them all."

"We had to limit your knowledge," said Melanie a little desperately. "If you'd known, you'd want to leave."

"You don't say!" said Asha. "So we're prisoners."

"You're *patients*," said Melanie firmly. "We're trying to make you better. The Waste hasn't killed you. If we can find out *why*, we can save the human species."

"Patients or guinea pigs?" said Asha.

Melanie's skin flushed a little.

"That's what I thought."

"CLAWS develops medicines that have helped millions of people," said Melanie. "You make that possible. And you"—she turned to Kobi—"you might be the miracle we've been looking for."

Kobi understood, sort of.

"Because I'm immune?" he said. "That's why you wanted to find me."

"Correct," said Melanie. "You can help us, Kobi. Help the world."

Kobi frowned. "I'm fed up with being lied to."

"You're not the only one," grumbled Asha, glaring ahead at Melanie. "You should have told us."

The director nodded. "Yes." She nodded to the guards. "Let's go inside, shall we?"

Back in Melanie's office, in clean jumpsuits, he and Asha sat side by side as Melanie had her back to them. She'd persuaded Asha not to say anything yet, but Kobi could feel her bristling, ready to explode. The window, which he now knew was nothing more than a projection, showed a beautiful mountain scene. A stag strutted under a glade of trees, and a waterfall tumbled into a sparkling pool.

Melanie touched the corner of the window and the view changed in a blink to the modern city. Cars zipped past, hundreds of feet up. Kobi saw a holo-ad displayed from some kind of drone. It showed a family facing each other at a table while they ate from cardboard cartons with chopsticks. The sight made him, for a split second, unbearably sad.

The director folded her arms and faced them. "Asha has a point," she said. "We should have told all our patients about the real world a long time ago. The longer you live a lie, the harder it is to tell the truth. You were all babies, at first, then toddlers. It never seemed the right time. And later, we weren't sure of the damage it might cause to pull the curtain away."

Asha grunted, clearly unconvinced.

The director continued to speak. "The work we do here is all that keeps this city alive," she said, waving a hand toward the outside. "We create all kinds of anti-Waste products. The sprays that kill Waste-carrying spores that are used on any goods coming into the city on trains or planes. Medicines that help stop Waste entering the body. We help treat those infected, extending their life spans, quarantining them in areas at the edge of the city. We produce detergent with anti-spore chemicals; we help protect food supplies. We help the government manufacture drones that sweep for contamination in our streets. We quarantine the Wastelands like Seattle, New York State, Louisiana and most of the South, Michigan. . . . We are everything! The research we carry out with our patients makes it all possible." She looked imploringly at Asha, who turned away.

Kobi really wasn't sure that made the lie okay either, but he didn't know what to say. He kept looking outside. A week ago, he'd thought he was alone. Three days back he'd found out there were some others. And now . . .

"How many people live here?" he asked.

"Just under three million," said Melanie.

Kobi sucked in a breath. He couldn't even imagine what such a number looked like.

Again, Melanie addressed herself to Asha. "We were worried that if you found out, the psychological burden of knowing how important you were, it might be too much."

"Whatever," said Asha. She nodded at the outside world. "Do *they* all know about us?"

Melanie pursed her lips. "A few," she said. "It's sensitive information."

"You don't say?" said Asha. "You need to be honest with the other kids. With everyone."

Melanie wore a pained expression. "Ask yourself, Asha. What would that gain?"

"The truth?" said Kobi.

Melanie's jaw tightened. "Perhaps you don't understand," she said. "Telling the other patients is one thing. There's no chance they can ever leave. They'd know what was out there, but they could never experience it. But if the general population knew about *you*, about actual Waste-infected individuals, in the heart of their supposedly safe city . . ." Her eyes flashed dangerously. "There's really no saying what might happen."

"Is that a threat?" said Asha, half standing.

"It's reality," said Melanie. "Fear and ignorance are just as dangerous as any disease."

Kobi watched the shifting emotions on Asha's face.

"But," said Melanie, suddenly more brightly, "if Kobi's blood samples confirm that he's as resilient as we suspect, this whole subterfuge might be academic. We *could*—and I pray it's true—we could be near to eradicating the Waste completely." Her gaze went over their heads. "Speaking of which . . ."

A woman in a lab coat knocked and entered, carrying a touchpad. She barely looked at Kobi. "Dr. Garcia," she said a little breathlessly, "I've got those results you wanted."

"And?" asked Melanie.

The scientist looked meaningfully at Kobi. "Are you sure you wouldn't rather talk in private?"

"No need, Ruth," said Melanie. "I think Kobi deserves to hear. Asha too."

The scientist nodded, and tapped her screen. At the same time, the desk display changed. There were several graphs that Kobi didn't understand, with incomprehensible units on the axes. The header read: "Epidemiology. Samples from Subject S374."

"As you'll see," said Ruth. "S374's blood shows no ill effects whatsoever from the Waste infection." She glanced at Kobi, then flicked onto a new page, with close-ups of what looked like blobs. "However, cell cultures show that he does carry a mutated form of the Waste proteins in his DNA, which forms a barrier against

Waste. It looks like his immune system has metabolized them, rendering their carcinogenic properties impotent. He retains the benefits of infection—able to harness the same strength and enhanced abilities of other subjects—but without the detrimental effects."

"Fascinating," said Melanie, but without much enthusiasm.

Ruth moved to a file that read "S591"—which showed an up-to-date image of Fionn.

"Hales did some remarkable work," she said. "He managed to isolate Kobi's antibodies into a solution that would be accepted by any host body. The antibodies effectively wipe out Waste from a subject's body. It seems it lasts only as long as the antibodies stay in the bloodstream—a few days—after which recontamination is possible. We've carried out routine analysis on S591—his Waste count is negligible. We're only in the early stages of investigating how that can be, but it looks like the anti-Waste cleanser Hales developed is a long way in advance of our own. It is entirely effective."

"So Fionn's going to be okay?" said Asha.

"Better than okay," said Ruth. "If he avoids contamination, he is entirely cured. No need for repeat doses or any kind of prolonged drug program."

"So one dose, and everyone will be better again," said Melanie. "As long as they stay in the quarantined city. One step away from a permanent cure, when we won't have to worry about Waste at all anymore." Her eyes flicked, lizard-like, from the screen to the other scientist.

The scientist's hands were shaking. "It's appears so, Doctor."

Melanie Garcia seemed to be in shock, glued to the spot like a statue, but finally she blinked a few times. "As you said, a . . . *remarkable* achievement."

"We'll need to run more tests—a lot more tests."

Melanie nodded and grinned widely, showing perfect white teeth. "Let's take this slowly. And strictly confidential for the moment. No one outside your team is to know. Kobi, I'm afraid we'll need to take some more blood. Enough for some continued testing. Is that all right?"

"Of course," said Kobi.

Melanie touched her lapel. "Assemble a medical team on the infirmary level. Omega protocols. Ruth, I can take things from here."

What does that mean?

"Wait a minute . . . ," said Kobi.

"Kobi, don't you see?" said Melanie as Ruth left the room. "You're the key to all of this. It's your antibody capabilities at the heart of everything. We're not taking any chances with your welfare. We need to wrap you in cotton wool."

"I guess so," said Kobi. "How long will it take?"

"Twenty-four hours, tops. Just until we're sure what we're dealing with." She gripped his shoulders firmly. "How does it feel to be the most important person on the planet?"

"Three days ago, I thought I was the only person. Along with my dad."

Melanie laughed for the first time since he'd met her, and it sounded as brittle as broken glass.

A few minutes later, Kobi was back in the elevator, this time with Melanie and the man called Krenner and one other Guardian. No one spoke at all. He really wished Asha were there too, but she was back in the dorms, having promised to keep her new secret under wraps. Kobi felt like there was a weight pressing down on him— now that he knew the truth, all of it, he realized how much they were relying on him.

The doors opened onto the infirmary floor, and Melanie took him past the room where Fionn stood behind the glass. Kobi managed a brief wave. He thought at first they were going all the way to Dr. Hales's chamber, but they stopped and entered a ward on the other side of the corridor, with four beds. Inside, a team of three doctors, their faces covered in masks, had already gathered around a gurney. A trolley stood beside the bed, with the glint of tools just visible beneath a covering sheet.

"Make yourself comfortable," said Melanie.

Kobi climbed slowly onto the gurney. She sounded businesslike, but there was an urgency in her voice. Almost like fear. Why wouldn't she look at him?

"What are we doing again?" he asked.

One of the doctors lifted a syringe. "We'll be injecting a dye marker into your bloodstream first," he said. "It will help us to find what we're looking for when we extract the antibodies."

"Will it hurt?"

"Not at all," said the scientist. "Just lie back and relax."

Kobi did as he was told but looked away as the doctor approached. "Don't like needles," he said.

"Who does?" said Melanie.

He felt the prick, and then an icy feeling coursing up his arm.

"Ooh!" he said. "It's cold!"

"It will be," said the doctor.

Kobi began to relax—the gurney bed was actually comfier than it looked.

"So, what will you do with the wolf?" he asked. "Can you cure it too?"

"I expect so," said Melanie. Again, her voice sounded off—like she wasn't really listening properly.

"It saved our lives," said Kobi.

"So I've heard," said Melanie. "A remarkable story."

He tried to lift his head to look at her, but he couldn't. His neck felt . . . heavy.

"Something's funny," he said, and he heard that his own voice was slurred. He was drooling.

"Nothing to worry about," said the doctor.

"You can go now," said Melanie.

"Yes, Director," said one of the doctors. A pause. "Someone

should monitor the drip though."

"We'll take care of that," said Melanie.

"Would you like us to—?"

"I'd like you to leave," said Melanie curtly.

"Yes, Director."

Kobi heard instruments being put down, then the suction of the door. His head flopped sideways. He tried to move, but everything was a dead weight. His heart rate quickened.

"What are you doing?" he said, but it came out *"Wharardin?"*

And he couldn't straighten his head at all. He watched helplessly as an IV tube was taped to the inside of his elbow, then Melanie appeared, crouching beside the bed. Her face was grim, and he saw the future in her emotionless eyes.

"Don't take this personally, Kobi. But CLAWS is doing very nicely providing drugs to keep people healthy. A cure doesn't really fit into our . . . corporate strategy." She stood up and moved out of his eyeline, but he could still hear her perfectly clearly. "Can I leave this in your capable hands?"

"Of course, ma'am," said Krenner.

Kobi wanted to scream and thrash and attack. He wanted to run. But as he tried to speak again, it was like pushing against a door that wouldn't move. Whatever drug the IV was feeding him kept him in a permanent state of paralysis, a limp body on the gurney. And though he was completely motionless, his mind raged with such turmoil it felt like his brain might explode. Who was lying to him, and who was telling the truth? He just wanted to be away, back at the school with the man who was not his father but who had never shown him anything but love.

Back when the world made sense.

He realized now. His father—Hales—*did* love him. He was protecting him. Protecting him from these people. From CLAWS and Melanie.

And Kobi had failed him.

22

KRENNER'S HANDS GENTLY STRAIGHTENED Kobi's head so he was looking straight up at the ceiling. The Guardian moved in and out of his peripheral vision.

Kobi knew he was going to die. He thought of Asha and the other kids, continuing their lives upstairs, and wondered what Melanie would tell them. That his immunity had been compromised, perhaps? That some sudden, unforeseen complication had arisen and there was nothing they could do? Asha and Fionn would probably be upset, but they'd seen others die. They'd forget in time. And CLAWS would continue to produce drugs to keep the Waste at arm's length and maintain their profits.

Kobi heard an electronic buzzing and the back of the bed he was lying on began to lift, raising his upper body into a half-seated position. His fears were confirmed—it was just himself and Krenner in the room. He was alone with his murderer.

The security guard raised his eyebrows and sighed. "Hales never liked the way we did things around here," he said. "I think he thought he was better than the rest of us—more noble in some way. I tried to warn the others that he was untrustworthy, but no one listened. Even after the others betrayed us, I knew he was behind it. They all said he was the most gifted scientist. They took their eyes off him." Krenner picked something up from the wheeled trolley, and Kobi's whole being flinched as it drifted into his line of sight. A bone saw. But as he panicked, he thought he felt a tingle of actual sensation in his right foot. Could it be that the drip was wearing off? Or maybe his body was fighting it. . . .

The security guard replaced the surgical tool, walking closer to the bed. He looked into Kobi's eyes with an unflinching gaze. "You look like him, even if you're not his son. Maybe it's because he brought you up. You've got the same sneaky look in your eyes."

Kobi stared back, hoping Krenner was paying attention to the rage boiling in the glare and not the slight movements of his foot, then his knee. He was definitely getting control back, but it was painfully slow.

"Determined too, I see," said Krenner. "Not that it'll do either of you any good." He disappeared, walking somewhere around the back of the bed. Kobi realized he could wiggle his fingers too. "You know, in the early days, I longed for a cure," Krenner continued. "As my parents died. My sisters. Friends. It happened so fast. I was lucky, in a way—the Marines kept me away from home in that first wave. But I felt so helpless. The Waste didn't seem to care who it took. The good and the bad. But as time went on, as we built this place, and as the new city grew, I began to see the positives. At least now we have order. People line up for their pills. We dish them out. Life goes on. It all makes a sort of sense. See what I mean?"

Kobi wanted to shout that Krenner could stuff his order. He felt the pillow pulled from under his head.

"That's all this is," said the head of security. "We're just keeping things . . . orderly."

Everything went black as the pillow pressed over his face. Kobi didn't even have time to draw a breath, and his heart pounded in panic. His arms moved weakly, reaching up, but Krenner was holding the pillow down tight. His legs kicked and thrashed as the pressure built up in his chest.

His hand hit something hard, and he realized it was the trolley. Scrabbling, his fingers closed on cold metal. Something heavy. Anything would do. With the last of his strength he swung the object at the place Krenner's head would be. It glanced off, but he heard a grunt of pain. He swung again, this time rewarded with a satisfying *thump*.

A flash of brightness as the pillow fell away. Kobi rolled off the gurney and landed heavily on the floor. Krenner was lying on his side, clutching his face, with blood pouring between his fingers, and moaning. Kobi realized he was holding some sort of gleaming metal hammer. He had no idea what it was for. He tossed it aside and ripped the Taser off Krenner's belt.

"You can't," groaned the Guardian.

Kobi managed to stand, then staggered toward the door.

I've got to tell the others!

Then he stopped and looked back along the corridor. Toward room six. *Dad . . .*

Kobi walked back quickly. His feet still felt a little strange—almost bouncy.

He reached the end room and saw beyond the glass screen that Dr. Hales was still hooked up, eyes half-open and dimly aware. Kobi entered the room, and Hales grunted. There was a pained look in his eyes, and they were moist with tears. Kobi didn't know if it would be possible to move him. There was no telling exactly what was in the drip, or what condition Hales would be in when he took it out. There was no time to think about that now though. He went to a set of wall-mounted cupboards, flinging them open. There were several boxes of various medical supplies—bandages, sutures, syringes, gloves, and actual medicines. He took a syringe, then sifted through the bottles and packets until he found what he was looking for—adrenaline.

He placed the supplies on a table, then turned off the drip tap, easing out the cannula from the back of Hales's hand. Hales grimaced slightly, and Kobi taped a dressing over the punctured skin.

"Just hold on," he said as he suctioned 0.5 milligrams of adrenaline, then leaned over Hales's arm.

The patient drew a long breath as the hormone entered his bloodstream, and his eyes focused. "Kobi . . . ," he croaked.

Kobi helped Hales off the bed like he was cradling a baby. He could feel his bony spine. The old man couldn't have weighed more than 130 pounds, he guessed. "There's no time to explain," he said. "We're getting out of here."

"Mischik," said Hales. "He's the only one who can help."

Mischik . . . but . . . how do we get him to come here?"

"There's a radio transmitter on level twenty-nine," said Hales through cracked lips, then, "No, they'll stop us if we do that. We have to get to level one—there's a parking garage underneath the building. We can escape through there."

"What about the others?" said Kobi, carrying Hales toward the elevator. "I can't leave them here."

Hales shook his head, an expression of despair. "We can't get them all out," he said. "Too many."

"Melanie tried to kill me," said Kobi. "There's no telling what she might do."

Hales's sickly eyes fixed on him with a look Kobi knew all too well. Pride.

They reached the elevator, and Hales said, "I think I can stand."

"You sure?" asked Kobi.

Hales nodded, and Kobi placed his feet on the floor.

As the doors opened and they stepped in, Krenner emerged, nose dripping blood, from the room farther down. "Stop!" he shouted, and began to run. Kobi hit the number *42* for the dorm level just as Krenner pulled his dart gun off his shoulder and took aim. The doors began to close. Kobi jerked back as a dart hit the rear of the elevator, and then Krenner was gone, hidden from view.

As the lift rose, Kobi wondered how long it would take for Krenner to raise the alarm. He brandished the Taser, ready.

The doors pinged open again, and Kobi saw an armed Guardian five feet away. Krenner's voice was coming through her communicator.

"... on their way up now! Take them out!"

She turned, her face registered surprise, then she raised her dart gun. Kobi charged, driving the Taser into her side and pulling the trigger. She spasmed and collapsed.

Everything looked normal. Behind the glass walls, four Healhome residents were playing a game of pool. Others were reading books on sofas, including Fionn. They looked up from their activities, staring in astonishment at him.

"Kobi?" said Asha, standing up. "What's going on?"

"We're getting out of here," said Kobi.

"What?" said Niki, coming to Asha's side. "Are you mad?"

"Who's that man?" said Leon.

The guard on the ground was stirring, with a grimace.

"You can't leave the facility," she said.

Kobi tossed the Taser aside and seized her rifle, pointing it at her. "I'm guessing whatever's in these darts wouldn't be good for you either," he said. "Open the panels."

The Guardian got to her feet and moved toward the controls on the wall, then tapped the screen a few times. The glass panels retracted smoothly into the ceiling. None of the kids stepped out.

"Kobi," said Niki. "The Guardians are our friends."

"They tried to kill me downstairs," said Kobi.

"That's not true!" said the injured Guardian.

"Shut up!" said Kobi.

Niki glared at Kobi. "You know nothing," she sneered. "Hales has brainwashed you. He stole you."

"I *rescued* him," said Hales. Kobi glanced at him. He looked so earnest, it was hard to accept Hales didn't at least believe what he was saying. Whether that was true or not, Kobi couldn't tell.

"Who's Hales?" asked Jo. All the other kids looked just as confused.

"He's a traitor," said the Guardian. "All he wanted was to make a name for himself."

"Dr. Hales is telling the truth," said Kobi. "It's Melanie and the Guardians who are lying. I've been outside—there's a city. With thousands of people."

Niki laughed uncomfortably. "What are you talking about?"

"It's true," said Asha, coming to stand beside Kobi. "I've seen it too. They lied to us."

The Guardian began to move toward her. "Kobi, the drugs Hales gave you have seriously compromised your brain. We can look after you, but you've got to stop this. Come on, hand over the— Uh!"

The dart from Kobi's gun hit her in the chest and she stumbled backward into the wall screen, then collapsed to the floor.

"No!" yelled Niki.

"Barricade the doors," said Hales. "They'll send more armed guards."

Kobi and Asha grabbed a sofa from one of the dorms and placed it against a door. Leon single-handedly carried the jukebox and blocked another. Kobi wondered, in the back of his mind, how much the boy could bench-press.

Most of the kids just stayed where they were, looking perplexed or muttering to one another. Fionn seemed to be communicating with Asha in hand gestures.

Niki remained where she was too, her expression caught somewhere between panic and contempt. The Guardian on the ground was lying still.

"I just stunned her," said Kobi. "She'll live."

Dr. Hales was shaken by a coughing fit and supported himself against a table. Kobi ran across to him. "Are you okay . . . ? He almost added *Dad*, but the word felt odd on the tip of his tongue.

Hales spat a mouthful of bloody sputum on the floor and wiped his lips. "We'll never get out through the garage now," he said. "They'll cover all the city exits."

"What about the transports on the roof?" said Kobi. "Could you fly one?"

"Perhaps," said Hales weakly. "I haven't in years, and the technology will have moved on a lot."

"Then we go to the roof," said Asha. "Come on, everyone!" She went to the elevator. One by one, the others peeled after her in a daze.

"Are you crazy?" said Niki. "Where are you going? There's nothing out there but Waste."

"You aren't safe if you stay," said Dr. Hales, leaning on Kobi's arm.

"I don't trust you," said Niki.

"You're asking a lot from us," said Leon. "The Guardians have cared for us our whole lives."

"Exactly," said Niki. "They took us in as orphans. They kept us alive."

"That isn't exactly true," said Hales.

"Is that right?" said Niki. "Care to explain?"

Dr. Hales looked ready to drop, his eyes watery and skin sallow.

"This may be difficult for you to hear," he said. "But you never had parents. Any of you."

Niki's mouth fell open, then she laughed. "Melanie was right. You *are* insane."

"You aren't orphans," said Hales insistently. "You were raised here from birth, grown from artificially fertilized embryos. Infected with Waste from the start. You're victims, but only because you were made that way."

Rohan said, "Is he telling the truth?"

"I don't know," said Leon.

"Believe me, I'm not proud of what we did," said Hales. "We all thought we were doing the right thing. It was the only option open to us to tackle the Waste."

"Human experimentation," muttered Jo.

"So we're guinea pigs," said Yaeko.

Hales was silent. Kobi looked at the man he'd once thought was his father, trying to reconcile what he was hearing with his previous life.

After a long silence, it was Asha who spoke first. "I don't care about any of this now. I've been lied to so many times I don't know what to believe anymore. What I *do* know is that I'm not spending another minute more in this . . . this *prison* than I have to. Niki, come with us, please!" She went across to the younger girl and reached out to take her hand. Niki, eyes welling with tears, let herself be pulled toward the elevator too.

Yaeko encouraged her. "Come on, Nik. We should get out of here."

But as Kobi pressed the call button and it didn't illuminate, he had a sinking feeling.

"They've deactivated it again," he said.

A series of loud bangs came from the barricaded doors across the room.

"We don't have long," said Asha. "If we can get into the elevator shaft there's a ladder."

"Allow me," said Jo. She came past them and extended a hand toward the closed elevator doors. Kobi watched, amazed, as her fingers stretched, splitting into vines, and feeding into the crack. The doors buckled, eased apart by her strange, organic power. When they'd opened a fraction, Leon gripped one and tore it off, shearing the steel with brute force. "Easy!" he said. The dark shaft was filled with cables and pipework. To one side, Kobi saw the ladder.

Asha gripped the rungs and began to climb. Leon followed. Rohan did as well, and Jo and Yaeko. But the other kids held back. "Come on!" Kobi shouted, but they shook their heads. Reeta, the red-haired girl, ran back into the kids' quarters, followed by the others.

"Leave them!" said Kobi.

Leon stared after the others, but Rohan said, "Come on, we gotta go!"

They all began to climb.

"I can't make it," said Hales.

"I'll carry you," Kobi replied.

He stooped, bracing his legs, and hoisted the weakened doctor over one shoulder in a fireman's lift. He couldn't help but recall one of his earliest memories, riding his father's shoulders through the school hall. Now it was the other way around.

"They'll be waiting for us up there," said Hales.

"No one's going to stop us now," said Asha grimly from above.

Kobi gripped the rung with one hand and then stepped across with his feet.

They climbed mostly in silence, and the stairs seemed to go on endlessly. When they reached the top floor, breathing heavily, Leon prized the doors apart. One at a time, they climbed out into the hangar. Apart from the ranks of Snatchers, it appeared to be deserted. A single transport sat on the launching pad.

"Come on—quickly!" said Asha.

They made their way in a huddled group. Kobi saw Hales gritting his teeth, as if each jolt as he was carried was causing him discomfort. When they reached the transport, the door was closed.

"Can anyone open it?" asked Asha. Her eyes flicked back and forth. "Wait, where's Fionn?"

Kobi looked around too, but the boy wasn't with them.

"He was climbing behind me," said Yaeko. "I'm sure of it."

Asha started back toward the elevator shaft. "He can't have fallen. . . ."

"Maybe he saw sense," said Melanie Garcia, walking on her own across the hangar from among the Snatchers. Everyone turned toward her.

Asha raised the dart gun. "We're leaving here," she said.

"Not like this, you're not," said Melanie. She spread her hands. "I don't know why you're pointing that at me, Asha, but I'd appreciate it if you didn't. You're right; we have to evacuate Healhome. But only because Dr. Hales has jeopardized everyone's safety."

"Stop lying!" shouted Kobi, shielding Dr. Hales. "Krenner tried to kill me!"

"That's right," she said, eyes flashing menacingly. "He did." The other kids were looking around at each other. "Because you and Dr. Hales have been working together to destroy us. Everyone, be careful. These two outsiders won't stop until Healhome is overrun with Waste."

"What Waste?" said Asha. "There are three million people

living on the other side of these walls."

"Asha," said Melanie softly. "I don't know what Hales has promised you to play along with his ruse, but it's not worth it."

"Then show them the view from your office," said Asha. "Show them what's really out there."

The other kids clearly didn't know what to do, and most remained where they were.

"She's not telling us the truth," said Yaeko.

"That's ridiculous," said Niki. "There's no way you could know that. She's not infected."

Rohan shook his head. "Asha wouldn't lie."

Kobi pointed at Melanie. "She has cleansers that can wipe Waste from your body. They're made from my blood. She doesn't want you to get better. Or anyone else."

Asha jerked the barrel at Melanie and glowered as if seeing the woman for the first time. "All CLAWS wants is to keep making products and keep raking in money."

"This is nonsense!" said Melanie. "Asha—I've had enough of your *ingratitude* and Kobi your fantasy stories. I've worked my entire life to battle the Waste. The rest of you, move it!"

No one did.

Melanie lifted her chin. "Very well. You've forced my hand."

Guards flooded out from between the Snatchers, where they'd obviously been waiting. There were five of them, dart guns half lifted in the direction of the kids. Krenner led them, his collar bloody, and a look of pure hatred on his face.

"Take Dr. Hales," said Melanie. "D-Six."

"No!" muttered Kobi, backing off. Two Guardians strode toward him, raising their guns.

The first one was ten feet away before a green vine curled around his legs and pulled him over. The tendril was snaking from Jo's arm. Another guard turned his gun on her, shouting, "Let him go!"

Leon lashed out, grabbing the barrel and twisting it back on itself. "Careful where you point that," he said.

"Stop it!" cried Niki.

A gun went off, and Leon stumbled sideways, a dart in his neck. The Guardian who'd fired was swinging the gun around when Rohan picked out a baseball from his pocket and threw it, knocking the weapon from the Guardian's hand. Kobi started to run at another, whose barrel swung to rest right on him. He saw the muzzle flash, but Kobi dodged and Yaeko sprung onto the man's back, clawing at his face. He heard a shot and turned to see Krenner with one arm around Jonathan Hales's neck, and a curved knife in the other hand. Hales was grimacing in pain.

"It's over," said Krenner. "All of you, lie on the floor, or your so-called savior is going to die."

Kobi looked at the others. No one was close enough to do anything. Krenner looked mad with rage and easily capable of cutting someone's throat.

"Listen to Mr. Krenner," said Melanie. "We didn't want any of this, but it's gone far enough."

Asha lowered her dart gun, defeat painted across her features. "She's right—we can't leave without Fionn anyway."

Melanie seemed to relax. "I'm glad you've seen—"

A deep growl echoed across the hangar. "What was that?" said Yaeko.

Silence hung over them all for a few seconds before another rumbling snarl broke it.

Light scuffling footsteps approached, and Fionn came running from behind the transport. Then a huge shape pounced on top, all four paws planted, and a long, wrinkled muzzle looked down. The wolf!

Melanie backed away. "Mr. Krenner!" she wailed.

Krenner pushed Hales off, and lifted his dart gun in a smooth movement. One hand moved over the buttons on the side that controlled the dosage, and from a crouch he fired three quick shots. The wolf jerked back as each hit, then toppled off the back of the transport and out of sight with a yowl.

"No!" cried Fionn, and his voice, so high-pitched and so clear as it echoed around the hangar, shocked Kobi.

Everyone froze, but a second later the wolf came bounding around the transport's prow. Kids scattered left and right as it barreled full pelt toward Krenner. He fired and fired, the muzzle flashing as darts discharged at the massive wolf. But even if they were hitting, they weren't slowing the wolf down. It threw itself at Krenner, knocking him to the ground, then set about the

Guardian with its teeth. Kobi heard Krenner's panicked screams and looked away.

The Healhome kids huddled together, and Melanie had pressed her body up against the side of the transport, hand over her mouth in horror. Thankfully, the sounds ended quickly, and when Kobi glanced back, the wolf stood over Krenner's body, a growing pool of blood around its front paws.

"What have you done?" said Melanie.

The beast staggered suddenly, almost falling, and Fionn rushed to its side. Several darts protruded from its fur, and Kobi could only guess the amount of tranquilizing poison in its system. The wolf's legs buckled, and it fell, head crashing into the ground with a thud. Dr. Hales moved slowly in front of Kobi, shielding with his arms. His gaze was fixed on the creature.

"It's all right," said Kobi. "It's on our side."

"Tame?" said Hales.

"Sort of."

Fionn's lips were moving a little as he buried his hands in the fur of the wolf's flank. *He's talking to it*, Kobi realized. Asha went across to him, stepping over the bodies of the other Guardians. All were moving, if weakly, on the ground.

"We have to go, Fi," said Asha. "They'll send more guards."

Fionn looked at her through tear-streaked, imploring eyes.

"We *can't*," said Asha. "It's too late."

The wolf lifted its head ponderously and licked Fionn's

forearm. Then, with a shudder, its muzzle sank and the creature lay still.

It died for us, Kobi thought.

Asha pulled Fionn away, and Kobi helped Dr. Hales toward the transport and Melanie. "Open it!" he said.

"Or what?" she said.

A dart pinged off the hull a fraction to her left, and Asha advanced with the dart gun. "I've set this thing so high you'll never wake up," she said. "We'll use your hand one way or the other. Now *open* the door!

Melanie, shaking a little, placed her hand against the handle, which lit up with a white glow, and the transport's side door slid open.

Asha pushed past Melanie and climbed in with Fionn. The other kids followed—some hesitatingly, others in a rush. Leon was leaden-footed from the shot he'd received but managed to clamber on board. Kobi came last with Hales, who hobbled weakly.

"It's done, Dr. Garcia," said Hales as they passed Melanie.

Two of the Guardians were groaning and writhing on the ground as they came around. The director's face quivered with rage. "This is not over, Jonathan," she said. "You crossed us once before and we found you. Remember that."

"I did what was right," said Dr. Hales.

When they were on board, Kobi looked back and saw that not all the kids had followed. Niki remained on the hangar floor, jaw gritted tight as she watched them. "Come with us," said Kobi. "Come and see the truth."

"No, thanks," replied the girl.

"You'd rather stay here?" said Asha. "Niki, can't you see? They're just using us."

"She's right, Nik!" said Yaeko.

"Dr. Hales can make you *better*," said Asha,

Melanie laughed and put a hand over Niki's shoulder. "My dear Nikita is right. We have the drugs here to keep you all alive. Leave, and you'll all die. Dr. Hales belongs in jail for kidnapping. He's the one who's using you—to escape justice. Look at him! You think he'll last long enough to work on a cure?"

Asha hit a button beside the loading door and the ramp began to rise.

"You'll regret this," said Melanie.

The ramp closed, hiding her, Niki, and the rest of the hangar from view.

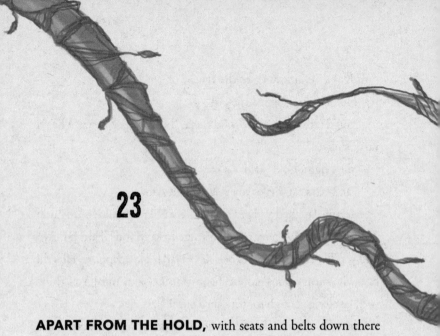

23

APART FROM THE HOLD, with seats and belts down there was a door leading to a cockpit area. Hales staggered through and fell heavily into one of the flight seats, eyes surveying the panel.

Reaching out tentatively, he began to pass his hands over various screens, and lights blinked on, showing an array of readouts. The craft vibrated and rocked as the platform beneath them rose. At the same time, a door slid closed, sealing the cockpit from the carrier section, and the wings on either side of the craft extended from their stubby housings.

"Get everyone strapped in back there," he said. On a camera screen, Kobi could see the Healhome kids all locking in. At the same time, the launch pad lifted them through the open hatch, onto the roof of the building, where he'd tried to escape before. The cityscape appeared ahead.

"Let's see if this works," said Hales.

He took hold of a lever and pressed it forward. The transport rose evenly on jet thrusters. "Kobi, seat belt," he said, and his tone of voice sounded just like old times.

And as Kobi clipped himself in with a chest harness pulled over his head, Hales squeezed the paddles on either side of the steering column, and they jerked forward. Kobi was pressed back into his chair for a moment, then Hales adjusted their speed, and they left the rooftop behind at a more even pace.

"Dr. Hales," said Melanie over the speakers. "You are in possession of CLAWS property. Return it at once, or we will be forced to . . ."

Hales dragged a dial down, silencing the voice. They climbed through the air, way above any of the other vehicles below, but still some way beneath the tallest of the gleaming towers.

"None of the kids have ever seen this," said Kobi. "They thought the contamination was everywhere."

"Yes, that was the protocol," said Dr. Hales. "If you control information, you can control people. I adopted the technique myself with you." He turned and looked at Kobi. "I want you to know that everything I did was to find a cure. To stop CLAWS's manipulation. I remember the first time I saw you as a baby. They told us to detach ourselves—to treat you like what you were: scientific experiments. Vessels for the development of drugs. But even before you showed no signs of negative Waste effects, I thought you were special. Whatever happens from here, I want you to know that you will always be my son."

Kobi's eyes welled up, and he wiped the tears away with the sleeve of his jumpsuit. "I can't forgive what you did," said Kobi. "All the lies. I still don't understand why it had to be that way. But . . . you are my dad. Nothing can change that."

A sob escaped Hales's throat and he smiled. "I don't deserve it . . . but thank you." As the vehicle sped faster, he leaned right across the panel, and his fingers flicked over several buttons. The parts of the cockpit that housed screens turned transparent, and the chatter from the back of the ship went silent. Kobi turned in his seat and opened the door to the carrier section. The Healhome kids were aghast, heads turning this way and that to take in the views through the windows. Rohan's yellow eyes sparkled, and Leon's sinewy muscles bulged as he gripped the seat restraints. "It looks kind of like the city in *Blade Runner*," Leon said. "But less dirty and eighties. A bit of Mega-City One and *The Fifth Element* in there too."

"Dude, stop talking about old movies!" said Rohan. "Anyway, this city is crazier than any of those places."

"Look, it's a park," said Johanna. "That skyscraper is bigger than the Empire State Building."

"I've heard of a million buildings higher than the Empire State," said Yaeko. "In Dubai and Shanghai and in India somewhere and one in Brazil. Hey, can we go to any of those places?"

"Private global travel doesn't really happen anymore," said Hales. "Unless you have a lot of money. Parts of northern India are Waste wildernesses. They were sold on the idea of GAIA and it was sprayed extensively over crops on the day of the global launch, before the initial reports came in. Dubai was quarantined easily in the desert, but it's still a lawless place, and Rio is booming, but Waste is slowly spreading through the Amazon. China destroyed most of its agricultural infrastructure thinking they were being attacked by a chemical weapon, and it's all cities now. The country is practically closed off. And they don't like Americans."

"What about LA?" said Leon. "Hollywood? Is Hollywood still there?"

"Parts of LA weren't destroyed. The foothills formed a natural barrier, and Waste found it harder to take hold. Plus they were ready with the incinerator drones by then."

"Cool!" said Rohan.

Kobi couldn't help smiling at the collection of bewildered, mesmerized faces. The streets below threaded in perfect geometric patterns around plazas dotted with green spaces and pristine blue pools with sparkling fountains. There was an airport near the center and aircraft circled it for landing. But as they climbed, Kobi saw the perfect modern city had its limits. Beyond the bristling buildings that formed the central district, the metropolis became a sprawl of mammoth warehouses in one direction. In another, several train lines serviced acres of uniform blocks of what Kobi guessed were apartments. Kobi could just make out what looked like barren desert outside the city, spreading far into the distance, filled with the detritus of burned buildings and roads. There were plains of shining solar panels and expansive wind farms and colossal industrial warehouses, and figures and vehicles milled around them.

It must take a lot to feed and power this place, he thought.

Beyond it all, he saw mountains on the horizon.

"This place has changed so much in thirteen years," said Dr. Hales.

"We've got a problem," said Asha. She pointed through the starboard hull, where three dots swarmed like distant flies.

"Snatchers," said Kobi.

Hales groaned, but Kobi couldn't tell if it was pain or despair. "They're coming after Waste-infected organic matter," he said, eyes flicking to the Healhome kids in their seat belts.

The drones were approaching fast, zipping after them.

"But they can't get us in here, can they?" said Kobi.

"They don't need to get inside," said Hales. "Melanie just wants to stop us. I don't think you understand the utter ruthlessness of the CLAWS organization. They will protect their secret and their power at all costs. Murder is nothing. They can always create more Wastelings."

The first Snatcher slammed into the back of the transport in an explosion of sparks, then fell like a stone, trailing smoke as it plummeted. The whole craft rocked, throwing Kobi around in his harness.

"Kobi, you need to take the controls," said Hales. "Swap chairs."

"Fly this thing?"

Hales nodded weakly, unfastening himself, as Kobi reached

across and took the flight paddle.

"I know roughly where Mischik's base is," said Hales, "but I need some time to reach him on a secure frequency. You can do it—just keep us in the air."

He sagged into the seat Kobi had vacated, rubbed his eyes, then began to move his fingers over what Kobi thought must be the communications systems. The transport began to tip.

Kobi's first effort to straighten the craft lurched the nose skyward and drew cries of terror from the rear. Next, he overcorrected. *Keep calm*. It was the first rule of a survival situation.

In a few seconds he had the transport leveled out.

Slam!

A second Snatcher careered into their side, spreading its wing at the last moment and clamping on to the outside of the hull. The glass panel distorted, flickering as cracks spread across one.

"What's it doing?" cried Leon.

Kobi, fighting for control, glanced back and saw the underside of the Snatcher's cavity opening. Then a buzzing sawlike appendage emerged. It tore into the metal of the hull, filling the hold with a screeching sound.

"It's going to get in!" cried Johanna.

"Come in, Mischik," said Hales calmly. "Can you hear me?"

All Kobi could hear was static and the terrible squeal of the Snatcher's claw.

"It's Hales, Alex. I've got the Healhome patients. Most of them. We need an extraction. Heading toward your position. Alex?"

Kobi heard a scream and looked back to see the Snatcher ripping a larger hole in the hull. Beyond was open sky. It squeezed a mechanical leg inside.

"What the hell is that thing?" shouted Leon.

The kids were trying to unfasten their belts in panic, pressing themselves farther from the attacking robot. Yaeko sprang across the craft and landed halfway up the vehicle's side, stuck there like a lizard. Then Asha was up and running along the center of the hold. She had a fire extinguisher in her hands. Just short of the encroaching Snatcher, she discharged it, blasting retardant over the drone. For a moment there was only white clouds of smoke and shouts of terror. Through the mist, Kobi saw her raise the extinguisher in both hands and slam it into the Snatcher's face parts. Once . . . twice . . .

With the third strike, she lost her grip, but Leon rushed forward and grabbed the Snatcher's last clinging leg, wrenching at it with a powerful jerk of his hands. It ripped away, and the gigantic metal monster seemed to be sucked backward out of the craft. Asha fell back in exhaustion as the Snatcher spiraled toward the ground far below.

Everyone cheered, and Kobi returned his attention to the landscape ahead. They were heading toward what looked like a low mountain, though the formation did not look entirely natural and he couldn't work out why. Beside him, Hales was still tinkering. "I can't seem to get a response," he said. "I don't even know if it's working prop—"

Another huge thud rocked them, and Kobi felt the stick judder in his arms. He fought for control, but the craft was listing badly to the right, pressing him into his chair. The lights across the panel were flashing, and he didn't need the alarms on the diagnostic panel to show him what was wrong. The starboard wing was on fire, and he saw the third Snatcher had latched on. It was clawing its way slowly along the wing's length like a spider coming inevitably for its wounded prey.

The altimeter display was spinning fast as they lost height.

"I can't hold it!" he cried, fingers sweaty. Asha leaned against the back of his chair, eyes glued to the approaching Snatcher. "Strap in!" shouted Kobi.

As Asha retreated into the main hold, a series of detonations seemed to come from deep inside the craft, and suddenly the starboard wing sheered away completely. The Snatcher dangled, half flailing in the wind, but somehow still holding on with just two legs.

Now that they were closer to the hill itself, Kobi realized the structures up its slopes were makeshift buildings, glinting with solar panels and scrap metal. There were people scurrying between them, barely visible from the air. It was some sort of slum.

And we're going to crash right into it!

"Down there!" said Hales, pointing.

Kobi saw what looked like a reservoir of water at the base of the mountain. Clearly man-made, it was threaded with several floating walkways and various small bubble-like enclosures. Crucially, he couldn't see any people. He pulled the stick hard, trying to keep the nose up, while also fighting the craft's tipping momentum.

"I'll kill the port engine too," said Hales. "It's the only way to stabilize."

With a few fluid movements of his fingertips, Kobi felt the power drain, and suddenly the stick was looser. Gusts buffeted them, throwing him around in his chair. He managed to level off, but they were coming in so fast and hard. He reached up and took the shoulder harness, pulling it into place. The whole transport was shuddering as if it would tear itself apart. Every instrument and readout seemed to be going into meltdown, but Kobi focused on the water ahead.

"Thrusters on!" said Hales.

"How?" yelled Kobi.

Hales leaned across, gripped the main lever with a wrinkled hand, and yanked it back, dragging back the main lever. The transport groaned horribly. At the same time, Kobi realized Hales wasn't secure—he had no belt on.

"No!" he cried.

And then they hit the water.

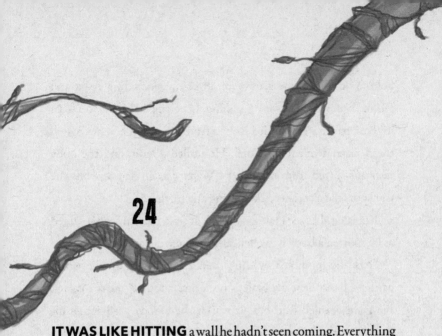

24

IT WAS LIKE HITTING a wall he hadn't seen coming. Everything went dark at the same time as tremendous force slammed Kobi in the chest. He heard crashing through the blackness, screams, and a succession of thumps. He was sure the harness must have broken, because he was being thrown around. Then he felt the cold surge of water around his legs. Something was pressing his face, making it hard to breathe.

Kobi opened his eyes and saw several inflatable balloons around his head. Heard the suck and slosh of fluid. As he wriggled to find the seat release, the balloons deflated to show what remained of the control panel and the collapsed windshield. Water was spilling over the controls, throwing up crackling sparks and smoke.

He shook his head to clear it and unclipped himself. His body was throbbing all over, but he climbed from the seat. In the back of the craft, similar inflatables were sagging from the walls of the hold. The Healhome kids were all secure, including Asha and Fionn. Some of them were groaning. Leon ripped his belt off with his bare hands, then pulled Rohan from his seat. Then he crossed the deck and opened a panel. He pulled a lever, and the body restraints lifted from the others. Water was ankle-deep, but the transport didn't seem to be sinking any further.

Kobi couldn't see Hales anywhere at first, then his panic surged as he spotted a body lying beneath the control panels.

"No," he mumbled, wading over. He crouched in the water, easing a hand beneath Hales's neck and another under his legs. He gently pulled him out. It wasn't the bloody gash across his temple, or the limpness of the limbs that told Kobi all he needed to know. It was the empty, staring eyes. Trembling, he felt for a pulse anyway. There was none.

Kobi felt his heart break.

"He's gone," said Asha quietly.

Kobi realized she was standing over him. Could she tell the truth through her telepathy, or simply by sight?

"We need to get out," said Asha.

The craft tipped suddenly, and more water began to gush inside. Kobi lost his grip on the body, which slumped into the rising water.

"I can't leave him," he said. He struggled back toward the body, even as the transport was being overwhelmed by the inflow.

"You have to," said Asha, tugging him. "Come on!"

"I think we better leave about now!" shouted Yaeko from the

passenger hold. Reluctantly, Kobi followed her to where Leon had managed to prize open an emergency door over the wing. He stood by as the Healhome kids shuffled out. His body felt like lead, and he could barely think. Tears stung his eyes.

"Focus, Kobi, never lose focus. The minute you lose concentration in a survival situation it kills you." Hales's words seemed to float into his head. Kobi felt oddly calm all of a sudden. He could hear cries outside—adult shouts of concern. When he reached the fresh air along with the other Healhome kids, he saw the transport was half-submerged, nose down and listing near one of the pontoons. There were people on shallow-bottomed motorboats cutting through the water toward them. As they closed in, Kobi saw they looked desperate, with drawn features and tattered clothes. But they were helping the others off the stricken aircraft. Beyond the rescue operation, the sheer scale of the shanties left him stunned— they rose high above on the slopes and for what looked like miles in either direction. It was so different from the sleek modern city where Healhome was based. There were no stories-high, flashing holograms here. No sleek steel and glass. The homes of the slums, their roofs broken with makeshift vents and chimneys, appeared to be built almost entirely of scrap and other detritus. He tore his eyes away and climbed onto a boat with Asha and Fionn and two adults, both women.

"Who are you?" asked Kobi.

"Friends of Dr. Hales," said one of the women simply. Kobi nodded. It's all he could do. Jonathan Hales's pale, lifeless face haunted his vision. It didn't seem real.

The other two boats were already heading for the strange lake's shore. The two women continued to throw worried glances upward as if afraid what else might come from the sky. As they followed the others, Kobi saw there were several people waiting on motorbikes, their faces concealed behind helmets, and engines running.

"Speed it up! Speed it up!" one yelled. "We can't stay out here!"

The Healhome kids were disembarking, and each was being directed onto the back of a bike. Asha looked as dumbfounded as Kobi felt, and she shrugged to Fionn. "I have no idea. But they seem to be expecting us."

Their boat reached the shore too. Asha helped Fionn off, then jumped over herself.

One of the women frowned over Kobi's shoulder. "What's—? Oh no!"

Kobi turned just as the boat tipped and the spray burst upward in a plume. Kobi's heart leaped in fright as something rose from the surface. *Snatcher!* The tiny part of him not consumed by fear told him it must have been the one that crashed with the transport.

Water spilled from the Snatcher's dented, scorched carapace as Kobi struggled and failed to keep his balance. He couldn't do a thing as he fell overboard. Plunged beneath the water into a chaotic maelstrom of bubbles, he saw the rest of the Snatcher's body. He fought his panic, kicking for the surface, then felt a hand grab his.

He was heaved up and managed to get the top half of his body into the pontoon before a viselike grip found his foot. Kobi strained against the Snatcher, but he felt himself slipping back. Asha had one arm. Fionn another, but they would never be strong enough. His fingers began to slide through theirs, and a fear he'd never felt before almost paralyzed him. *If it gets me under the water, I'm dead . . .*

"Help us!" roared Asha.

He heard pounding footsteps, saw his own terror matched in the stares of his friends as they clung on. They knew it too. It was only a matter of time. His ankle screamed in pain as the claw bit deeper into his flesh.

A hollow *whoosh* went past his ear, followed by an explosive bang. Suddenly the pressure on his foot vanished and he flopped onto the pontoon, yanked up by his friends. He looked back and saw the Snatcher smoking on the water before it slowly sank beneath the surface in a slick of bubbles and swirling oil. His relief quickly changed to confusion. Had it somehow malfunctioned?

Then he saw a tall man in a helmet on the jetty, with his visor up to reveal glinting blue eyes. He carried some sort of tubular weapon on his shoulder, like a bazooka but smaller and more lightweight, with dials on the side.

"Where's Hales?" he shouted.

Kobi took a moment before replying. "He didn't make it." It sounded cold and emotionless coming out of Kobi's mouth. He felt leaden with shock. He kept thinking Hales was actually on the jetty, his brain and body confused. *It shouldn't have ended like that.*

He saw the man's gaze soften as he took a deep breath, but then he regained his composure.

"Come on," he said, slamming down the visor of his helmet.

Kobi, soaked to his skin and limping, followed them along the pontoons to the bikes. His feet left bloody puddles on the pontoon. Asha and Fionn both climbed on behind other riders, and Kobi took the back seat on the tall man's own bike. The man folded the weapon and slid it into a harness across the handlebars.

Kobi noticed hundreds of faces looking out from the slopes—men, women, and children—watching the scene. And when he looked back across the lake, where the bow of the transport was still just visible above the water, he saw a swarm in the sky above the city. More Snatchers. Perhaps thirty of them! Kobi could barely comprehend the vision.

Kobi's savior twisted the bike's throttle, and the whole band of riders headed for the slum city.

They traveled at breakneck speed, plunging into narrow alleyways between shacks large and small, bouncing over the uneven ground. The air in the alleyways was thick with the scent of burning fuels and cooking smells. They dodged dogs and cats and chickens, but most of the people seemed to be keeping well out of the way, crouched in doorways and leaning through hatches. A few cheered as the bike convoy roared past. It was like some sort of peasant village from the Middle Ages, but instead of wooden buildings, everything seemed to be scrap metal or tarpaulins. There were odd signs of tech too—bright screens glimpsed through windows, or tottering droids, parts of harvested engines powering mechanisms Kobi didn't have time to understand. The people he saw were mostly normal, but from time to time something not quite right caught his attention. A man with a single eye in the middle of his forehead, or odd furred features. He could have sworn he saw a toddler with a pair of diaphanous wings flickering from her back, but perhaps it was just a costume. Could these people be fugitives from the Wastelands too, or sufferers of Waste mutations like the Healhome kids?

What he didn't see any of was plant life.

After they'd been traveling for two or three minutes, around countless twists and turns, through patches of light and dark, the bikes began to slow. Up ahead, the leaders seemed to simply vanish, and when Kobi reached the same spot, he saw a large hatch open in the alley, and a ramp leading downward. His stomach flipped as they descended quickly underground. His mind and body remained in shock, and he could barely take in his surroundings, only to wonder if his dad had ever been here, of what he might say if he was with him now.

It seemed at first like a network of bare earth tunnels, but there were cables and pipes too lining the walls and ceiling. Dim lights stationed at regular intervals lit the way. Guards too, standing at archway openings, waved the bikers through. They weren't in the open anymore, but the feeling wasn't pleasant at all. The walls seemed to press in, and all Kobi could think of was how far from daylight they were traveling. Just as the claustrophobia was getting unbearable, the tunnel opened up into a larger underground chamber, and the bikes drew together and killed their engines. Kobi's rider climbed off after him, then tugged off the helmet. Beneath, he saw those startling blue eyes were set in a hard, grizzled face, topped with salt-and-pepper hair. And Kobi recognized it at once from the hologram projection from the GrowCycle lab.

"You're Mischik," he said.

"Correct," replied the man. He held out a gloved hand. "Nice to meet you again, Kobi."

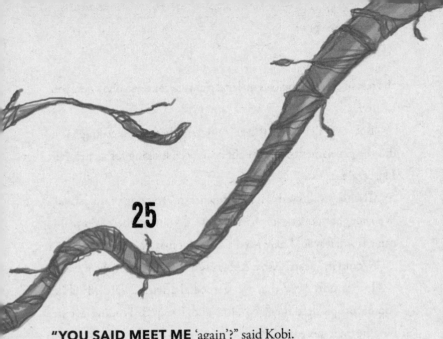

25

"YOU SAID MEET ME 'again'?" said Kobi.

He was lying on a medical bed, with a masked nurse dressing the wound on his lower calf where the Snatcher had grabbed him. All around, the other Healhome escapees were being seen to. The infirmary looked more like a military field tent than a real hospital.

Mischik nodded. "You didn't have a name back then. You were just a baby, like the others, but I'll never forget your label—S374. Dr. Hales was astonished when he realized what you represented. An end to Waste, an end to CLAWS. He named you Kobi. It means 'supplanter.'"

The grief welled up again. Kobi had to squeeze his fist to stop the tears. "Did he tell you he was going to kidnap me?" he asked.

Mischik grinned. "*Kidnap* is the wrong word. That's what Melanie called it. But yes, Jon told me. We both realized the threat you posed to the company. The experiments were top secret. You, the rest of them—you had no legal rights because no one knew you existed."

"But you still worked there?" said Asha, her tone accusing. "You did the experiments. You might have been looking for a cure, but I lost *friends*."

Mischik swallowed, his eyes downcast. "You don't understand. We thought you *were* orphans—if we'd known where you really came from, it would have been a different matter."

"Would it?" asked Asha. Kobi could see how angry she was.

"It was only later that we learned the truth," said Mischik. "Some people left then, but Jon and I stayed. Finding a cure became even more important.

"But you changed everything," Mischik said to Kobi, eyes intense. "We guessed CLAWS wouldn't want you to exist. Our old friend Melanie—we went to university with her in Seattle—had climbed to the top of corporate leadership at CLAWS, and she became more and more ruthless, more and more . . . inhuman. We knew that she wouldn't let you survive. We finally saw what we were doing for what it was, who we were working for. I left then and formed Sol."

Kobi frowned. "Sol?"

"It's Latin for 'sun,' a symbol of enlightenment and a new dawn."

"Very noble," said Asha. She stood up and went over to speak with Fionn, who was with one of the medical staff. Despite his injury and the danger of the escape, he looked better than ever.

The nurse treating Kobi's injury looked up, removing her face mask. "It looked like you'd need twenty stitches, but I've only had to put in five," she said. "Your healing metabolism is like nothing I've ever seen—remarkable!"

"Yeah," said Kobi. "That's what Dr. Hales . . . Dad used to say."

The nurse's eyes softened. "He was a good man." She finished up and went off to look after the others.

"Something tells me you're going to prove interesting in lots of ways," said Mischik. He took off his glasses, rubbing the lenses absently. "You know, Dr. Hales did care for you like a son. You should never doubt that."

Kobi lay back on the bed, thoughts swirling. "I know. I just wish he'd told me the truth."

"He was going to," said Mischik. "When the time was right."

"When the experiments were complete, you mean?"

"Not just that," said the doctor. "When you were older; when you were ready."

Kobi smiled. He remembered how protective Hales had always been. That's what had started all this—the day Hales had insisted he stay behind at the school. If Kobi had gone too, perhaps none of this would have happened. Maybe he'd be back there now, in a classroom at Bill Gates, eating baked beans and thinking they were on their own.

"I was ready," he said quietly.

Mischik reached across and tapped his shoulder comfortingly. "For what it's worth, I think you probably were. Question is, are you ready now for what needs to be done?"

"What do you mean?" asked Kobi, suddenly on edge.

Mischik replaced his spectacles. "CLAWS is *the* biggest corporation in the world. They have influence everywhere—police, government, resources. They have the ultimate product"—he reached into a pocket and took out a small plastic pill pot, shaking it—"life." Mischik's eyes gleamed, and Kobi thought he saw a tinge of yellow in the whites. "That's where you come in," he said.

"Go on," Kobi said.

"Until CLAWS intercepted our communication with Hales, they assumed you were dead," he said. "They didn't know about your immunity, and they thought Hales had just grown too attached to you when he stole you. But now they know you're very much not dead . . ."

"They'll come after me."

Mischik stared at him. "I won't lie to you, Kobi—like you said, you're ready to hear the truth. They won't stop until you're eliminated. They'll hit us with everything they've got. We've got to be smart, cautious, and probably lucky too. But we've got the advantage—the ultimate weapon."

Mischik took Kobi's arm and pointed to a blue vein. "Your blood holds the key to defeating the Waste, and without the Waste, there's no CLAWS."

Kobi swallowed, and whether it was the feverish way Mischik looked at him, or the almost reverent way he spoke, he finally understood the reason Hales had taken the risk he did. But he still had so many questions. He glanced around at the makeshift infirmary, the pieced-together tech.

"I don't get it," said Kobi, recalling too the odd mutations he'd seen on the motorbike ride. "This place—these slums—they're not like the rest of the city."

Mischik nodded. "New Seattle is a capitalist society like any other. The poor—those who can't afford the best pills—end up on the periphery, living in squalor like this. Waste infiltrates the borders of the city sometimes, and in increasing amounts. We're losing the war. The slums are cordoned off with quarantine barricades. There's a black market for medicine here, of course—because people are desperate. But you can change that. We can create our own medicines, flood the market, and undermine CLAWS."

"Melanie Garcia won't like that," said Kobi, feeling a little afraid. "And if she's as powerful as you say . . ."

"We need to spread the word without the whispers drawing attention back to us," said Mischik. "We're just a seed at the moment, and it won't take much to snuff us out. But if we play this right, if we nurture it, we can grow into something unstoppable."

Kobi felt it right then, in his chest, exactly where the pain of grief had sat like an indigestible ball. Hope. He saw it too in the eyes of the other fugitives around him, torn from the only existence they had known and thrown into a fight they never asked for. A war Jonathan Hales had given his life for.

I didn't ask for this. It was just fate. Genetics. But I can't walk away from the responsibility. Hales never did. He made mistakes, but he tried to do what was right, and I will too.

He swung his legs off the bed, flexing his healing leg.

"Okay. Where do we start?"

THE ADVENTURE CONTINUES IN

Keep reading for a sneak peek!

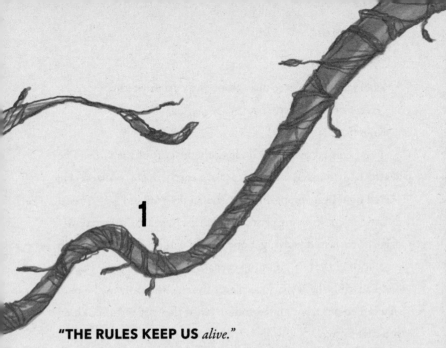

1

"THE RULES KEEP US *alive.*"

He'd heard it a hundred times, so why hadn't he listened? Why hadn't he stayed put like he was supposed to?

"Dad?" Kobi whispered. He cut a path through coarse grass as tall as his shoulders, using his machete, then climbed a tangle of roots twisting out from the enormous trunk of a cedar. His eyes darted around the mutated undergrowth, searching for movement or for a sign his father might have come this way. There was nothing.

"*I scout ahead; you stay exactly where you are until I come back and give you a signal. It's how we move safely. Got it?*"

Kobi had begged his dad to take him along, to let Kobi go with him out into the Wastelands, train him how to survive. "I'm nine years old, Dad," he'd said. "I'm ready."

He'd been so stupid.

Kobi raised an arm to push through a curtain of leafy vines.

"Examine everything. Never move without looking."

Kobi froze.

Tiny serrated teeth edged along the lengths of the vines. The Waste had mutated them into flesh-eaters, Kobi realized. He peered up. High among the branches, a massive gull was trussed up inside a crisscrossing prison of tendrils. Acid sap dripped slowly over the carcass, dissolving it one feather at a time. Kobi saw a rib cage, melted flesh, a gleaming eyeball. He remembered what his dad had said: the ivy Chokerplants weren't as deadly as the ones that lashed out from underground, but if they got you they killed you a lot slower.

Trembling, Kobi crouched beneath the Choker. He glanced up at the sharp-bladed feelers, inches from brushing his back. He stumbled.

"Never rush, Kobi!"

Kobi screwed his eyes shut for a moment. His heart pounded like a drum in his ears, and he worried the feelers would sense the tremors.

After a minute, he moved off again, taking each step with careful precision, until he was finally out of the Choker's reach. "Dad?" Kobi called out as loud as he dared. "Where are you?"

He wanted to shout, to scream so his dad would hear him. But that would be suicide. Anything might hear. Chokers, wasps, wolves, bears, eagles.

Snatchers.

His dad had said the drones could pick up audio from five miles away.

Kobi bit his lip to stop himself whimpering. He was lost. Alone.

"Out here we're prey, Kobi. Remember that. There are a hundred things that can kill us."

It had been going so well, their first training session. But Kobi had gotten scared. When his father hadn't returned after ten minutes, he'd rushed after him. Betrayed his trust. That was the worst thing—worse even than the ball of fear building in his gut now. *I've let Dad down.*

He heard a noise, to his left. Just a rustle.

"Dad?"

He walked quickly, placing each foot with care on the spongy, moss-covered ground. He ducked under a branch, feeling twigs scrape at his hair. Sunlight trickled through a break in the foliage just ahead. The clearing where he was supposed to wait! He'd managed to circle back. He could wait here for his dad. Kobi wiped his tears away and hurried on. It was going to be okay. His dad might never know he hadn't waited.

Kobi burst through the veil of branches, tearing aside leaves bigger than his head.

His feet skidded in the mud as he stopped. It wasn't the clearing at all. It was a rocky wharf.

He gazed out over the largest expanse of water he'd ever seen— stretching out for miles.

"Elliott Bay," Kobi whispered. He'd seen it on maps. His breath

3

shuddered in his chest at the size of it.

Huge patches of phosphorescence shimmered like spilled oil, and lily pads several feet across floated on the surface, sprouting flowers of every hue. Shreds of dense mist drifted in places, hovering over the surface. In the distance, on what must have been the far shore, colossal green monoliths soared into the clouds. *Downtown Seattle.* Bill Gates High School, where Kobi and his dad had made their base, was in West Seattle, a formerly residential area of the city. Unlike his dad, he'd never crossed the bridge to the downtown area, but he'd heard it was once home to two million people, before the Waste had wiped out the population and the genetically modified vegetation and animals had taken over.

Kobi was about to retreat from the bay and continue searching for his dad when his ears caught a sound: the soft slap of water. Then ripples began to pulse from a patch of mist, furrowing the surface until they reached the bank near his feet. When Kobi squinted, he could just make out a dark shape in the center of the lake, moving steadily parallel to the shore. His knees almost buckled as he took a slight sudden step forward. *A sail? A boat!*

His dad had always been so sure there were no other survivors, and if by a slim chance they *were* out there, they would be too hard to reach. But Kobi had always hoped. He could never get rid of the thought, a lingering, impossible dream that one day they might find others like them—kids his age, other families, people who they could rely on. And now, almost like a miracle, that day had really come. Here they were: survivors, just a few hundred yards away. Kobi found his voice. "Hey!" he called.

The boat kept going, drifting away into the mist.

"No! Wait!" Kobi shouted, waving his arms.

But the ship maintained its course, becoming a ghostly shape in the mist before disappearing entirely from view.

Kobi looked around for something to throw—a rock or a branch. Anything to get their attention. But there was nothing. He watched the mist again, pleading in his heart for them to turn around and come back. How could they not have heard him?

"Kobi!" called a distant, frantic voice. *Dad.* "Kobi, where are you?"

His eyes still on the water, Kobi shouted back. "I'm fine! I'm by the water. Dad, I—"

A vast gleaming fin sliced up from the depths, twenty yards out, and the surface ballooned upward as a massive body followed. Kobi staggered back.

What he'd seen, he realized, hadn't been a boat at all. A wall of water overwhelmed the bank and crashed over him, freezing and sudden. The ground turned to slick mud, and his feet slipped out from beneath him. Kobi felt the current snatch him up and suck his legs into the shallows. He twisted and clawed at the bank, but his fingers slid over the ground. And then he was under.

Kobi flailed. Water burned up his nostrils and into the back of his throat. He scrambled for purchase, but the bank dropped away suddenly. The churning water dragged him deeper. He couldn't swim. He couldn't breathe. But rearing above both of those fears was a greater terror: the creature looming out there in the murky water. His fingers brushed something slimy, and he recoiled, kicking out and striking a harder surface. A low, mournful sound—an eerie call—seemed to come from every direction at once. It was impossible to pinpoint. He felt the water stir again below, and looking down into the depths, he saw a flash of silver flesh, rolling, then a sickly yellow eye, watching him. It rolled back in a fleshy red socket, and the creature rose. The scale of its body seemed impossible. Frozen, Kobi took in the scarred flesh of its head, a blunt nose, a mouth that stretched open like a crack in the ground. Rows of jagged teeth, each curved fang long enough to pierce right through Kobi's body. . . .

Something clamped his upper arm, digging into the flesh, and pulled. Suddenly he was out of the water, being hauled to shore, slithering across the muddy bank. The water exploded upward, drenching him in its spray as a black-and-white body rose, then crashed down again. It was some sort of orca, Kobi realized, its skin gouged with scars and patches of red, raw flesh. Kobi watched it disappear beneath the surface as he was dragged farther from the water's edge.

His dad was here, hands clamped on Kobi's shoulders, pulling him to his feet. His eyes searched Kobi's body frantically.

"Are you hurt? Did it bite you?" he was saying.

"I . . . No . . . I'm fine," Kobi managed to reply.

His dad crouched in front of him, a look of utter panic on his face. "What the hell were you doing, son?"

"I . . . I thought it was a boat. Survivors."

His dad looked incredulous, shaking his head. Then he pulled Kobi into an embrace and held him firm. Kobi could feel his father's heart rattling.

"Never run off again," he said, squeezing more tightly. "Got it?"

"Got it," said Kobi.

His dad released him, staring hard and angry until Kobi couldn't maintain eye contact. His face flushing red, he glanced down.

"Look at me, Kobi," said his dad.

Kobi raised his gaze. His dad's face wasn't furious anymore. It was resigned. Sad, even.

"Son, there aren't any survivors," he said. He pointed at the city skyline across the bay. "I've been there. I've seen it. There's no one."

"But *we* survived," said Kobi. "Maybe there are others. If they had a home and could get food like us—"

"There *aren't*," said his dad. "Trust me. Even if the predators didn't get you over there the Waste would. There's no medicine. The air is toxic. A human wouldn't last a week."

Together they watched the surface of the lake for a few seconds. It was completely still again, with no clue of the horror that lurked within. Kobi wondered if he'd ever get chance to go into the city. Probably not, after today.

"Come on," said his dad. "Let's get back to base."

He stood, and helped Kobi to his feet as well, then folded an arm over Kobi's shoulders. "I thought I'd lost you," he said quietly, then sucked in a breath as if trying not to choke up. "I thought I lost you, son."

Kobi reached up and touched the rough skin of his father's hand on his shoulder, sliding his fingers through his dad's. They felt real, but he knew they weren't, and that made his heart ache too much to bear.

Kobi awoke from the dream. Though it wasn't a dream. It was more than that. A memory. A flashback. Kobi had been having them often. Like his past invaded the present whenever he was most vulnerable. He pushed his legs out from under the sheets and sat up, visions of the Wastelands still around him, cast against the gray concrete walls of his bedroom. There was no natural light, only a blue night-light. Kobi didn't like much other decoration. A few books, a couple of posters of his favorite movies he used to watch with Hales—classic black-and-white ones from almost a hundred years ago. Hales had liked those the best. Kobi realized his cheeks were moist, and he brushed the tracks away with his pajama sleeve.

"I thought I'd lost you. I thought I lost you, son."

Hales's words echoed again in Kobi's foggy brain, causing him a spasm of hurt. "I was never your son," he replied out loud.

"Kobi? You awake?" There was a knock at the door. Kobi wasn't allowed a lock, and before he could say anything the steel door swung open. It revealed Asha, watching him with dark eyes filled with worry. Her thick, black hair was hanging to her shoulders, bunching at the collar of a beige fleece and drifting in the air over her scalp, from the static, Kobi guessed, of putting on the sweatshirt. In the blue lamplight, her brown skin shone the color of dusk.

"I sensed you," she said. She tapped her temple. "This dream was really vivid."

Kobi just nodded. Asha was a Receptor, a telepath who could sense the thoughts and emotions of all organisms contaminated by the Waste. Without waiting for an invitation, she strolled in and sat beside him. "You saw an orca? That's what that thing was in the bay."

"Yes," said Kobi. He cleared his throat. "That was my first day training outside the school with Hales. After that we didn't go out again for months. I still don't like water—the ocean or lakes or anything. Not many of those around here." He smiled at her.

She returned the smile for a second before looking away, wistful. "I'd like to see the ocean one day. We never saw it when we were with you in the Wastelands."

"I guess there wasn't much time for sightseeing."

She sat down on the bed. Kobi didn't need Asha's telepathic powers to read the guilt on her face. "Not really," she said. "But that's the past now. We need to focus on the future."

Like Kobi, Asha had grown up believing human society had been completely destroyed by the Waste after it was released into the environment over twenty years ago—the chemical that had been intended to accelerate the growth of crops but had instead spread through the environment, mutating plants and animals and killing humans. Until six months ago, she'd lived her whole life in a secure facility called Healhome. The scientists there, led by Melanie Garcia and calling themselves "Guardians," had told Asha and the other kids that they had a natural resistance to the Waste. They said they were studying the kids' resistance to find a cure. But it was all lies.

The truth was, only pockets of the world had been ruined by the Waste. Those had been cordoned off in quarantine zones; the rest of the world was intact. Healhome was really hidden away at the top of a skyscraper in the city of New Seattle—a hundred miles from the city now called *Old* Seattle, built as a symbol of humanity's defiance against the Waste. Melanie had told the truth about one thing: she was CEO of CLAWS—the Corporation of Leading Anti-Waste Scientists. But they weren't trying to find a cure. They just wanted their drugs to work well enough that the people of New Seattle would keep coming back for more. CLAWS had been experimenting on human embryos, contaminating them with Waste on purpose. Most died, but some survived, the Waste's mutations giving them strange, superhuman abilities.

Kobi had been one of those embryos too, and the only one to develop complete Waste immunity. So when he was a baby, Dr. Jonathan Hales, a CLAWS scientist, had kidnapped him and taken him to Old Seattle, the heart of the Wastelands. He'd thought they would be safe there, long enough for Hales to develop from Kobi's blood a *real* cure for the Waste. Hales knew that if CLAWS realized Kobi was entirely immune, they would kill him rather than see their empire threatened. Hales told Kobi he was his father so Kobi would never question anything he said.

Six months ago, CLAWS had dispatched Asha and two other Healhome kids to the Wastelands to find Kobi—an eleven-year-old boy called Fionn and Niki, who was fourteen like Asha, a year older than Kobi. After finding Kobi's dad's secret lab, Asha had called in reinforcements from CLAWS. Kobi didn't blame her anymore—she had been manipulated. But Asha still found any mention of it awkward.

"Sorry. I don't always mean to listen in on your dreams, you know," Asha said. "I can't control my powers when I'm sleeping. It's not actually fun to live other people's nightmares."

Kobi nodded. "Right. You don't have to apologize."

"Have you told Mischik about this memory?" She pointed to the journal on his desk, where Kobi had been ordered to write down anything he remembered about Hales's work. Next to it lay a map of Old Seattle that Kobi had labeled with all of Hales's labs and supply caches.

"I've told Mischik about everything, just like he asked. But he doesn't seem that interested."

"He just wants you to keep focused on the plan," said Asha, echoing what Mischik had repeated over and over to Kobi.

Right. The plan. The one that means I'm stuck waiting around here.

He'd thought that joining the resistance against CLAWS would mean *doing* something. But so far all he'd done was wait.

Kobi stood up and moved to his small wardrobe. "Let's head to the game room. I need to . . . *do* something. Blow off some steam."

Asha watched him. "I know you're frustrated, Kobi. I'm sure this place is pretty claustrophobic to you, coming from your old life outside. But we have to stay strong."

"I know," Kobi grumbled. The longer he stayed in this base, the less *strong* he felt: his body felt tired, his mind foggy. "I need to get changed."

"I'll wait outside," Asha said.

As soon as the door shut behind her, Kobi sighed. He couldn't go anywhere without someone accompanying him. It felt like he was being watched every second of the day.

And he was. In the corner of the bedroom, the small red light of a camera blinked. "We can't risk anything happening to you, Kobi," Mischik had said. "We need to keep an eye on you. Just in case."

Kobi changed and left the room, brushing past Asha to lead the way through the base. Hales had taught him to imprint safe routes into his memory; it meant he could navigate the maze of tunnels toward the game room without thinking. Kobi heard the gushing of running water above him, and for a moment he felt himself transported back beneath the lake: the current rushing in his ears, drowning his scream, heavy clothes pulling him down, a giant yellow eye watching him through the murky depths. His step ceased, his boot making a heavy clang on the metal floor.

"You okay?" Asha asked. Kobi felt his head prickling as Asha read his mind.

Kobi squeezed his fists. "Yeah, it's just the water pipes."

Asha looked up. This facility had once housed machinery for generating, storing, and transmitting hydroelectric power from the nearby Columbia River dams, before the tech was made obsolete by the biofuel plants of CLAWS. But the underground tunnels had never been removed. There were enough secret access shafts that Sol's resistance fighters could stay hidden but also move around the city, like rabbits in a warren, out of sight of CLAWS and the New Seattle authorities.

A few Sol scientists wearing lab coats paused to watch him, muttering. Maybe with excitement or maybe with worry. Kobi knew their work wasn't going well—synthesizing his antibodies to increase production of their new anti-Waste cleanser, a drug they'd called Horizon.

When they reached the main set of corridors, Kobi pressed his thumb onto the scanner, and the doors slid apart in a hiss of air, revealing a large central atrium space with corridors and gangways leading off it at various heights. Metal mesh stairs climbed up to the different levels, encircling the space like an amphitheater, or a prison. There were scientists, tech guys, and Sol field agents everywhere here—perhaps a hundred altogether, striding back and forth between meeting rooms, weaponry stores, and labs. They watched Kobi with awed faces as he passed.

"If it isn't our savior!" Kobi turned to a young man with straggly hair and thick hexagonal glasses. He was eating a giant baloney sandwich. Some of the filling had fallen down the front of his shaggy Metallica T-shirt.

"Hey, Spike," said Kobi with a grin.

He caught a flicker of movement just behind him. He turned and found Asha shaking her head insistently at Spike.

"Uh, or not-savior," Spike said.

"Don't worry," said Kobi, rolling his eyes. "Asha just wants to take the pressure off me as much as possible." Kobi lowered his voice. "Affects my production of antibodies."

"Hey, that's not the reason," Asha protested.

Spike gave a toothy smile. "Hey, we're all stressed." He pulled out a small metal object from his jeans pocket and threw it into the air. It uncoiled into the shape of a metallic insect, which began to hover in the air on a blur of buzzing wings. "I'm about to show off this new hacker bug to the bigwigs."

"Cool!" said Kobi. Spike had been helping Kobi catch up with modern technology—VR goggles, holo-tech, drones—taking apart machinery and showing him how it worked. It helped Kobi relax, like he was back helping Hales in his workshop.

"We call it the dragonfly," said Spike. "It locks on to drones and hacks into the CLAWS comms network. We'll get the lowdown on their plans—plus we might even be able to use their drones to send our own messages to everyone with a CLAWS app on their device. Which is basically everyone in the world. The signal won't get blocked if it originates from CLAWS tech. We'll finally be able to get the truth out there. Neat, huh?"

"You're a genius, Spike," Kobi agreed, grinning.

"You said it." Spike took a bite of the sandwich but almost spit it out again as he caught sight of something over Kobi's shoulder. "Sorry, gotta go. Boss is here." A cluster of important-looking adults was pacing through the atrium, including the tall figure of Alex Mischik, leader of Sol. Spike quickly grabbed the dragonfly from the air and stuffed it in his pocket. "Probably shouldn't be showing this thing around just yet." He slapped Kobi on the shoulder. "See you—savior." He grinned at Asha, who shook her head, letting out a disapproving sigh.

"You've got to give Spike a break," said Kobi as they walked away. "At least he doesn't treat me like some kind of prophet, or like I'm going to fall apart if people come near me."

"People just want you to be focused," Asha told him again. "They stay away so they don't distract you."

Kobi didn't reply. He'd been focused on supplying his blood to make the Horizon drugs for going on six months now, and it didn't feel like Sol was any closer to breaking the stranglehold CLAWS had on the city.

"We have to have faith," said Asha. "Put our own discomfort aside for the greater good. I'm sorry, Kobi. I know it's frustrating, but soon we *will* win. One day CLAWS, the Waste—all of it will be gone. Things will be like they were before the Waste disaster."

Kobi listened to her, trying to picture it: being a normal kid, going to school, hanging out with friends. Having a family. Where would he live? With Mischik or the other Healhome kids? Would someone adopt them?

The only thing he could come up with seemed cheesy and fake—like a commercial. A laughing family sitting around a dinner table in a neat kitchen. The real problem was that every time Kobi tried to imagine the future, the past invaded, and one face was stranded there forever: Jonathan Hales. The only family Kobi had ever known.